Books by
A. Claire Everward

The First

Oracle's Hunt
Oracle's Diplomacy

Blackwell: A Tangled Web

D1292170

A. CLAIRE EVERWARD
A TANGLED WEB

Author & Sister

First published in 2019 by Author & Sister
www.authorandsister.net

Print ISBN 978-965-92584-5-1
eBook ISBN 978-965-92584-4-4

This one is for you, my sister. I will write them as long as you want me to.

Chapter One

Twelve years. More than twelve, spring was already here and her count began in the dead of winter.

That was a long time. Still, even now she couldn't bring herself to think she might be safe. It never even began to feel that way, safe that is, but then she hadn't expected it to. That was why she still lived as she had back then, had never really made a home for herself. Home was something that would be hers, that could never truly be taken from her. She didn't believe she could have that. Not anymore. Not since. Not all considering.

Too much, considering.

Still, she had begun to think that this was where she would stay. At least she had a friend here. And her job, which she liked. She was good at it, too, one of the best. And she knew everything and everyone around her. That counted for a lot, it counted toward her ability to correctly assess the people she met, their intentions. Situations she encountered. To maybe be safe, even if she could never truly feel safe.

She read the email again. Monday, nine-thirty in

the morning, at the office of the transition team's screening and vetting officer.

The one who had been tasked with conducting the background checks that would thoroughly comb through all their lives before the security clearance would be granted and the company's takeover—and their relocation—would be completed.

She had until Monday morning to find a way to disappear.

"You're out of your mind." Robert Ashton fell back into the chair, slack-jawed. "This is madness."

The man sitting behind the heavy desk leaned back and looked at his friend and attorney with no humor in his eyes.

"Why on earth would you choose to do this?" Robert couldn't wrap his mind around the request.

"Freedom," was the answer.

"Freedom? You?"

They were sitting on the top floor of Blackwell Tower, the building that housed the San Francisco headquarters of Ian Blackwell Holdings. And the man behind the desk was Ian Blackwell himself.

"You're rich, you're powerful, you're respected, you're one of the most sought-after bachelors in the country. In the world!" Robert said. "What more do you want?"

"That last one is becoming rather annoying. At least the more publicly visible part of it." Ian stood up and walked over to the floor-to-ceiling glass that spanned the wall to the left of his desk, overlooking the great city. As he neared it, its tint lightened just enough to allow him a clear view to the outside in the bright midday sun. "Robert, I can't go anywhere without someone blabbing about it on some snooping media, social or otherwise, and it seems that every single woman I encounter nowadays wants to be the one who snared Ian Blackwell, the coveted bachelor."

"That's not new."

"No," Ian conceded, and turned to Robert. "But ever since that gossipmonger Cecilia Heart put me at the top of her Pounce-For Bachelors list, my social life has been nothing short of a circus. My public relations department is constantly finding photos and videos of me, taken everywhere I go. My administrative assistant gets emails and letters with proposals for me. And so do *her* administrative assistants." He turned back to the spectacular view outside. "Some peace and quiet on the women front would be nice."

"Yes, it's very tiring to be chased by gorgeous actresses and models and whatnots. You never know who you'll have in your bed in the morning, and trying to remember all their names, it's absolutely exhausting."

A frown passed over Ian's face, and Robert looked at him with interest. Maybe he really was getting tired of his way of life.

"I like to choose for myself who I sleep with,"

Ian said. "And I very much like my sexual endeavors to start and end at my own leisure."

Or maybe not. Robert sighed. "And you think this crazy idea of yours will divert the unwanted attention away from your social life."

"Yes."

"Why don't you just do what everyone else does? Go out on real dates with women you have genuine interest in. Who knows, you just might fall in love. Get married. Live until you're old and creaky with the same woman, if you're lucky."

"That was more of a possibility a decade ago. It's far less feasible now that I am . . ." Ian indicated the office around him.

"Ian Blackwell," Robert completed the thought.

The man himself nodded. "And after all the women I've been with, face it, Robert, I have yet to encounter one I cared to stay with. Nor am I likely to. People like me, they stay alone and get heckled by the Cecilia Hearts and the wannabe billionaire wives of this world. Or worse, they marry and divorce the latter in a tiring row. And that is not who I am."

No, he wasn't, despite appearances. Robert contemplated him. "So what you want is the freedom to continue sleeping with whomever you want to, but without cameras following you around because everyone will believe you really are married. Cameras will always follow you around, Ian."

"I'm used to cameras, to the mainstream media.

It's the gossip chasers I want gone."

"They will still chase you and the woman you marry."

"To a more controllable extent. With the bachelor part of it off the table, much of that unwanted attention will be gone."

"So, no more bedmates of your choice?" Robert asked innocently. He still couldn't believe his friend was serious. "Like that brunette last night?"

"She was boring," Ian said absently. She was fine in bed, and ultimately it was her body he had wanted, but still, she had bored the hell out of him. "No, I will still sleep with whomever I want to. The arrangement I have in mind will allow it. I'll just have to be discreet about it."

"Damn, you're serious. You want me to find you a wife."

"I want you to hire me a wife," Ian corrected him. He walked back to his desk, a towering man with thick black hair and dark gray eyes that were forever calculating, more ice in them than warmth. Even without his habit of wearing black, a black suit, a black shirt with its top button open as if to mislead an onlooker into thinking there was anything even remotely off-guard about him, he was a formidable man.

Robert shook his head. He didn't like this one bit. Not because he didn't think it would work. Ian had made things work his way long before they had first met. But Robert cared about his friend and didn't like the idea of him sinking even deeper into the personal—or rather impersonal—life he was already leading.

He himself was married, had been for a little more than ten years now, and had two kids, a boy and a girl, both in elementary school. Five years older than Ian, he was a young attorney in his father's modest law firm back when he had drawn the first business contract for the ambitious man when Ian was barely twenty-one, doing so pro bono, and had continued to stand by his side after that day without asking for anything in return, believing in him, in his relentless drive. Twelve and a half years later, he was still Ian's best friend and his personal attorney.

He was also the general counsel for what had since become Ian Blackwell's multinational conglomerate.

"Fine," he finally said. "What am I looking for?"

Ian considered him. "A socially adept woman. Tasteful. Intelligent—it would be nice if she could hold an at least coherent conversation when I entertain a business associate, as it would obviously reflect on me. And keep in mind that I would necessarily have to spend at least some of my time with her, since we would be living in the same house." His brow furrowed. That unavoidable proximity, in fact, was one of the main reasons it had taken him this long to make the final decision to go forward with the idea.

"And you have no patience for stupidity," Robert

remarked dryly.

Ian raised an eyebrow.

"Sorry. Yes, I understand what you mean. Looks, I suppose, are a requirement?"

Ian forced patience into his voice. He could understand Robert's frustration, but that didn't mean he intended to let it influence his decision. "Only to the extent that she needs to be presentable, as would be expected of my wife. I don't need beauty to represent me."

"And if you want it for other purposes, you'll just get it elsewhere."

"Yes." The eyes that came to rest on Robert's were impassive.

"Come on, Ian. You should have better. You deserve better."

"You're a good friend, Robert. But we are not the same, and we are not meant to have the same." Ian turned his attention back to the Alster report on his dual computer screen. "I have no time for this. You deal with it."

"You mean you want me to choose by myself?"

"You know me better than anyone. Draft the contract, choose the woman."

"And you'll abide by my choice?"

Ian didn't bother to answer.

Robert looked at him with exasperation, but said nothing. Despite his misgivings, he would not hesitate to do as he was asked. He was one of a rare few who knew the man behind the carefully cultivated image, and he would follow Ian Blackwell to the end of the world.

He got up to leave.

"By the way, you're flying with me to Denver tomorrow," Ian said, still not looking at him.

"Denver. InSyn?"

"Yes. I want to have a look at the damn thing myself before I tear it apart."

Ian raised his eyes to the door as it closed behind the attorney. It was, indeed, enough if Robert dealt with the matter. After all, it wasn't as if this woman would be his wife in the true sense of the word. She would, in essence, be nothing more than a business partner who would be sharing with him the more personal aspects of his life. All barring the physical, of course—he had no intention of sleeping with her, in any sense of the word. That would cause complications he did not intend to allow, since the arrangement he had in mind would be expected to last for some time. As long as its purpose would serve him, to be exact.

He didn't have to be told that his was an unusual plan, all the more so in this day and age. But it wasn't a spur-of-the-moment idea. In fact, it had been forming in his mind for quite some time now. Nor was it purely the result of his irritation at the outside disruptions to his social life, as he had told Robert, although that was certainly enough of a reason. No, the fact was that at his age he had never been in a long-term relationship, or had even been seen with the same woman for a duration, and Heart and too many others were using this to depict him as a playboy, a womanizer who wasn't likely to ever settle down. Which he wouldn't give a damn about, except that he wasn't only a billionaire who could do whatever he wanted. He also headed a multinational company of a considerable size, one that he himself had built, and as such he was acutely aware that he was responsible for tens of thousands of jobs, both in his company and in others that depended on its business. Families depended on him for their livelihood, and that mattered.

He had a solid image in the business world, that of a ruthless, yes, unrelenting, no doubt, but also fair and responsible man. His work had nothing to do with his personal life, and he had always been careful to keep the two apart. Yes, he had his choice of women. Obviously. And he slept with them. Sometimes he even dated them, albeit briefly. But that was it. No playboy life for him, no frivolous partying. His company, that was his sole focus, and he intended to keep it that way.

But social media was a powerful thing, and social media didn't care who Ian Blackwell really was. Its followers, at least those who had come to matter in his case, the ones who were proving to be a disruption for him, didn't watch business news or listen to finance and economy journalists. They only followed the likes of Heart like a captive herd, and they knew nothing about him but what she chose to show them. And what she showed them was an irresistible—and irresponsible—playboy.

She created interest, and in the era of smartphone cameras in everybody's hands the attention quickly became a nuisance. He was photographed everywhere he went and with anyone he happened to be with at the time. Including with business associates. He found himself having to conduct all his meetings under a blanket of secrecy, even the ones that didn't warrant it.

And then the previous week a major real estate developer he had been considering a transaction with—he wanted to build a technology campus for one of his subsidiaries, Pythia Vision—had joked about a photo of him leaving a restaurant with a woman, which that damn Heart had posted in her unfortunately widely read blog and had spoken about with relish in a morning show that had her as a regular contributor, claiming the photo was proof of yet another fling he was supposedly having. Which brought on countless of snide responses within the hour, and it wasn't even true. The woman was the chief operating officer of one of his foreign subsidiaries, a valuable asset who had flown to the United States to discuss with her colleagues at Ian Blackwell Holdings' headquarters and finally with him her plans for the assimilation of a recently acquired startup, and who had almost quit because of what Heart had done.

The real estate developer had, naturally, lost the deal and was already being taken over by his biggest competitor in a process initiated by Ian and that would end with his ousting from his company. But Ian was sick and tired of this. It was irritating and disruptive. He was getting fan mail, for heaven's sake. Fan mail, women *worldwide* offering themselves to Ian Blackwell. And hate mail, of course, that went without saying. This had gotten ridiculously out of hand.

He wanted it to stop.

The gossip chasers didn't seem to give a damn about the truth, so he would create a new one for them. He knew there would be rumors and speculations once he carried out his plan, but that didn't matter. These would wane with the marriage lasting, and with the right wife, which Ian was certain Robert would choose. And when Ian did decide to womanize some more, which he would, he would make sure no one knew about it. He would have his way—out of the public eye.

Impatience surfaced again. He was overthinking this. The Alster acquisition, that was the only matter he should be giving his attention to right now. He leaned back in his chair, the frown on his face deepening as his thoughts turned to the troubling issue that had been plaguing him.

Jeremy Alster was sixty-four, happily married to his high-school sweetheart, with no children or any other family members to whom he could pass his

Oakland-based company, Alster Industries. The company was privately-held, like Ian's was, but it was far smaller, nowhere near the size of Ian Blackwell Holdings. It was also highly inefficient. Alster kept subsidiaries that no longer had place in the fast-advancing industrial world alongside companies that could easily become industry leaders. There was no business sense behind this, but then Jeremy Alster was not a strategist. He was all about protecting his employees. He kept unprofitable subsidiaries running at the expense of profitable ones in order to keep the employees of the obsolete businesses from losing their jobs, and didn't do nearly enough to try to turn around the failing subsidiaries. His was undue sentimentality combined with a business practice that was doomed to fail, and that was fast depleting the company's resources.

Now, finally, Alster was considering selling, but he had stated that if it came to that he would only sell Alster Industries as a whole, and only to the right buyer. He knew well that if he delayed much longer his company would run into the ground, and still he hung on, refusing to sell to a buyer he would not approve of.

Ian wanted something Alster Industries had. A subsidiary that had originally been formed on the basis of an idea for a breakthrough virtual interface developed by an Alster employee who was also a gamer, and who had been fired for it—games had apparently been more important to him than getting to work on time. But the guy had been smart enough to approach Alster himself, and the latter had recognized the potential of the concept and had registered patents on it in his company's name. Unfortunately for Alster, so far he hadn't been successful in turning the idea into a viable technology. Alster Industries just wasn't that type of a company, it didn't have anywhere near the required set of skills or the necessary resources.

But neither was a problem for Ian Blackwell Holdings. It had the perfect home for the interface, the perfect place for it to become a reality. Pythia Vision, a subsidiary that Ian had formed and was putting substantial resources into, intending to make it his company's forward-looking artificial intelligence arm, a hub of technological brilliance. Pythia Vision was already working on a number of commercial applications, but its aim was to ultimately develop complex civilian and defense systems that would require the participation of both humans and machines to achieve optimal results. And the attainment of this, Ian believed, depended on two crucial components that existed in two companies, one of them Alster's.

The other he had already acquired a few months earlier. InSyn, or Intelligence Synergy, which was what he thought it should have been called—why the founders had decided to shorten the name into an unintelligible assortment of letters was beyond him. InSyn was a company in Colorado, in the Denver

Technological Center, that was working on creating the algorithms platform for a synergistic human-machine interface. One that would one day, once the required technologies advanced enough, allow humans and machines to work side by side seamlessly in dynamic multitask decision-making situations.

InSyn's algorithms were his, but in order to implement them in an actual interface in a way that it could be used by Pythia Vision, he needed the Alster virtual interface. The problem was that the interface was too skillfully patented, and, anyway, Ian wanted the developer, too, and the team the guy had already assembled.

He had no interest in the rest of Alster Industries. Still, he was willing to buy the entire company, if needed, to get that one subsidiary he wanted. And if he already had to buy Alster Industries in its entirety, there was another aspect of it that interested him. As a result of Jeremy Alster's treatment of his employees over the years, they were loyal to him. And loyalty was not easy to find these days. Employees who invested back in a company that invested in them, who chose to remain with it and to grow and develop according to its needs, that was an asset of great potential if one handled it correctly. Training new people took time, and time was competitiveness and money.

Ian knew the plans of the other contenders for Alster Industries, plans they tried their best to hide from Alster. They would get rid of the weak and keep only the strong. That wasn't quite what he had in mind. He would take Alster Industries apart, yes. It would effectively cease to exist. But while the more successful subsidiaries would be added to his own or merged into them—for the most part, he didn't mind having them in Ian Blackwell Holdings' extensive portfolio—the failed ones would not be eliminated, not exactly. He would use their employees. They weren't stupid, they knew their time was up and had known for a while that Jeremy Alster was carrying them on his back. Concern was widespread, and Ian intended to use that to his advantage. He would inject new businesses into any subsidiaries he could, and where that wasn't a viable option, he would relocate useful employees. He would then take the others, compensate those he had no need for in a way that would undermine any dissent, and teach those who could be taught, to enable them to join Ian Blackwell Holdings. Give them all peace of mind, give their families a future, and shift their loyalty to him and to his company.

He had already decided on the team that would be in charge of the human resources part of his plan, and intended to have Alster himself work alongside it. The man knew everything about each and every one of his employees, and that was invaluable and would make the process more efficient. They would be interacting with Alster, rather than with the unfamiliar representatives of the company that would by then have taken over their livelihoods. The way Ian planned it, the transition would be far more likely to succeed.

Money was not an issue for him. He was not Jeremy Alster and Ian Blackwell Holdings was not Alster Industries. Ian never compromised, and every takeover he had ever completed, friendly or otherwise, had been carefully thought out. As a result, he was not only the only one offering this ambitious plan to Alster, he was also the only one who had the ability to carry it out without it causing too much of a dent in his own company's very deep pockets. Failure would hurt but not destroy him. Success, he knew, meant that Ian Blackwell Holdings would skyrocket to new heights.

The problem was that Alster was hesitating. People did not usually hesitate when Ian Blackwell came after them. It was known that if he wanted a company, he got it. But Alster was different. He would fight to the end to protect his employees, which was why Ian had approached him in the first place in a different manner than was his convention. He had stayed back, letting others bid for the company, not letting anyone know he too was interested while learning their intentions. When he had finally entered the arena, it was quietly, and he had approached Alster directly. His offer was a number, and a plan. The number was less, much less, than the others had bid, which he had ways of finding out. The plan was for the failing companies, and for each and every one of Alster Industries' employees.

Alster had not made the offer public, which was a good sign. And yet he wasn't going forward with it, either.

Ian had an idea why. And he was hoping his plan to get married would go some way toward solving that.

Chapter Two

Victoria Davis glanced at the man she was walking beside. She was more nervous than she'd ever been. If he would not be pleased at the end of his visit, it would be her job that would be lost, her career that would end. Although she wouldn't mind that as much as she would not having a go at getting Ian Blackwell.

This wasn't her first time on one of his post-takeover transition teams, but it was her first time as the administrative head of one, and she was determined to show him she was a team player. She would, simply said, do whatever he asked, and if she was lucky maybe he would be open to more. She let her eyes roam over him, discreetly so. That's one hell of a man, she thought. Put him in a crowd and he would stand out, a striking man by all standards. By all standards indeed. She sighed inwardly. She followed the gossip, knew every item her boss appeared in, had heard of his feats. She had a photo of him tucked away in her bedroom, where no one would see it. Everything she wore now, and the hairstyle she had done as soon she got the call informing her that he was coming to see InSyn, it was all meant to attract his attention.

So far he hadn't so much as looked. And right now he didn't seem pleased, to say the least.

Ian finally had an insight into what was happening in his most recent acquisition. On the flight over to Denver he had read once again the reports he had been getting from the transition team and had gone through the original due diligence report prepared for the company, which had been unfailingly thorough. And yet none of these had given him any idea as to why all efforts to successfully integrate InSyn into Ian Blackwell Holdings' companies portfolio had failed.

But this visit had.

"Sir, I know you originally intended for InSyn to be an independent subsidiary of Pythia Vision," Davis said, "that you wanted it to retain enough of its operational freedom to continue doing its work the way it always has. But that's just not working. These people are impossible. I have to say, I have no idea how this company has managed to get this far." She glanced at him. He didn't bother to return the look. "And I think you're right. I mean, of course you're right. It can't stay here. It's best to just dissolve it, as you said. I tried everything, they're refusing to cooperate. Even after I told them what you've decided, that because of their behavior we're shutting them down. And even after we've already began the preparations for the relocation of the employees we plan to keep."

Ian frowned. He hadn't approved that. InSyn was not supposed to know what he had planned for it until he would make his final decision, after this visit. It made no sense to tell them yet.

Davis continued, nervousness clear in her voice. "We didn't even ask them for much, just to understand that they're now a part of a bigger company, your company, and to act accordingly. But they're constantly objecting to me and to my administrative team, and even the technology coordination team, the one from Pythia Vision, I don't understand their problem with it."

InSyn and Pythia Vision had worked together in the past. Pythia Vision had been using InSyn's machine learning algorithms in its artificial intelligence applications for more than a year before Ian decided on the takeover, and InSyn had advised Pythia Vision on a number of occasions. But now Ian wanted more than that, he wanted InSyn to fully align itself with Pythia Vision's technology development plans in order to focus its expertise accordingly, and, at the same time, to prepare to translate its algorithmic platform into reality with Alster's virtual interface. Evidently, neither was happening.

"I mean, it's been three months since we . . . since you took them over," Davis said, "and, sir, nothing has been going as scheduled. Nothing. This has never happened in any transition I've been a part of." She hurried on, defensive. "Instead of synchronizing its administrative operations with those of Pythia Vision, and increasing its cooperation with the technology development teams, the same teams it has already worked with so well before, it's just . . . it's like it's increasingly withdrawing into itself." She shook her head in exasperation, managing to make eye contact with Ian. "I'm sorry, sir, they're simply impossible."

Ian had to contain his impatience. He knew all this. It was why he had finally decided it would be better—and certainly easier—if InSyn would be dissolved. The small company would be stripped of its assets, its technology experts moved to Pythia Vision as its direct employees and the rest made redundant. Ian wanted this to be done without further delay so that the elements he was interested in would be assimilated into the context he had intended for them, to be ready when he put his hands on the patents owned by Alster Industries. Which he had no doubt he would.

Still, he was hands-on, and had his own way of looking at companies, down to their very core. The way an engineer would look into a complex machine and know, simply know all about it, he could look at a company and know its strengths and its weaknesses, its potential and its risks. And so before making his final decision what to do with his rogue acquisition, and for the first time ever for this company, he flew in himself and walked its hallways.

And now he knew.

The problem with this company was its people. InSyn was, quite simply, resisting its takeover, long after it was a done deal. Normally that wouldn't be a problem, Ian Blackwell Holdings had more than enough experience—and ways—to deal with that. But InSyn wasn't the maker of a technology that could be placed in the hands of an external development team if necessary. It was people, brilliant minds who had spent years creating machine learning algorithms, analyzing the responses of human operators in their work with machines, and developing algorithms designed to balance all elements of the human-machine interaction in order to optimize it.

And that meant that InSyn's value lay in both its algorithms and the people who made them and on whom they were built being taken together. And if the people didn't want to be a part of Ian's company, despite what it was offering them, the very function he needed from them was under the threat of being rendered useless.

He could understand their shock. They had had no idea that one of InSyn's two founders had made failed financial investments in an attempt to make enough money to buy out the only other shareholder in InSyn, a venture capital fund. In a bout of greed, the man had wanted to reap the fruits of the small company's success after he'd realized it was becoming a valuable subcontractor for Pythia Vision and had suspected that a takeover by Ian Blackwell

Holdings—a high-premium one—was only a matter of time. The guy should have stuck to what he knew best, but he didn't, and this resulted in his financial ruin. His and InSyn's, as he had dipped into its financial reserves. And no one in InSyn had known, no one had any idea.

Ian did. And he had used that fact to buy the man, then an emotional wreck, out. Or actually, Ian Blackwell Holdings had bought him out. Completely out. Ian no longer needed the guy for the company and didn't want someone as unreliable as him in it. He had then bought out the other founder, too, but that one was easy. The man loved InSyn, and all he wanted was to remain with it into its future, to continue working in the company he had founded. And since his technological contribution was of value, Ian didn't mind letting him do so. The money was just an added benefit for him. He liked to live well, and the purchase offer had given him just that.

This meant that Ian Blackwell Holdings owned the two founders' shares in InSyn. The rest were still owned by the venture capital fund that had made a series of investments in InSyn over more than a decade, ever since the algorithmic platform it had ended up developing was not much more than a theory. The fund had made the investments quietly and patiently, and it deserved its shares, no doubt, and the substantial gain it would now make from Ian Blackwell Holdings' acquisition of InSyn and its planned use of the small company's know-how.

And so it was a good thing that Ian himself was also the sole owner of the venture capital fund and was the one who was providing it with its investment money, which not many knew, not even in his company. He doubted the greedy one of the two founders would have sold him his shares in InSyn as easily if he had known. Which didn't matter, Ian would have ultimately bought him out anyway. He always got what he wanted.

And he would solve the InSyn mess, too. He already had an idea how.

"This way," Davis said, and Ian turned his attention back to his surroundings. They were going down the stairs to the only part of the building he hadn't been in yet, the basement level.

"This is where they keep their mainframe," Davis said, "and they use this place to store their data, too, there's storage media here. And also a library of sorts, books and files." Her voice took on an irritated edge. "I kept finding here some of the people who belong upstairs. Apparently they were trying to form another team or something, I'm not sure what that was. I put a stop to it immediately." She shook her head, displeased. "I made it clear to them that we're now making the decisions who works where, and that we'll decide everything with Pythia Vision. They argued, but they always argue. They'll simply have to get used to the way things are now. I know you wouldn't want them to stand in the way of your plans, sir," she added, "and I will do everything necessary to bring them in line before you relocate them."

Ian's brow furrowed.

The basement was cool and silent but for the constant hum of the powerful mainframe. The light came from evenly distributed, recessed LED light fixtures overhead and from long, narrow windows at the top of the external walls, hugging the ceiling. It was a good setup that prevented the sickly lighting that normally characterized such places, making it a friendlier work environment. The entire floor was an open space, and the only dividers were created by the cabinets holding the equipment, right of the stairs, and shelves holding books and storage media in orderly, clearly marked rows on their left. Several desks stood at convenient intervals, some with sophisticated workstations on them, although there was no one there to use them.

Davis turned right at the bottom of the stairs, and Ian followed her deeper into the floor, between the sleek dividers. Everything here was state of the art, as he'd expected, and extremely well maintained. It seemed that the founders had at least done that right, even though they had not been smart with their funds, wasting money they didn't have. He looked around him, assessing every element, every part of the place's layout. He knew, of course, about all of it, every piece of equipment and every mind this company had. But he was seeing it first hand for the first time.

The sound of someone speaking had Davis and him walking on to the end of the floor. Near the wall up ahead, a man sat behind a desk, where light from the early afternoon sun fell on him. As they watched, the man, black, heavyset, and in his late fifties, Ian judged, threw his hands up in frustration and then typed fast on the keyboard detached from the set of screens before him, speaking to himself in the process.

"No, no, no," he was saying, apparently reacting to something on the screens. "If you do this the loop will be too quick for the human operator. What on earth are they thinking up there?"

"Excuse me." Davis took a step toward him, glancing back at Ian.

The man didn't answer, intent on his work.

"Excuse me," she said again, her tone hard. Perhaps she thought this approach would appeal to him, gain her his respect, Ian thought with distaste.

"I told you," Davis said, looking at him. "They don't listen, that's what I've had to deal with ever since my team and I got here. It's as if they don't understand that they're now under a different ownership, that we're the bosses now. They just keep trying to—" Her voice took on a shrill edge. "This disregard is annoying," she continued, turning back to the man. "You there," she called out to him.

"Just a minute, please, we almost have it. I do apologize but this has to be done properly," the man said, his eyes on the screens.

"That I agree with. Damn it, you will come when your bosses call."

A dark expression crossed Ian's face. He did not approve of her speaking to this man, or to anyone for that matter, in this way. He had seen how everyone he had met in the building so far had reacted to her.

And she was taking some liberty putting herself in the same level as him. This visit had already shown him she was the wrong person for the job, and his transition teams coordinator would have to answer to him for that. He was angry, certain that if things here had been handled properly, the drastic change he had come to consider for this company, or his involvement at all, might never have been required.

The fact that Jeremy Alster had called him two hours earlier to tell him he was not likely to accept his offer because, in his words, Ian would not be the appropriate person to care for his company, and that Ian suspected this had something to do with the story a morning show had run earlier that day, a gossip item involving his date with the brunette, which they had elaborated to include his "feats" as depicted by the enthusiastic interviewee, Cecilia Heart herself, was not helping his mood any. That's what happens when there's no real news to report, he thought to himself with irritation. He hoped Robert would solve his problem soon, but at that moment Robert was right there, following him and Davis around InSyn in this visit that shouldn't have been necessary. And so he could expect a delay on that, too.

It would, it seemed, be a day of delays for him. And he hated delays.

"This is an interactive session with the balancing algorithms team upstairs," the man was saying. "If we stop working on this now we'll have to start over again. And this is an important loop for the—"

Davis didn't give him a chance to finish. "I don't care what you're doing, it will wait."

"You don't understand," he tried to explain, finally looking up. "I'm sorry, Ms. Davis, I don't mean to offend you. I know you're not a tech, maybe I can speak to someone in your technology team? They will understand, they can help—" He saw Ian beside her and obviously recognized him. He stood up. "Mr. Blackwell, sir, you understand, you need me to continue this now, as it is with the transition we are losing time—"

"Excuse me, you will speak only to me. Mr. Blackwell is not here for this, and you may not address him," Davis said indignantly. "You know what, that's it." She was shouting now. "You'll be the first, maybe this example will straighten out the others, which is long overdue. You're fired. You will transfer your work to Ms. Andrews and leave."

"Please, you can't do this!" the man blurted out and stood up.

"But I can do whatever I damn well want." It

was Ian who answered him, the anger in his voice unmistakable. He'd had enough of this. Of Davis, of this man, of this shouting and the unprofessional conduct. Of people around him being complete idiots and standing in his way. "InSyn is mine now and I'm sick and tired of you people telling me what I can and cannot do with it—"

"That's enough." The voice was quiet but left no place for argument.

Ian turned around. And froze. Before him stood what could only be described as a classic beauty, the kind of beauty that would unfailingly stand out, even in the understated way she was dressed, too understated for his taste. In a long sleeve, navy blue pullover, one size too big—there was no way she would need that—and a pair of jeans, plain blue ones. Plain, that was it. A woman who looks like that shouldn't be dressed this plainly, the thought went through his mind. And she certainly shouldn't be hidden away in some basement. Tall, slim, her hair pulled back in a ponytail. Auburn. No, a true dark red, the mix of lights in this underground hideaway playing with its hues to confuse him. And her eyes, those beautiful eyes that rested on his, full of fire, were a piercing gold amber.

"God." That came out involuntarily.

"No, just me," she said and turned her back to him.

Anger flared. At her, and at himself for reacting this way. He wasn't used to being taken by surprise.

Nor was he used to being slighted.

Beside him, Davis gaped. And in the shadows behind them, Robert watched with growing interest.

"Jayden Rees," the woman said, walking to the shocked man standing at the desk. "That's his name, and he's been with this company since its inception, no one knows it as well as he does. What you need from InSyn wouldn't be if not for him. Although" —she turned her angry gaze to Davis—"apparently loyalty doesn't matter now that you have what you want."

"Do you know who this man is?" Davis was appalled.

"No, I don't know." The woman turned back to Ian and he was hit by the force of that golden gaze again. "Who are you for him, Ian Blackwell?"

The eyes that met hers narrowed, gray ice meeting her fire with equal force.

"You will be fired for this!" Davis was nearly screeching.

"Couldn't care less. I wouldn't want to stay in the type of place that treats good people this way," the woman said, never raising her voice, never taking her eyes off Ian's. "Of course, now that you're firing me, you can't fire Jayden. He's the only other person here who can keep the data function working." And with this, she turned her back on both of them again and went over to Rees.

Davis was about to follow her, seething with anger, but Ian motioned her not to, a deep frown on his face. Instead, he turned to leave, Davis following him after a last hateful glance behind her.

Hidden by a divider to their left, Robert moved back, wanting to remain unseen. He had watched the exchange between his friend and the woman, had seen his reaction to her. Under any other circumstances Ian wouldn't let things get this far, nor would he react this way, knowing intimidation came too easily for him. But he was in an extraordinarily bad mood. And it showed.

And yet this woman, whoever she was, had easily stood up to him, to his anger, not in the least caring who he was.

And Ian Blackwell had backed down.

Robert looked on as the woman walked up to Jayden Rees and spoke to him. Rees gestured toward Ian's and Davis's distancing backs in obvious shock and disbelief, and she put her hand on his arm and spoke quietly, soothingly. Inconsolable, Rees shook his head, but she continued to speak, her voice gentle. Robert moved a little closer to hear better. She was assuring him, letting him know everything would be all right. Promising him it would be. And he seemed to take her word for it, breathing in deeply, calming down. Sitting down again.

Robert turned and left, unseen.

He waited until he was alone to check InSyn's employee register on his laptop. Then he took out his phone and made a call. The report was in his private email early the next morning. It was prepared by the only person Robert would trust with this, the man who headed IBH Internal Security, the Ian Blackwell Holdings company in charge of integrated security in all its subsidiaries, including the vetting of its employees.

Tess Andrews had no skeletons in her closet, that was Ira Gold's bottom line. She was adopted as a baby and raised in Denver as an only child by an elderly couple who died less than a year apart, her father first and her mother just after she graduated from high school, at seventeen. This had left her all alone. She had joined InSyn almost immediately after, choosing not to go to college. Twelve years later, she was still at InSyn. And she still had no one, no family. Nothing to stop her from moving to another city, another state. Good.

When InSyn was awarded its first IBH Pythia Vision contract, Tess Andrews had undergone a preliminary background check, the only one needed at the time by all InSyn employees and that Gold had attached to his report. Skimming over it, Robert nodded to himself, pleased. Among other things, the background check, which included both information she provided and some information collected about her without her knowledge, disclosed also her personal status and living arrangements, and required her to provide changes in these while InSyn worked with Pythia Vision. This provided Robert with some insight into her personal life.

Not that she had one. None to speak of, anyway. She lived in the same address she had moved into when she had joined InSyn and spent her entire time at work. The only people she was in any sort of contact with outside work seemed to be Jayden Rees and his wife, her only pastime the gym around the corner from InSyn, which she went to most days before working hours.

Not married, and no boyfriend, neither at the time of the initial background check nor currently, according to Gold. This suited Robert's purpose, but it also interested him. A woman like her, who looked like she did, leading a solitary life. He thought about the way she dressed, understating her own femininity. He looked again at her employment record, at the hours she kept. Workaholic, it looked like, work for her superseded everything. Just like Ian.

Except that she didn't push to advance her career, although she could have. She had taken courses over the years, some InSyn had offered, others she had asked for. Yet she had never made an effort to get a formal degree and had refused any promotion that would have taken her outside her comfort zone, it seemed to him. Certainly nothing that would have led to her working with anyone outside the small company. Nor had she responded to persistent attempts by headhunters to lure her to other companies. Still, her status at InSyn was that of a valuable asset to be retained, and so she was left to decide her own and do as she pleased.

There were some questions there, no doubt, and some curious gaps. People usually had more of a life to show, a life they shared with others. They had friends, hobbies they engaged in. Presence in some social media or other. It was odd that she didn't have any of that. She was somewhat of an enigma at close scrutiny, Robert mused. A very solitary enigma. But the fact was that, according to Gold, she was clean. He remembered the way she had intervened in favor of Rees, protecting him, the way she hadn't hesitated to stand up to those who had the power to fire them both. The way she had spoken. Quietly, not once raising her voice. Assertive but never aggressive. The intelligence in her eyes. The gentleness in her voice when she had soothed her upset friend.

The way she had been with Ian. The way he had been with her.

Gut feeling, he had long ago learned from Ian Blackwell, had a crucial role in one's fortunes.

Robert made his choice.

Chapter Three

Tess Andrews looked out of the window of her tiny living room, her gaze thoughtful. Outside, her view in the quiet Greenwood Village neighborhood, just south of Denver, consisted of the house her apartment was a part of, on top of its detached garage. The house, and the man who was just then coming out of it. Jayden Rees was on his way to his Saturday morning golf game, the only outdoor activity he thought was worth his time. As he was leaving, his wife Aisha hurried out of the house after him, holding a light sweater in her hand. She wrapped the sweater tightly around him and tipped her face up for the kiss Jayden never failed to give her on her cheek. Then they went their separate ways, she back into the house and he to his game, both with smiles on their faces.

Tess's brow was furrowed, her eyes full of worry. She needed to find a way for this not to have any repercussions for them. Jayden and Aisha were the best people she knew, and she would not let them be hurt by their association with her. She had hoped the events of the day before, her run-in with

Davis and with Ian Blackwell, would lead to her simply being fired, which would, in a way, solve her problem. But to her surprise she found out later that neither she nor Jayden were being fired. She was happy for Jayden, but for her this was the worst thing that could have happened. She'd certainly not meant to antagonize Blackwell, but once she had, she had hoped that her clash with him would have the windfall of allowing her to disappear without too many questions being asked.

Blackwell. The mere thought of him infuriated her, because of the way he had spoken to Jayden. She didn't like people who talked down to others, and Blackwell and especially Davis, whom *he* had sent to head the transition team, had done just that. She knew who he was, of course, he'd been the most talked-about person in InSyn's hallways since the takeover, and Jayden had told her he was in the building, that he'd finally come to see them himself. She didn't care, but Jayden had been excited at the prospect of meeting Ian Blackwell, and even more excited that it was his company that had taken over InSyn, if that was the way it had to be. And that's despite the conduct of Blackwell's transition team, and especially Davis. He is a brilliant business man, Jayden had told her every chance he got. There's no way he would allow Davis to do this to us, he'll fix this, you'll see, that was what he had said to her that very morning. Blackwell was a fair man, Jayden seemed to think.

Some fair, she thought angrily. Jayden had been terribly hurt by the way Blackwell had treated him, and by what he had allowed Davis to do. As far as she was concerned, Ian Blackwell was just another one of those domineering people who were used to nothing and no one daring to stand up to them. Everyone at InSyn certainly seemed to cower when he walked by and he didn't even seem to notice, walking around with the arrogant confidence of a man who owned the world.

Her mind unwittingly brought up his image. He was younger than she had expected, but then she didn't really know much about him. She didn't watch television, had no patience for it. Or for spending endless hours online, for that matter. Nor did she have any inclination to join social media, the exposure it brought with it wasn't for her. She liked her privacy, and she preferred to read. Reading was solitary, quiet, and allowed her mind to go where the words went rather than where her thoughts wanted to take her. She didn't even keep a television here, in her apartment. The laptop was enough.

And she had never bothered to check out Ian Blackwell when he had taken over InSyn. She already knew the company he'd intended InSyn to work under, Pythia Vision, from InSyn's ongoing cooperation with it, and anyway it was only his plans for InSyn that mattered to her, and that information she could get most efficiently from inside InSyn itself.

It was just that she'd thought he was older. And

not looking like . . . that. Nor had she expected to meet him. She'd been busy, working in that part of the building that had become her hiding place, where she liked to work alone, away from everyone. And then he was there, she'd heard the exchange, had heard him side with the head of his transition team as Davis treated a good man unfairly. In the time it had taken her to get to Jayden, she'd heard Blackwell's tone of voice, the same icy anger he then had in his eyes for her. He had expected her to yield, just as Davis had expected her to.

But she hadn't yielded, she thought with satisfaction. The arrogance! He seemed to expect everyone to kowtow to him, just as Davis had expected them to do for her. She was angry that InSyn's founders had sold out to this man who didn't seem to bother to listen to those who really knew the company and what made it so good at what it did, and who thought he could treat his employees the way he had, the way the people he had sent to take care of the transition had. She couldn't believe this guy.

Restless, she went to her laptop, which sat on the small coffee table. She looked him up, then closed the browser tab before the search results even came up. What was she doing? She didn't need to know anything about him. She'd already seen enough. She remembered his eyes, gray ice that bored into hers, which she imagined answered his with just the right amount of fire. She'd infuriated him. And surprised him, too. That one almost pleased her. It would have, if she wasn't so worried.

Which brought her back to her most urgent problem. She wasn't fired for angering Ian Blackwell. And although the relocation was off, for now at least, InSyn would still become a subsidiary of IBH Pythia Vision. Which meant that her life was still about to be scrutinized along with those of the rest of its employees, by Blackwell's background investigators, people who didn't know her and who worked within a system she didn't know and had no control in whatsoever. It was going to happen, and she had run out of time.

She closed her eyes. What on earth was she going to do now?

The ringtone made her jump. Her phone. She didn't have a landline here, only her smartphone, and the generic ring let her know it wasn't Jayden or his wife, nor anyone from InSyn. She picked it up and looked at the screen. A blocked number. She considered rejecting the call but then answered anyway. Maybe someone was calling to fire her after all, she thought with some cynicism. And some hope.

"Yes?" she said.

"Ms. Andrews?"

The caller was a man. Couldn't be someone trying to sell her anything, she thought absently. Her number wasn't listed, and not for that reason.

She didn't answer, and the caller continued. "I'm sorry to disturb you, Ms. Andrews, but I need to speak to you. I'm an attorney."

She focused instantly.

"There is a matter I would like to discuss with you, a matter of a personal nature."

"What is this about?" She kept her voice calm, guarded.

"Nothing that can be explained on the phone, I'm afraid. I know this is highly unusual, but I wonder if you might give me a few minutes to explain, face to face."

When she said nothing, the attorney continued. "I would appreciate it if you could meet me at the law offices of Parker and Williams." He gave her the address, in an area that housed mostly law and accounting firms in Denver's Central Business District.

"And your name is?"

"In fact, we can meet there in, say, an hour, if that's all right with you. I happen to be on my way there right now," he continued without answering her question.

"You don't really expect me to agree to this, do you?" she said.

"Please, Ms. Andrews. I know it's a lot to ask." The attorney's voice remained calm, confident. Not angered in any way.

Tess closed her eyes. After a lengthy pause during which the man on the other end of the line remained silent, she confirmed she would meet him. She didn't want to, but knew she had to, had to know why an attorney was calling her out of the blue, refusing to identify himself or to explain what he wanted unless she met him. And this wasn't about curiosity.

It was about survival.

In InSyn's too cramped a conference room for his taste, Ian was sitting with the transition team. The administrative part of it, not the techs. And the new administrative part of it, not the one originally assigned to this company. The latter no longer worked for him, and the former were an experienced bunch, who'd worked well together on several of his previous acquisitions and had done an excellent job. He had them flown in overnight on his company's executive jets from a number of locations, taking them away from well-earned vacations. Now that he had a good idea of what had been going on at InSyn, he had changed his mind about how to approach its integration into Ian Blackwell Holdings, deciding to give another try to his original plan of letting it stay as it was, in Denver. And this team, they would do the job he needed them to.

He glanced at his watch. Robert was a no show. He'd called, said he had something to do and that he would update Ian later. Ian didn't need him for this meeting, now that the original strategy for InSyn was back on, but since they were both due to head back to San Francisco in just a few hours, he wanted everything that might necessitate their presence here in Denver to be sorted out before that. He had no patience for any more delays.

At least it was the weekend and InSyn was nearly empty. He hoped this meant that woman wasn't somewhere in the basement two stories below him.

She was the last person in the world he wanted to see.

The building was one of those bleak concrete and metal affairs built when someone still thought impressing meant trying to intimidate. Tess stood on the sidewalk and looked up at it, she had no idea for how long, then lowered her gaze to the simple glass door set in the somber exterior. She wasn't in a hurry to go inside, but then the idea of staying out here didn't appeal to her, either. Denver's bustling Central Business District felt to her far too crowded.

She took a deep breath, walked up to the door, pulled it open resolutely and walked in. Inside, the building had been renovated recently enough to be bright and almost cheery. Almost, but not quite, but then again maybe that had more to do with her state of mind than with anything else.

There was no one in the lobby, and she went ahead and took the elevator up to the seventh floor as the attorney had instructed. The entire floor was occupied by the law firm of Parker and Williams. She breathed in again, bracing herself, and walked on the colorful checkered tiles toward the receptionist's desk, also empty.

"Ms. Andrews?"

She turned around to see a man coming to stand a distance from her. He was thin, delicate almost, and the same height as her. His face was longish, clean-shaven, his blond hair slicked back, every strand in place. There was a smile on his face, a friendly expression, but he was clearly scrutinizing her. Which was only fair, she supposed, since she was scrutinizing him, too.

There was nothing threatening about him, in fact he seemed amiable enough. But not for a moment did she forget that this man was an attorney. And a high level one, quite obviously. His three-piece suit was meticulously pressed, custom-tailored, and very expensive. Too expensive for the offices they were in, that much was certain. This man didn't belong here. Not in this building, and not, she thought, in this city.

He approached her with a measured step, extending a well-manicured hand. His shake was light and formal.

"Thank you for meeting me, and at such a short notice," he said and led her to a large office at the end of a wide corridor. The name on the door was that of Gerald A. Parker, Senior Partner. The photos along the corridor walls were enough to show her that this man was not him.

She declined his offer of a refreshment and waited, standing, facing him. Careful. She had long ago learned to be careful.

"May I close the door?" he surprised her by asking. "Several of this firm's attorneys are here, in their offices, and I would like to have privacy for this conversation, if that is all right with you."

She nodded. He closed the door and came to sit not behind the desk, but on one of the chairs beside a long, rectangular table that stood not far from it. The chair farthest from the door and from her.

Making sure she wouldn't feel threatened, she thought. This man wanted her to listen, and to focus on what he was saying, not on anything else. And he was aware that for her he was nothing but a stranger who had called unexpectedly on a Saturday morning, so far giving her nothing in return for the trust he had asked of her.

Now she was curious.

She took a seat opposite his, the closest one to the door, putting the table between them.

He nodded. "I've asked a lot of you. And yet I have two more things to ask."

She waited.

"First, I would like you to hear me out before I tell you who I am." He gestured to indicate the office around him. "You've quite obviously noticed that this is not my office and have guessed that I don't work in this law firm, although I can tell you that Gerald Parker is a trusted colleague, which is why we are sitting in his offices on a Saturday."

She considered this. "And the second thing?"

"I need you to promise me to keep this conversation between us. Regardless of its outcome."

She frowned. "Why not simply have me sign a non-disclosure agreement, then?"

He wasn't surprised at her familiarity with the option, considering her work. "This matter involves a great deal of trust. That trust has to begin somewhere," he said evenly. It was, in fact, the most crucial element in their conversation.

She contemplated this, and him. He found the eyes that held his disconcerting. Highly intelligent, calculating. Not unlike his client, he thought. And there was something else there, too, something he couldn't quite put his finger on.

Finally, she nodded once. "You have my word."

He was taken aback at her choice of words, and she saw this.

"I apologize, it's just that I don't usually hear people say it quite that way. My client does, too," he chose to tell her. "Which brings me to the crux of the matter. I have a proposal for you."

She waited, intrigued. She'd already understood that, contrary to her initial concern, this had nothing specifically to do with her, her work, her life. Her past. All that was left, then, was her curiosity.

"As I said, I am an attorney. For one client. A very rich and powerful client." He watched her. She watched him back. Good. Most people had some reaction to those words, usually fear or greed. Or both, in most cases. She had neither.

He paused, not sure how to do this. It was, he realized, more complicated to put it forward than he had thought it would be. Both because of the nature of the proposal he was making to this woman, who was not quite the type he had thought he would be making it to, and because of the necessity to hide his client's identity.

He considered his words carefully, not wanting to point her in the right direction. In the past weeks alone his client's name had been constantly on the gossipers' lips, mentioned too many times for it to be missed. And as it was he had worried, before their meeting, that she might recognize him, and thus understand who he was representing in this matter. After all, he occasionally joined his client in business meetings, or at certain social functions, with his wife. And his photo appeared on Ian Blackwell Holdings' website, since he was its general counsel. She would have seen him if she had in fact followed his client on the media, or, frankly, had simply looked deeper into the company that had bought InSyn. Apparently she hadn't done either, which he found interesting.

"Because of his status," he proceeded to say, speaking slowly, "my client's relationships with women are too often too closely watched. In addition, my client finds that at times it would be easier to have a woman by his side, to . . ." He struggled to find the words.

"You're having quite a bit of difficulty with this, aren't you?"

He started. Then he laughed. He hadn't expected that. "It shows?"

She nodded, a shadow of a smile on her face. "Just say it like it is. What's the worst that can happen?"

"Right," he said. "Right. Here it is, then. My client wishes to marry a woman who will not be his wife in the . . . biblical sense of the word, if you will, but more like a business partner. Someone who will be present at the various social functions he is required to attend, with him or in his stead, someone who will, for all outward intents and purposes, be known as his wife, taking the . . . eligible bachelor title away." He risked it, willing to bet that she had no idea who Cecilia Heart was.

It was her turn to be taken aback, but she collected herself quickly. "A contract marriage. In the twenty-first century."

"The twenty-first century with its media and social media frenzy, the too readily, too immediately available information that is all too often inaccurate, can pose quite a lot of difficulty for a man like my client. It has become very disruptive, if I do say so myself."

She tilted her head slightly, and Robert allowed himself a smile. The reality he was describing wasn't familiar to her. Good. It seemed that this world, the world of gossip, of celebrities, of runaway impressions, did not appeal to her.

"The outside world will not know that this is a business arrangement," he continued. "It is quite easy to say that you two have been meeting in secret for a while." Especially since she worked in one of Ian's companies, although this was something Robert could not yet say. "If they believe it, fine, if they talk, then they will, but at least, whatever they think, he will still have a wife, and even nowadays that counts for something. Especially if the marriage lasts, and follows a set of careful guidelines, which I have already drawn in detail."

She wasn't telling him he was crazy, nor was she running away. By now he found he wasn't surprised. Whatever the outcome, this woman would hear him out as she had promised.

"You would be married in a private civil ceremony. The media will talk about that, too, the absence of a big wedding, but they will talk no matter what my client does. I'll make sure they blame their own prying behavior for this. You will move into my client's home, where you will have your own room, your privacy, of course. At no point"—he emphasized, wanting her to understand, to be sure, wanted her to be the one to accept the proposal—"will you be required to be his wife in any way other than outwardly. In other words, he will not touch you."

She had understood that part from the outset, which was why she was still there.

"However, the two of you will be putting up the facade of a married couple, so you will need to get to know each other. To learn to be comfortable around each other, at least to the required extent. I have therefore inserted a clause requiring the two of you to spend at least one meal a day together, when you are both in the city." He was careful not to say which city. "I have also added another clause requiring my client to refer to you in your conversations as Mrs. . . . let's say X, for the time being, and you will refer to him as Mr. X."

When she frowned, he added, "You are strangers who will need to prove to the outside world that you are far from it. This clause is meant to ensure that you get used to the new arrangement as quickly as possible. This simple form of address will remind you constantly of what you had both agreed to and will therefore reduce the risk of slip-ups during your appearances in the outside world." He couldn't tell her that he suspected she and his client would not be assuming the comfortably familiar use of first names anytime soon. "Outwardly, when speaking to others, you will refer to him as your husband, and he will refer to you as his wife. At least until we convince the outside world of the authenticity of the marriage."

"What about outward affection?"

"My client is a private man. He doesn't normally exhibit physical affection when he goes out with a woman. It would, I imagine, be accepted that he would adhere to the same privacy in his marriage."

"Good," she said. That, no displayed affection in this deal of a marriage, was certainly acceptable to her. In fact, it would be a deal breaker if it weren't so, and she said so now.

He nodded. Interesting that this was her emphasis. He wondered about her, but the fact was that the more he sat here with her, spoke with her, saw her reactions, the more he liked her for his client's wife.

"You've thought this through." She contemplated him.

"Necessarily so. This is quite a complex matter."

"That's an understatement," she said.

"Please understand, this idea was not arrived at lightly. And yes, it will be complex, you would understand why if you knew who my client is. Also, you should know it is intended to be a long-term arrangement. The contract will not set a term in order not to limit either of you, and if you absolutely do not get along or if anything else happens that would require it to be voided, this can be done. But obviously this is something my client wishes to avoid. The chosen wife would be expected to remain by his side for a significant term."

"The chosen wife." Her brow furrowed. "Your client doesn't know about me, does he?"

"No more than you know about him."

"What kind of a man sends an attorney to choose his partner in marriage for him?"

"But that's just it. I am choosing a *partner* in marriage, a business partner."

"Still." She considered this, not quite sure what to think. But then the entire situation was surreal. "To come to this."

He let her think about it for a while. Digest it. "This won't be easy for whoever accepts this proposal, either, not only for my client, please don't think either I or my client are overlooking this fact," he finally said. "For you specifically it would mean leaving your job and your home, and moving to a strange city to live a strange life in a strange house with a stranger."

"Well put," she said, and didn't tell him that the first three she'd been planning to do anyway, and, in any case, she had never called this place home. There wasn't, for her, any place she could call home, hadn't been for too long for her to remember what it was like for it to be any other way.

"My client acknowledges this," he continued. "He wishes to provide you with at least some sort of a safety net, other than the contract, of course. Something that would be yours without any precondition, and that you can use as you wish if you ever feel the need to. For this reason, he has instructed me to open, when the time comes, a bank account in your name only, with a substantial sum that would make you quite comfortable. It would be yours to do with as you please, no questions asked. But note that you will not need it while this arrangement is in effect. As his wife, you will be provided with everything you need or want. My client insists on it."

"This shouldn't be a part of your proposal," she remarked, preoccupied with what she'd heard so far, putting things in context. Hers.

"I'm sorry?"

"Too early for you to say this. The promise of wealth can't keep a woman in the type of situation you're describing, unless she is greedy for it, for the status, for the opportunities that would benefit her. And that, I think, is not the type of woman you want to trust with keeping your client's interests."

"At this moment I'm hoping I won't need to make this proposal to anyone else," he said frankly. "In truth, I believe you are it."

She looked at him in surprise.

"I consider myself a good judge of character, Ms. Andrews. It comes with the territory. And with the personality, or so my wife says."

She smiled at that. She found she liked him. And unfortunately, she had also had to learn to be a fair judge of character.

"It is clear to me that it is not the money that would appeal to you, Ms. Andrews, which is why I wanted to get it out of the way. Truthfully, I don't know why you would wish to do this, to enter into this contract, and I'm not asking. I just think that you are the right person for it. For my client."

"You need a woman with social skills, a woman who has already been a part of the society you're describing, the rich and famous, if I understand correctly. Who would know how to play the role of a socialite alongside that of the wife of a wealthy business man."

"I thought so too. That was my original plan, the

socialite part of it, I confess. But I think"—he considered how best to put it—"I think that aspect of it can be learned, and I think that what you specifically will bring to this role is just what it may need."

She frowned at that, but this, this he would say no more about.

"Allow me another caveat at this time," he added with a bit of hesitation. "You must understand that the requirements of this arrangement are quite strict. While you are married to my client, you will not be able to date. To . . ."

"Sleep with anyone," she said with some humor. "And I assume he will?"

Robert was finding this more difficult than he had imagined he would. And not only because of the task itself. This extraordinary woman deserved more than this. "Yes, he will. But when he does, he will do so discretely, and never in the house he will be sharing with you. That too is in the contract. He is not one to humiliate a woman, any woman, and he will act toward you with all due respect, Ms. Andrews, that much I can promise."

"In this era of the constant exposure that you yourself have mentioned, things come out eventually. I wouldn't want to be blindsided. That, whether your client intends it or not, would be hurtful."

He nodded. "He is a powerful man. Power can do a lot."

She said nothing.

She has no reason to trust either me or my

client, Robert thought. "I cannot ensure that he will tell you if and when he chooses to . . . date. But if I assure you of a certain openness in this matter, such as if there is any concern of . . . let's call it a breach of discretion, will that be satisfactory?"

After a slight hesitation, she nodded.

"You are concerned about that, but not about the fact that this arrangement would require you to be alone? You are, if I may say so, a young woman, you turned twenty-nine about . . . three months ago, did you not? You certainly have all the qualities that would give you more than enough chance of being in a true relationship, a real marriage."

"And yet you chose me," was all she said, indicating that she presumed he had checked her out, knew the solitary life she led. Which she was not inclined to discuss.

He nodded. This was purely his curiosity about her speaking, not the necessity of the matter at hand. Still, he thought he should be more perturbed than he was about what he was getting his client—what he was getting both these two—into.

He wasn't. She was perfect, perfect for the man who was, indeed, his client, but first and foremost his closest friend. And he knew now what it was about her that he hadn't been able to put a finger on earlier. Yes, she was highly intelligent, like Ian Blackwell, and calculated, like Ian Blackwell. But she was also, where it counted, completely and entirely inaccessible.

Just like Ian Blackwell.

He thought she would need time. Not to absorb the proposal. That she already had, this was quite clear. But to decide. This was not an easy choice to make.

Instead, she went straight to the point. "What if I refuse?"

"I have your word that you will keep this conversation to yourself. It's enough." He found he didn't even need to think about it, which only increased his hope that she would say yes.

"And if I agree?"

"I have the detailed contract here."

She nodded slowly, a slight furrow in her brow. He got up and took a laptop out of a briefcase that sat on the desk behind him, brought up the document and put the laptop on the table in front her, then went back to his seat. "If there are any changes you wish to make, mark them in there." He thanked heavens he was professional enough to contain his excitement. Was that a yes?

True, he had expected her to think about it. And he might have prodded her to do so himself. But this woman, his gut told him not to let her go.

Chapter Four

Tess parked at the curb in front of Jayden and Aisha's house. The car would be taken away by the company InSyn had leased it from on Monday morning, by which time she would no longer be InSyn's employee. From now on—from an hour earlier, to be exact—her life would be dictated by the arrangement the attorney had proposed.

That was the deal. She had not signed the contract yet but had consented to do so. The attorney had answered all her questions enthusiastically and had made changes where these were required, where the contract now pertained specifically to her. The document itself was extremely well thought out, extremely thorough. It spelled out the next day of her life and onward. Her life, and that of the mystery man she would be marrying.

The irony did not elude her. She was marrying an unknown man and walking into complete uncertainty. Her. Yes, the irony was certainly there. Even the attorney was still an unknown. He had begged off telling her his name until the next time they met, and she had agreed, thinking that the unknown she had already agreed to would not be reduced by her knowing who he was. And it didn't really matter. Nothing did, not anymore. What she had done was, quite simply, the only course of action she could have taken to keep Jayden from harm. It was the perfect solution to avoid hurting the one man who had been protecting her all these years, and for her it was no worse than what she had already been through.

It had to be done, and she would go through with it. The next morning, in fact, when she would be flying by private jet to wherever it was she would be living in from then on. The jet, the attorney had explained, was also where the final contract would be signed.

She got out of the car and stood looking at the main house. After a long moment she took in a deep breath and went inside to speak to Jayden and Aisha. Her words were simple. She was leaving. They could contact her on her phone, which she would be taking with her. Whatever they would hear in the coming days, they should speak to her about it directly, ask her anything they would like to know. She didn't have to ask them not to listen to rumors, she knew they wouldn't, not when it came to her. Nor did she have to ask them not to speak about her, about what she was doing, to anyone, not even at InSyn.

She said nothing else, not wanting them to have to lie. She wanted them to be able to say they knew nothing and for this to be the truth. She knew they would accept was she was saying and doing. They had never questioned her before, and never would. They cared about her for who she was, and she trusted them for a reason. At least, she thought with some relief, there was no longer need for her to cut them out of her life.

After leaving them, she went to her apartment and packed one bag, a small suitcase she'd borrowed from Aisha. For weather that hadn't been much different in the past days from the weather where she was now, that much the attorney had told her. Just enough for a few days, he had assured her all her needs would be taken care of within as short a time as possible. Anything else she wanted to take would be packed and shipped to her, with Jayden and Aisha's help.

As for the abrupt termination of her employment at InSyn, it would be dealt with, the attorney had not elaborated how. There was the matter of her bank account, but the attorney had assured her that it too would be taken care of. She lived modestly and had rather substantial savings, since she had been paid well by the company that appreciated her, and while the arrangement made sure she would not require that money, it was hers, well earned, and it would be transferred into her new account.

With everything being taken care of for her, there was nothing else she needed to do. The last thing she did that day was decide what she would wear the next morning. She settled for simplicity—a pair of blue jeans, a simple shirt, an equally simple jacket.

This was her they were getting, it would still be her no matter what.

She barely slept that night. In the morning she was as ready as she could be, had only to take a last look around the apartment she had lived in for the past twelve years and say her goodbyes to the only two people she cared about.

A black sedan with tinted windows and an impassive driver arrived at the assigned time to take her to the airport. Centennial Airport, the driver informed her when she asked, and she was relieved that it wasn't Denver International. She didn't think she could face the bustle of a large airport, not that day. The driver took her suitcase without another word and put it in the trunk of the car, then opened the back door and waited. She hesitated, and turned to look at Jayden and Aisha, who stood before their house, their arms around each other, concern for her on their faces.

She got into the car.

As it took her away, she turned back and looked at the place she had lived in for almost half her life as it grew smaller. Her gaze turned up to the open sunroof, to the sky passing overhead, fast, faster, as if in a hurry to have her gone.

She closed her eyes.

They made it to the airport in no time, then drove straight through to the hangars. Tess had never been there before, but she didn't look around her, didn't care to. Alone in the back seat, she tried to relax, failing miserably. Not surprising, considering that she was walking into a whole new dimension of unknowns.

The car approached one of the hangars, drove around it and stopped in the back, near a door that opened to reveal the attorney. Tess heard him instructing the driver to put her luggage on the jet, and then he opened the car's back door himself.

"Ms. Andrews, good to see you again," he greeted her with enthusiasm as she got out.

"I think under the circumstances you can call me Tess," she said, her voice quiet.

"Very well. And under the circumstances, by the way, I am about to officially become *your* attorney, too. So I should probably finally introduce myself." He smiled. "My name is Robert Ashton, but do call me Robert."

She gave no indication that she recognized his name, and his smile widened. "This way," he said, and led her through the door into the hangar.

She stopped in the doorway. In the middle of the hangar stood a large aircraft, silvery white with a black stripe curving smoothly along its side, shiny in the internal light of the vast closed space. Its door was open, the stairs down, but there was no one around it, they were alone. She stared. She had never seen a private jet before, not this close up.

"This is my client's personal jet," Robert said, kindness in his voice. He could understand the reaction. "He prefers to use it rather than his company's jets, he likes his privacy. Much like you, I believe." And he guided her to the aircraft.

Inside, Ian glanced irritably at the time on his laptop. He wanted to be on his way. As it was he hadn't planned to stay the extra night in Denver. He had concluded his business at InSyn the previous evening and could have been in his office by now. Robert could have flown her, whoever she was, in one of the company's executive jets, and they would have met later in the day to conduct their . . . business. He didn't like wasting time.

Although he had spent at least part of the night working at his hotel suite and the past few hours working here, conducting a conference call with his London office. So time, a small voice in his head argued, was not really wasted. He refused to admit to himself that he was, quite simply, nervous because Robert had refused to tell him who the woman was whom he had chosen or to provide any details other than to say that she was perfect, or that it bothered him that Robert had made such an important decision so quickly. He had read the draft contract, and, yes, it was as good as he had expected the attorney to prepare. It also showed him that, not surprisingly, his friend had an accurate understanding of his needs and his reasoning. But to settle on a woman, a *wife*, this quickly?

He shook his head and focused on his work again. Or at least tried to.

Tess walked up the narrow stairs. Slowly, bracing herself. Robert followed a few steps behind her, giving her space.

She walked in. The jet was empty, as Robert had requested it to be. Empty except for the man who sat on one of the plush seats just ahead and who now raised his eyes from the laptop he was working on.

He stood up in surprise just as Tess froze in place.

"Tess Andrews, Ian Blackwell," Robert said earnestly.

The two stared at each other. Then they both turned to Robert, who took a step back at the anger in their eyes, raising his hands with his palms outward.

"Wait, just hold on. Hear me out." He motioned Tess inside. "Please."

She hesitated, then finally took a few more steps into the cabin while Ian remained where he was.

"I think . . . no, I'm sure, that the two of you together can pull this off perfectly—"

"So you're here to have another go at me?" Ian interjected icily, his words aimed at the woman who just wasn't supposed to be there.

"Why, are you planning to get all big and

powerful again when you talk to a loyal employee? Any other companies you plan to destroy while you get your way?" Tess answered his ice with her own fire.

"You have no right to interfere in what you don't understand."

"I will interfere in what I damn well please, and it is you who had no understanding of the situation. Funny, I thought they said you're a competent businessman. Or is running over others enough to build fancy conglomerates nowadays?"

Ian laughed mirthlessly. "You're who he chose? And I'm supposed to trust you by my side when we can't even spend five seconds together?"

The slap of a magazine on the table Ian had been working on made them both jump. The glossy affair was one of those print issues still popular even in the days of digital access, full of the type of gossip that would always have enough appeal to sell.

They were on the cover. Both of them. Someone had taken an image of a moment they had stood close enough to each other and had manipulated it to look as if they were, in fact, standing together. Tess recognized the setting immediately. InSyn's basement. With its spanning security camera coverage, of course.

"Allow me," Robert said with exaggerated politeness. He picked up the magazine again, every move deliberate, opened it, then cleared his throat with a dramatic flair and read, "And who is that with our

yummy Pounce-For Bachelor this time? The myste-
rious beauty is undoubtedly his latest—"

Ian raised his hand, indicating for him to stop.
Tess could do nothing but stare.

Robert put the magazine back down, open to the
colorful double feature. "This is from the one time
you met. One time. You met, you had a fight, you
moved on, all in the basement of an obscure building well away from where you live your life, Ian.
And yet this photo came to be, an entire piece in a
gossip magazine came to be, and, I've got news for
you two, it was already mentioned on two shows
this morning and social media is having a ball. I'm
guessing Davis was angry because you got rid of her
instead of Tess here, Ian, but that's just me."

Ian was seething. "I'll deal with her."

"I have no doubt you will. But, Ian, this is exactly the type of thing your idea, this arrangement, was
intended to stop. And Tess"—he turned to her—"I
really don't know anything about you. Despite the
report I have on you, and you know that I do. I only
know two things. One, there is a reason, and I'm
not asking you what it is, nor will I, because, frankly, I trust you, but for that reason you've agreed to
replace your life with a completely different one with
a man whose identity you didn't even know, and
without so much as flinching. And two, you can do
this, and you can do this like no one else can. She
can, and I'm telling you she is the right person to,"
he addressed Ian again, and the way he said it made

Ian stop and focus on the friend he trusted like he trusted no one other than less than a handful of other people in the world.

"Fine," he said. "I'll do this. We'll work it out. Let's sign the damn contract."

"Fine," Tess said, thinking about her reasons for having to do this. The attorney was, quite simply, right.

"Fine with me, too," Robert said. "The magazine article will, I believe, add in this case to the facade you two will be putting up from now on." He went over to his briefcase, which was sitting on a seat across the aisle, and took out three copies of the final contract. One for each of them, and the third for him, the official one. He placed the documents on the table. "Here," he said, handing Ian his pen.

"Right," Ian grumbled. He took the pen from him and signed all copies.

"This too." Robert flipped to the last page of his own copy. A marriage certificate was attached to the contract, already filled in, signed by a judge and authorized, including Tess's name change.

Ian looked at him.

"I arranged for it last night. I thought it would be more convenient than having a judge actually be present for this." The things money could do. "Sign."

Ian did so with a finality to it that had a pang of regret go through his friend, and then handed the pen to Tess without looking at her.

This is the only way, she said to herself one last

time. The only way.

And she signed.

Robert witnessed the signatures. "One more detail," he said, pushing away the last of his regret. It was done, there was no going back now. He took a small box out of his briefcase and held it open for them to see.

They both stared.

"It will do what you want it to do. That is, if the two of you behave as agreed. It will convince everyone around you that you are married. People still tend to think of this one small symbol that way, and regardless of what they think of this marriage, your wearing this will go a long way toward convincing them."

Neither moved.

"Go on." He took the rings out himself and handed each of them one. Without looking at each other, they put the simple gold bands on.

"Simple, yes, devoid of emotion, I would think. But then so is this marriage ceremony, isn't it?" he couldn't help saying.

They both shot him poisonous glances. He didn't care. Marriage, to him, was sacred. He had fallen in love and had courted his wife for a year before she'd even agreed to date him. His marriage was his life. His wife and two kids, they were his life. The man and woman before him were giving that up far too easily.

"And this one is also for you," he said to Tess and

handed her the third item he had in the box.

This ring was different. Delicate, it boasted a series of small stones. Tess frowned at it.

"It's your engagement ring. I chose it myself," Robert said dryly.

Not looking at either of them, she put it on.

The jet took off shortly after Robert called the crew in. The silence in the cabin was deafening. Ian sat in his accustomed place, his wife in the seat opposite his, where Robert had insisted she sit. He himself had moved farther away after hammering into them the precise rules he had set for their marriage.

"So InSyn will need to replace you after all." It was easier for Ian to think about business.

"Jayden can take care of things in the meantime, we've been working side by side for years and he knows what I did there, he knows everyone and everything at InSyn. If need be, he can call me."

"You're no longer an InSyn employee."

"True, but I'm leaving, quite suddenly, a good company with good people, and I will do all I can to help them."

"I'm sure my company can do without you," Ian said with sarcasm he did not really intend. But then she seemed to provoke something in him, something that made him react.

"It can," Tess retorted. "But I can make things easier for it. As it is the takeover has been far more difficult than it should have been." The insinuation against him was clear, despite the quiet voice, or perhaps because of it.

"My transition team knows how to do its job and Pythia Vision is by now experienced enough in its work with InSyn."

"Your previous transition team brought in Davis. You brought in Davis." Maybe she didn't feel like being subtle after all.

She was right. Ian didn't need her to tell him he had allowed a grave mistake to be made. "She may have done what she did, but she knew her job."

"She acted in a way that has impaired InSyn's ability to function properly. And all she did the day before yesterday was react emotionally to a business situation and threaten to slow InSyn down to a crawl by getting rid of your two data experts just to impress you." Tess's eyes narrowed. "And you know what, forget that Jayden is the best person you can have working at InSyn. For him what he does there is his life's work, he's been with it from the very beginning and has put everything he is into it. He loves that company, and it needs him. InSyn, its people, they rely on him. Firing Jayden was the worst thing Davis could do." Thinking about her friend only made her even more angry at this man who had allowed Davis to hurt him. "And then when you fired her she apparently turned on you, too, acted against you in the exact same way that got you into this marriage plan in the first place."

"You are good at stating the obvious," Ian said

icily, but all she did was raise an eyebrow at his tone of voice, which only irritated him more. Still, he was taking pleasure in the fact that he was obviously irritating her equally effectively. "Davis is no longer an employee of Ian Blackwell Holdings, and her actions will have consequences. As for InSyn, the new transition team will do its job well, and InSyn will thrive, as all my subsidiaries do."

Tess shook her head. She cared about InSyn and didn't want to see it harmed. "InSyn has a complex personality and operating structure. If you fail to maintain it, it will fall apart and what you need from it will be useless. You need to take care of the people and let them do their thing." This came out more harshly than she had meant it to. All she wanted was to explain what she knew about the unique company, but his arrogance was getting to her.

The ice in Ian's eyes only grew colder. "See? It's a good thing that you explained this to me since this is my first day on the job. Oh wait, I built a multinational conglomerate worth a small country's GDP over less than a decade and a half. I might actually know what I'm doing."

Robert's jaw dropped at the exchange. They were at it again. Damn, he thought. I really did make the right choice. He didn't know Tess well enough, but he had certainly never seen Ian react to anyone this way. Nor had he ever seen anyone who matched him, or dared to.

"Now now, kids," he said. "A honeymoon is not

supposed to be this prickly." He was, and sounded, amused.

They both turned to him angrily.

"Ah, see? Now you two agree on something."

With a double icy stare at him, they turned back to face each other again and fell silent.

Chapter Five

The back of the car had never been as uncomfortable for Ian as it was now. He had sat here alone countless times. He had sat here many times with business associates. And he had sat here quite a few times with some woman or other beside him, and those times there had mostly been some touching involved, naturally. But he had never sat here with his wife. Nor had he ever been so distant, in every possible way, from whoever had shared this space with him.

He glanced at her. She was looking out the tinted window, her gaze distant, her expression blank. He wondered what was going through her mind. What kind of a woman was she to do this, he asked himself for the hundredth time since they had signed the contract. When he'd thought Robert's choice would be what he himself had dictated, he'd known the answer to that. A woman who put her societal image first, who wanted to enjoy, if not to share, the wealth, the power, the status that came with being Ian Blackwell's wife.

Tess Andrews seemed to be nothing like that, and

he couldn't begin to make sense of her or of why she would be here with him now, a wedding ring that matched his on her finger. He thought about what Robert had said to her before the impromptu ceremony—it seemed to him that his friend didn't know much about her either, and yet it was her he had chosen, and seemingly without hesitation. Ian looked forward to reading the report on her that Ira Gold had put together, which Robert had told him about but had refused to send him until after he met her. Should he? the question came to his mind. Of course, was the immediate answer. After all, she wasn't his wife, not really, not a woman he had chosen to get to know, fall in love with, start a relationship with. She was a business partner, and he always ran a check on business partners.

It would also go toward ensuring the success of this arrangement that had to last, he reasoned with himself. It had already gone this far, too far, and there was no going back, so it might as well be proceeded with in the best way possible. This had to be done. It had been his choice to begin with, his idea, and he would make it work.

He cleared his throat and tried this, in the way Robert had set out in detail in the contract, one of the habits that needed to be adopted by them both to allow his plan to proceed in a believable manner.

"Mrs. Blackwell," he said, keeping a carefully neutral tone.

She started and turned her head to look at him.

Well, it worked, he thought. She did respond.

"Are you okay?" he surprised himself by asking. But then it made sense for him to do so, he reasoned some more. He at least was coming back to his life. Hers had already changed completely in a matter of hours.

She contemplated him, tilting her head just a bit, her eyes a soft dark amber in the dim light of the car. "I'm somewhat out of my depth here," she finally admitted.

He waited.

"Mr. Blackwell," she added, and the slightest furrow appeared between those pretty eyes.

He nodded. "As promised, I will ensure that you are as comfortable as possible," he said, making an effort to sound amiable. "Everything else will come with time." At least he hoped so. He couldn't see this woman who worked in a basement in a plain shirt and jeans mingling with the rich and famous in an evening gown, or, worse, facing those damn gossip reporters and bloggers and their pushy questions, or the far too many cameras everywhere. Nor was he sure that she could handle the business media or stand by his side when he hosted his business associates.

He wasn't at all sure about this.

He sighed inwardly and focused on the more immediate reality this woman would be required to deal with. "I live in Woodside, about half an hour south of here. That's where we're headed." They had landed in San Francisco International Airport and had disembarked inside his private hangar, alone again except for his trusted aircrew and the driver of the crystal black over gray Bentley Mulsanne that had come to stand beside the jet. The woman he had married just hours earlier had said nothing, had asked nothing, as they entered the car and set out to his home.

"My household comprises two live-in staff," he continued. "Everybody else lives in town and comes in as needed. I prefer it that way. Graham Eaton runs the house, in fact he runs my entire domestic life for me. And Lina, Lina Mills, she helps Graham, and now that you're here, she'll make sure you have everything you need, much like Graham does for me. They are the only two people you will regularly have around you, the others you won't know are there if you don't want to. Graham and Lina are used to ensuring no one interferes with my routine and they will do the same for you." He was giving her quite a bit of information, but she was clearly absorbing every word. "I don't usually entertain in my home. I like my privacy, which is severely lacking outside it. So you will have all the time you need to get used to the house and to everyone in it. What's wrong?" That slight furrow appeared in her brow again. That, and a bit of apprehension in her eyes, it seemed to him.

"Nothing, I just . . . I guess I didn't expect more people around us."

"You'll get used to it, to being taken care of. Money has its perks." He stopped. He hadn't meant to sound cynical. Shouldn't have. This woman obviously didn't care about wealth or status. She was not about greed, that much he could tell, and, in fact, seemed wary of the luxury that now surrounded her.

When he spoke again, his voice was somewhat softer. "Graham has been with me for over a decade now, almost since the beginning. And I hired Lina when I bought the house a couple of years ago." He hesitated, then continued, giving something of himself. He was, after all, determined to give this a real chance. "I got tired of living in a condo in the city where I could too easily be found and bothered, and I happened to drive through Woodside one day, it seemed quiet, out of the way. My house is in the hills, it's surrounded by expansive grounds and is very private. I have everything I need there, for my —our use." He frowned. She would see for herself soon enough. She would, of course, have unlimited access to the entire house, no sense setting undue restrictions that might antagonize her.

"The only other person you will encounter regularly is the chauffeur of this car, Jackson Green. Like the jet, the Bentley—this car—is owned by me, not by my company, and Jackson works directly for me. He lives in town with his family, but has always been unfailingly available when I needed him. Now that you're here I would prefer that you use him, so when you need this car I'll be using a company limo or one of my other cars."

"I can drive."

"You won't have to, and I would rather you be accompanied by a professional driver. And Jackson is also a trained bodyguard."

She frowned. "Bodyguard."

He let her absorb the implications of what he'd told her. "I realize it's overwhelming," he said quietly. "Just let them all do their jobs. They know what to do."

"Do they know . . . about us?" she asked in a low voice, looking out of the window again.

"Graham knows everything, he is crucial to the success of this arrangement. And I trust him," he added, stressing the point. For her sake. "Lina and Jackson know of the nature of this arrangement, of course, since we will not actually be living as husband and wife. But they only know what's necessary. Graham will make sure they know more if the need arises. And they all know that you are a complete stranger to this life." He watched her. "They are good people, Mrs. Blackwell. They've been with me long enough to understand why I'm doing this, and they will help you."

What will they think of me? Tess wondered, but said nothing. The notion of living not just with this man but with a staff, his staff, was daunting to her. She hadn't considered the possibility. She had lived by herself for so long, just her in that tiny apartment on top of Jayden and Aisha's garage, and had always taken care of herself. Been alone. And now. . .

Ian saw the anxiety, the struggle. Watched her win it. She was, he thought with interest, quite a fighter.

The bustle of the city soon made way to quiet hills, and for a time they traveled on gently winding roads, with scenery that might have soothed Tess if it wasn't for the circumstances she was in. Soon enough, too soon, the Bentley slid smoothly through heavy gates with the name Blackwell embossed on them in brass letters. They drove down a path that took them to the heart of the exclusive property, winding through woods that cast gentle shade on the car as it passed through, with the occasional meadow in between them, green ruling at times, colorful flowers dominating in places. It looks peaceful, Tess thought, wondering in the silence of the car if birds were singing outside in the lively sun, but she made no move to open the window, to let life in.

She finally saw the house peeking among trees in the distance as they came around a hill, seeing more of it as the car rounded a lake that wound lazily on their left. When the car finally stopped in front of the house, he—her husband, she had to remind herself this was how she should think of him for this facade to work—got out of the car without waiting for Jackson to open the door for him, then walked around it to her side and held the car door open for her.

She got out slowly and looked at the house she would be living in from now on. It wasn't what she had expected. She had thought it would be cold, formidable, as overpowering as the man who lived there. And it was big, yes, what this man had described as his sanctuary. No doubt about that. She had seen the sprawling size of the two-story house as they drove toward it. But the stone cladding and the gable roofs spoke, most of all, of a warmth that fit this peaceful place she never would have imagined he would be living in.

Her husband stood quietly, patiently, a distance away. Giving her time, she supposed, which she needed. When she finally turned to look at him, he gave a slight nod and guided her to the front door, which stood open. The man who waited there was in his late forties, early fifties perhaps. Burly, with a face that made her think he might have been through his share of fights in his day. But his eyes were clever, and impassive. If there was judgment there, he hid it well.

When her husband introduced Graham, she nodded, a little overwhelmed. A lot overwhelmed, she had to admit. This brought home most acutely the need to deal with people other than the stranger she had married, which would be difficult enough. She had no idea how to begin doing this.

It was Graham who made the first move. "Mrs. Blackwell," he said and moved aside, welcoming her into the house.

He watched her as she walked in and stood just inside the doorway, looking around her. Hesitant, yes, but her head was held high in determination. He hadn't known, of course, who the woman would be that Mr. Blackwell would bring home, and all he could do was wait and see what he would think of her. Mr. Blackwell had certain standards when it came to women, and so he knew to expect nothing less. Mr. Blackwell was also quite diverse in his tastes, and so he had kept an open mind as to what he might encounter when Mr. Blackwell finally brought the woman home. And, of course, knowing all too well Mr. Blackwell's reasons for this rather unusual arrangement, and what it required, he had expected a confident social shark to come out of the Bentley and rush into the house, clad in fashionable attire and very meticulously made up, ready to have attention bestowed on her and her opinion heeded and obeyed. He had expected . . .

Not this. He hadn't expected this. The woman Mr. Blackwell had married was beautiful, but not just in the usual sense of the word. She had an elegance about her, something one didn't see much these days. And the eyes that were now taking in her surroundings and that had met his just moments before with uncertainty and, he thought, some wariness in them, were gentle and inquisitive. Nothing eager about her, nothing of what he had worried would be, the victory of catching a man like Ian Blackwell.

He had thought he would feel disdain, perhaps, certainly no respect, for the woman Ian Blackwell could buy. He was surprised that he felt nothing of the sort. What he felt, most of all, when he finally met the woman, *this* woman, was curiosity.

The company limo dropped Robert Ashton at his home, in the neighborhood of St. Francis Wood in San Francisco. He barely got out of the car before his son, Ben, opened the front door of the house with some difficulty and ran out to meet him. Robert swooped the five-year-old into his arms and turned to his wife, who followed the young boy, a bright smile on her face.

"Where's Emily?" he asked. Emily was their eight-year-old daughter. Almost nine, as she constantly reminded them, too eager to grow up.

"Pool party at a Gina's. We weren't entirely sure when you'll get back."

"Neither was I." Inside the house, Robert set his son down and gave his wife a heartfelt embrace. "They are going to kill each other," he said. "I let them go to Ian's house by themselves and they're going to kill each other, I tell you."

"That bad?" Muriel Ashton looked at her husband with concern.

"Worse."

"Really? What's she like?" Muriel asked.

"She was made for him," Robert answered, a wide grin on his face.

Tess walked in, her husband a measured distance behind her. Like the exterior of the house, here too, although it was clearly the house of a man who had it all, it was, first and foremost, a home. The floor was hardwood, in light tones. The entire hallway, in fact, was in light, inviting hues. To her right, an elegant wooden staircase with finely detailed ironwork railing wound gently to the left, up to the second floor, ending in a corridor that extended to both sides. Ahead of her she could see all the way to the other side of the house, where a trio of French doors stood open, giving her an enticing view of green foliage over garden furniture beyond and letting the smell of spring in.

Ian tried to put himself in her place, and found he wasn't entirely sure what he should do or say, which he wasn't used to. He knew what he would do if she were his real wife, if things were the way they should be, if they were each other's choice. But this was certainly far from the case. He also knew how he would act if she were the woman he had expected Robert to choose for him. For one thing, Graham would be the one conducting this tour, not him. The man who managed his household would be the one taking her through her first steps in the life she had been contracted to assume, he would be settling her in and familiarizing her with her husband's routine, his life inside and outside his home.

Ian wasn't entirely sure why he felt the need to give her the attention he was.

"Your room is this way." He led the way up the stairs and left, to the closest door. "It's one of the guest suites. The master bedroom, my room, is to the right of the stairs, in a separate wing from this one." He opened the door and walked in, the woman who was his wife following him. He took in the room and nodded, satisfied. "I had Graham and Lina prepare it as soon as Robert had informed me he had found someone to . . . fulfill the contract. It was prepared somewhat in a hurry, but I do hope it will suit your needs."

He turned to her. She was looking not around her but at him, and he suddenly realized the situation they were in.

No. The situation *she* was in, with him here, in what was to be her bedroom.

"I will not be coming in here again," he said firmly, his eyes on hers. That had to be made clear for this to work. "No one will, except for Lina, and except for anyone else authorized by you to do so." He paused, but she said nothing. "This is your home now, Mrs. Blackwell, and you will be made comfortable here and treated with due respect, as my wife," he added with finality. And with this he left, closing the door behind him.

Alone, Tess sat down on the edge of the bed, her heart racing. She took in a deep breath, and then another, but her hands wouldn't stop shaking.

Outside, Ian stood at the closed door, trying to get a hold of himself.

Both shared the same thought.

What the hell was I thinking?

Chapter Six

A knock on the door brought the woman who was now Tess Blackwell back to this place, to this moment, to the decision the consequences of which she had no choice but to face. She stood up and crossed the room to the door, which opened when she called out for whoever it was to come in.

Graham did not enter the room. Instead, he only placed the small suitcase Tess had brought with her immediately inside the door, and then motioned in a full-figured woman in her forties, a half a foot shorter than Tess, with a friendly expression and warm, matronly eyes.

"Mrs. Blackwell," Graham said as the woman entered the room, "this is Lina. She and only she will be in charge of this room, if that's all right with you."

"Thank you," Tess said to the woman and received a wide smile in return.

"Anything you need, you just tell me, ma'am," Lina said, her voice as cheery as her expression.

"Or me, where that is more convenient for you, ma'am," Graham said. "If I may, ma'am, you have an appointment with the personal stylists tomorrow, at ten in the morning."

"Stylists?"

"Yes, ma'am. Jackson will take you there. Also, Mr. Blackwell would like to have dinner with you this evening, if that's all right with you."

As per the contract, Tess thought, and nodded her consent. Might as well jump straight in.

"Until then, would you like something to eat, a light meal perhaps? I can prepare anything you like," Graham added.

"Thank you, but I'm not hungry," Tess said. Food was the furthest thing from her mind.

"Very well, then. I will leave you to get settled in, ma'am," Graham said and left her with Lina, who stood rooted in place. Waiting, Tess realized, for her instructions.

"I would appreciate your help here, Lina," she said to her. "You know the workings of this house, and I don't."

As she'd hoped it would, her frankness had the same effect on the other woman. "Don't you worry about a thing, ma'am," Lina said cheerily. "Anything you want to know, just ask me. May I?" She indicated the suitcase.

Tess nodded, feeling somewhat embarrassed. She wasn't used to this.

Lina opened the suitcase and walked around the room, efficiently placing each item where it belonged while chatting happily. Tess finally allowed herself to look at this place she would be sleeping in, her corner in the house she now shared with the stranger who was her husband.

It was spacious, the biggest bedroom she had ever seen. It was also tastefully furnished, the luxury understated, allowing cozy comfort to dominate. The colors were all white—walls, carpet, curtains and furniture alike, and even the television screen that hung in a recess in the wall. All except for the decorative pillows on the plush bed that stood with its headboard against the wall opposite the door and on the wingback tufted armchair that stood to one side with a low ottoman before it, beside a low round table, and except for the heavy curtains intermixed with the delicate white ones, to the right of the bed. These were all in soft magenta hues, bringing life to the room. The curtains were open to reveal dual French doors set in matching glass paneling, which led to a balcony overlooking the back of the house. The doors were open, and the room was airy and full of light, the gentle breeze from outside warm and fresh. The entire property, located where only the truly rich lived, those who valued their quiet sanctuary in a hectic life they had little respite from, seemed to be just that, a corner of peace.

She followed Lina through a door far to the left of the bed and found herself in a white and marble bathroom that looked to her like something from a luxury hotel, and then to another door that led to a walk-in closet, where Lina put in place what little clothes she had brought with her. The closet was huge, and she couldn't imagine being able to fill it. God, she thought, this bedroom is bigger than my entire apartment was.

"Don't worry, ma'am. This will be all filled up in no time."

Tess colored, realizing her awe and concern were showing.

"We'll make you feel at home here, Graham and I." Lina smiled.

"Why would you?" Tess asked. They had no reason to make her feel comfortable there. They knew perfectly well the arrangement she had entered into with the man they worked for, and no clue as to why she would do such a thing.

"You seem nice," Lina said simply. "And life has taught me, you see, so much can happen that we don't plan on. Not everyone judges, ma'am." And you look sad, she didn't say. You don't look greedy and pushy and arrogant like I was afraid you would be. You look lost.

Alone once again, Tess went out onto the balcony. She approached the railing and breathed in. Before her stretched the endless hills of woods and flower-spotted meadows that surrounded the house, giving it an isolated feel, a peaceful ambience. Below her, through the thick foliage of the trees, she saw stairs going down through thick grass to the lake, which shimmered in the sun, its water calm. She thought she saw a waterfall in the distance, but wasn't sure.

She didn't know what she had expected, but this place wasn't it. Here, even if only for a moment, she could forget it all, forget the deal she had made that had taken her from the only life she had known for so long to this house, to the man who was somewhere in it, waiting for her to be what he needed, and to a life she had no idea how to begin living.

This was a completely different world she was now in.

Ian went straight to his den. He would have liked to go to Blackwell Tower, even though it was Sunday, since he had been away for two days. But under the circumstances it made sense to remain in his home, make sure that his wife—he had to get used to thinking about her in this way—was comfortably settled in. Not only that, Robert and Ian Blackwell Holdings' public relations department would have already begun to circulate the rumor that he had gotten married, and they would have enough to deal with, with his surprise marriage to a woman no one had known he had in his life, or the fact that he had chosen not to take his new wife on a honeymoon, without him also showing up at his office on his first weekend home as a married man.

Work distracted him, to an extent. The rest was taken care of by his determination. He had done this for a reason, he reminded himself, and would stick to the plan, his plan. Although, perhaps he should have chosen his wife himself, considering Robert's choice, which was interesting, to say the least. Tess Andrews—Blackwell, he reminded himself—was far more of an unknown than he had bargained for. And he could not simply throw her into his world and let her contend with it, as he should have been able to do with a well-versed socialite. There was no doubt his wife would need to be helped, watched, controlled.

In fact, all considering, it looked as if he would have to control the entire situation more carefully than he had thought he would have to. But he was used to that, to exerting control. He was a powerful man for a reason. He left nothing to chance, and he had long learned to carefully plan all his moves well ahead. No, there was no reason at all to be distracted. He could handle anything that came his way. And that included her.

He returned to work, but the furrow in his brow remained.

He came to the dining room at the assigned time, as did she, and they stood facing each other. She was with those damn jeans again, a simple white shirt, her hair up in a ponytail. It wasn't that he minded, not too much, but it was a constant reminder that the woman he had married was nothing like he had thought she would be, what he needed her to be.

She was eying him impassively, and he realized his displeasure must have been showing. Forcing himself to behave, as Robert had so eloquently put it to both of them when he had seen them to the car earlier that day, he indicated the table.

Saying nothing, she approached it, and him. As she walked by him he reached out, without thinking about it, not meaning anything but to guide her to her place, and put his hand on the small of her back, as he had done with so many before her.

She stiffened and recoiled away from him, and he immediately removed his hand from her back. They stared at each other. She, with the shock of the touch she had not expected. He, with the shock of what he had seen in her eyes even as he had felt her reaction. Surprise. Surprise and . . .

It couldn't have been fear, he told himself. She had no reason to fear him, no reason for that or for the startled, quite nearly panicked reaction, yet she had flinched away from him, from his touch. Whatever it was, she had hidden it quickly. But it was too late. He had seen it and he had felt it. And it stung.

"I gave my word. As the arrangement that binds us dictates, there will be nothing between us." She didn't budge, and he felt rage threaten. He would not be perceived this way, not by anyone. Least of all by the woman who was meant to share too much of his life. "Let me make this clear. I have no wish to touch you." He no longer tried to hide the ice, the disdain in his voice. "But you do realize that, outwardly, there will have to be some proximity between us, no matter how much we both dislike it."

No, she hadn't realized it. Not really. There was

the contract, there were its terms, but reality had been too far away to imagine at the time, and she had not, never had the chance, never really had a choice, to think it through. And now this, that fleeting touch, brought reality home too sharply.

"I assure you such proximity will not go beyond standing close to you or touching you as I have just now," he was saying. "It is the least that would be expected of us as a married couple, even under the guise of privacy we are claiming."

She was barely listening, too busy trying to regain control of herself. It was nothing. This man could have any woman he wanted, he didn't need her. And in any case, it was, she remembered Robert explaining to her, in his interest to keep this arrangement viable for the long term, and he needed her to put up a facade that would not be marred by something that would not be appropriate between them.

Logic and the words the man she now had no choice but to call her husband was saying were hard at work, trying their best to calm her. But they were working against the fact that she was standing here, alone, with this man who was nothing like she had somehow, stupidly, thought—if she had thought at all, that hadn't been her focus at the time. Who was young, not that much older than her, who was in his prime and so much stronger than her. They were working against his touch, still fresh on her back.

And they were working against who she was.

No. She knew how to deal with this. She had

certainly had more than enough practice. And this man, he wasn't a threat. Not an immediate one, anyway. And if anything, she realized, finally managing to move beyond her own reaction, if anything, he seemed offended.

Dinner was even more strained than it would have been without yet another clash between them. Neither was particularly hungry, and neither wanted to be in that dining room. Both were there only because that was what the arrangement they had agreed to had dictated. And they were there, yes, but well away from each other, on the opposite ends of the dinner table, and with new uncertainty in each of them as to the other.

Ian, for one, had no idea what to think. He had never had such a reaction from a woman, hadn't expected it. He had never touched a woman against her will, he wasn't that kind of a man. Nor had he had any reason to expect such a reaction from the woman he had married, to whom the terms of the arrangement had been made clear, with emphasis on that specific aspect of it. In the time since their arrival at the house he'd had the chance to go over the report on her and there was nothing there to explain what had just happened.

Even as the thought passed through his mind, it slowed, came to a stop, and he contemplated it from all sides. That was just it. There was nothing in the report that could explain anything about her. Her life, her simple, very solitary life, presented nothing but questions.

He raised his eyes and looked at the woman he couldn't begin to figure out. Control the situation, he told himself. "Following your appointment tomorrow morning, I imagine you will have more suitable clothes to wear."

"There is no need for personal stylists. I'm perfectly capable of shopping for my own clothes," she answered.

"Perhaps. But while you might have a sense of fashion, which remains to be seen, you have not been a part of the world I live in. I have, and I need . . . my wife," he stressed the words, "to be suitably presentable."

He had a point. But she still had to fight her own indignation at the implication that she had no idea how to dress. "I assume, then, that you will be joining this little excursion to pick my clothes for me?"

He didn't miss the edge of fire in her voice. Control, he reminded himself. "No. Get acquainted with your new stylists. They will show you what you need to know, and then you can choose your clothes yourself." He paused, saw the temper, and couldn't resist. "If, later, I believe anything needs to be changed or added, or eliminated, for that matter, I will say so."

"Of course you will."

He didn't miss that either. Irritation crept into his voice when he spoke again. "In the house, you can dress as you wish. Outside it, you are my wife with all that this entails, as was agreed."

He was looking at the glass of white wine he was holding, and so he missed the slight narrowing of her eyes. But she said nothing. Once again, he had a point.

He did infuriate her, though.

Exerting control and making sure he got what he wanted from her was one thing, alienating her was another, Ian reminded himself. He needed this arrangement to last, at least for the required minimum amount of time, and he needed to get his way while it did. And that meant ensuring her compliance. "I did think, though, that it might be more comfortable for you if you don't do this alone. Robert's wife, Muriel, will be here in the morning, she will spend the day with you. She's a good friend, and she will help you in any way she can," he added before she could object, with what he hoped was a more agreeable tone.

She remained silent.

Dinner was as awkward as was to be expected, under the circumstances. The food was excellent, Tess had to admit. It was like dining in a Michelin-starred restaurant. But more than anything she wanted to withdraw to her room, have a moment to herself, try to ground herself with something, anything, before the onslaught of the days, the life, ahead.

Try to brace herself for the consequences of her decision, which were now her reality.

When Tess finally returned to her room, she closed the door behind her and locked it without thinking. Realizing the automaticity of the act, she stared at the door.

And left it locked.

She looked around her. Lina had been in here. The doors to the balcony were closed against the evening chill and the delicate curtains were drawn. She walked over to them, moved one of the curtains aside and looked through the clear glass at the world outside, now dark but for the gentle throw of lights scattered across the grounds closer to the house. Her gaze moved up to the night sky, to the gently glittering stars in the silent darkness. She stood this way for a long time before she finally moved away, letting the curtains fall back into place, leaving her in here alone.

Sleep did not come easily that night. Nor did it last.

On a television screen in his den, Ian watched the shocking news being reported by, well, pretty much everyone. Ian Blackwell had gotten married. Under the guise of a business trip, no less. No one knew who the woman was, no one had even glimpsed her yet. No one had known he'd been dating anyone. Why, only a few days earlier he was seen leaving a restaurant with someone else, yet another in a long line of women, and there was that magazine photo of him with another just the day before. Surely, then, the rumor wasn't true?

And yet Ian Blackwell Holdings' public relations department had issued a brief statement to that effect. Too brief and extremely unrevealing, but it was an official press release. So did he get married? And who was the woman? And why no wedding—this one actually backfired on the gossip reporters and bloggers. It was no wonder Ian Blackwell had chosen to get married this way, was the consensus, what with the relentless social media campaign that had been hounding him. It was their fault, everyone agreed. There was actually widespread sympathy for him. Love, marriage, there was always a soft spot for them.

The speculations flowed, as Ian had known they would. Good, Robert had done well. Ian didn't care what they said. They would continue to talk, to speculate, to dig, no matter what he did. The difference was that now it wasn't one of their bogus stories out there, for them to spin against him. Now the ball game was his. They would talk about his marriage, but time was now on his side. If he could show a stable relationship, as he intended to, eventually those rumors, too, would be controllable, would be where he wanted them to be.

An interviewer was speaking to a harried Cecilia Heart. Heart looked crushed. The magazine she had written that last gossip piece for and the television station that had her as a regular contributor were the only ones that didn't get his public relations department's press release. She had been the last to hear that her most lucrative Pounce-For Bachelor was now off her list. He had, in fact, ruined her plans, cut from under her the wave of attention and fame she had been riding on.

At least that, Ian thought with some satisfaction. He logged out of his laptop and turned off its adjoined screens, the exact same setup he had in his office in Blackwell Tower. The main wall screen, which doubled as his television screen, was the last one he turned off, for once. Then he left the den and walked to the stairs that led up to the second floor, ascended them slowly, and turned right to where his bedroom was, glancing toward hers. This time of night the house was quiet, deceptively peaceful. Nothing was indicative of the fact that, just that morning, he had gotten married.

He walked into the master bedroom and closed the door behind him, then stood where he was and looked around him. At the dark shades of the bedroom of a man, a bachelor. At the bed, in which he would invariably sleep alone from now on. At Ian Blackwell's personal life.

He let out a breath and dropped back on the bed, fully clothed.

Chapter Seven

"What the hell were you thinking?"

Robert had expected this. He had avoided Ian's calls all morning precisely because of it. Finally the man who headed Ian Blackwell Holdings simply summoned him to his office, and that Robert could do nothing about.

"I'm surprised to see you here," Robert tried. "I thought you might stay at home for a day or two at least, get to know your wife."

"She's spending the day with yours. Robert," Ian's tone was dangerous. "Her?"

"Come on, it makes sense. If you didn't react to each other in this way, you would see it too."

Ian's eyes narrowed, and Robert took a step back, raising his hands in surrender. "Okay. Look, she is honest, she is reliable, and, come on, you've got to admit she is bloody gorgeous. I knew she didn't follow your business ventures, otherwise she would have recognized me. In fact, she didn't seem to know anything at all about you, and she certainly didn't seem to follow gossip, which, under the circumstances, is priceless. And the way she stood up for her friend, well, if she does that for you..."

"She would rather throw me off a cliff."

"Yes, and *you* would rather throw *her* off a cliff. But you're both adults and you both got into this with your eyes open."

Ian shook his head and turned to look at the familiar skyline of the city he had built himself in. Right now he felt more inclined to deal with the Cecilia Hearts of this world than with the woman he had in his own home.

"She fits your shopping list."

"She is its opposite, Robert."

"She certainly has the looks," Robert argued. "She's intelligent, in fact she's no less intelligent than you. And she won't bore you, I'm betting you'll have a lot to talk about." If they could let go of each other's throats for long enough. He sighed inwardly. He'd gone with his gut feeling when he chose Tess, but that didn't mean he had an inkling of an idea how to make this work. How to make *them* work.

"What about socially adept? With an impeccable fashion sense and an ability to hold her own under the onslaught of just about everyone she will meet?" Ian said, not at all amused.

"Perhaps not, but you can teach her that. And Muriel can help, you know she will, and so will I."

"Robert, she has no idea what to do in this world of ours. They will eat her alive."

Robert wasn't so sure. "I guess we'll see."

Her husband wasn't in the house when she came downstairs in the morning. Relieved, Tess went directly to the kitchen, determined to get to know the people who were tasked with taking care of her.

The kitchen was all wood and stone, all but the marble work surfaces along two walls and the one on the island in the middle of the kitchen. It was the biggest kitchen she had ever seen, and it was certainly more equipped than any other kitchen she had ever been in. But everything had its place, nothing was there just for show. And it looked convenient. No, not convenient. It looked comfortable, and the smell of strong coffee and the sight of jars of recently made jam near the stove only added to the ambience.

Graham was sitting at the kitchen island, reading aloud something from an online newspaper he had on a tablet, for Lina, who stood at the kitchen sink. Surprised at her appearance there, they both turned to her, exchanging a glance between them.

"Ma'am, we would have come to you, all you needed to do was call," Graham said, standing up.

"I didn't want to put you out." She looked from him to Lina and back. "Unless, of course, you're uncomfortable with me being here. I'll understand if you are." She said it kindly, and she meant it. She was the intruder here, the unknown wife they were forced to accept and serve.

"Not at all," Graham said. "You're welcome here whenever you like, ma'am. In fact, if I may, your being here will give us a chance to find out your food preferences. Beginning, I think, with your tea or coffee preference."

"Coffee, if I'm to have any chance of waking up in the morning," Tess said with a smile, and Lina nodded vigorously in agreement. "And is the ma'am necessary? I know you're not allowed to call me by my first name, but the ma'am sounds like . . ." She searched for a description.

"An old matron. All stiff with that bluish hair," Lina said, laughing.

"Lina!" Graham said to her in reprimand, but then turned back to Tess when she pitched in, not at all angry.

"With a far too critical eye and a shrill voice," she agreed. "Exactly. No, I don't think I could be that formal, if you don't mind."

"Just Mrs. Blackwell, then," Graham said, nodding.

"Still better than ma'am," Tess agreed, noting that they were already relaxing.

She ended up having her breakfast in the kitchen with them, coffee with light cream cheese on fresh bread that Lina had just taken out of the oven, and the jam that turned out to be blueberry jam that she had made, some of which was still cooling on the stove. Graham and Lina used the time to ask her everything they could think of that they needed to know, that was relevant to them for running the house with her now in it. And she answered, although it felt strange for her to do that, to let others do things for her. It only brought to a sharper light the drastic change in her life.

And she learned quite a bit from them, too. She learned that while Lina made the homier food in the house, a lot of which reminded her of her childhood, she said with some nostalgia, Graham was the chef who cooked the excellent dinners Tess had been eating, which he had learned to do while working for Mr. Blackwell and was clearly proud of. They spoke of the house and its workings, and about their life with Mr. Blackwell, giving her some insight about the man she had married, through the eyes of those who were privy to what no one else was.

She learned from Lina that he never raised his voice, that he was patient, that he had been unfailingly kind to her since she had come to work for him in this house. From Graham she learned that he rarely interacted in his home with anyone other than the two of them, that for the most part everyone else who worked in this house and its grounds did so when he wasn't there. That most days, including weekends, he left for his office early and returned late, choosing to make the drive to this place where his privacy was not disturbed. That on the rare occasion he would spend the day in the house, where his den provided what he needed to do his work, and that it was important for Graham to make sure he could do so uninterrupted. That he worked too hard, Lina said, a worried tone to her voice, as she sat down near Tess with a cup of coffee. That those things all those people had been saying about him ever since that horrid Cecilia Heart had begun to bother him weren't true, they didn't know him at all. That he went out, yes, to charity functions, or to meet business associates, friends rarely, the Ashtons of course, he was the godfather of both their children. And yes, there was a woman now and then, why not, a young man like him.

And that was what stayed with her when she left them. That they were endlessly loyal to Ian Blackwell. And that they loved him.

She was in the morning room, looking at the sunny day outside and contemplating what she had learned about her husband, when Graham came to tell her she had a visitor waiting in the living room. Here we go, she said to herself, and went to meet Robert Ashton's wife.

Muriel Ashton was a head shorter than her husband. Tastefully dressed and meticulously made-up, with straight blond hair that framed her face and blue eyes that looked at Tess with open curiosity. Graham left them alone, and the two women looked at each other in silence.

"Expecting criticism. And judgment. Yes, you are, aren't you?" Muriel's voice was mellow, with a touch of an accent. Something southern, a remnant from a past long gone, Tess thought. "I suppose that's to be expected."

Tess only nodded.

"You are not one for pretenses, are you? You're perfectly aware of your position and accept it because it was a choice *you* made. And just like Robert said, you're not about the frills and money and society and what being Ian Blackwell's wife gives you, are you?" She shook her head in wonder. "No, you're not."

"You sound like a therapist." Tess didn't like this. She felt exposed.

"Worse." Muriel sat down with an audible sigh. "I'm a mother to a girl who is in a rush to grow up and to a boy who has not long ago discovered there's a world beyond his mommy. Which also makes me a certified mind-reader and spy. And," she added in a more serious tone, "I'm a part of that societal circle you're about to find yourself thrown into. And while the people in it don't know the facts and likely never will, sooner or later the rumors about you and Ian will start. Probably later."

"Later?"

"Ian is a very private person."

Tess tilted her head slightly.

"He really is. Despite appearances. Think about it. You've seen him in business contexts, and you've seen him with the occasional woman, and he does catch the eye, true, but he is never the one to seek the publicity. It always seeks him. Initially it was because of who he is, and that was fine, that's just the way it is, but now gossip is constantly at his heels. And I suppose that in the era of that dreadful social media this cannot be avoided. But what do you really know about Ian Blackwell the man?"

"I don't."

"I'm sorry?"

"I work, or used to, in a demanding job. I read books. No television, it bores me. And I've never liked gossip. I never paid any more attention to his name than I did to others in the news, or in business contexts, as you call it, and I didn't hear much about him at all until he bought the company I worked in and everyone started talking about him and before I met him there I wouldn't recognize him if I bumped into him on the street." Tess breathed in. It felt good to finally let it out. "Ian Blackwell, your husband, you, you all seem to expect me to know who he is. But I don't. I don't know him, and I don't know what kind of life he leads."

Muriel's jaw dropped. "Wow. Robert wasn't kidding. Okay. Honey, you're going to have to learn all about him. And yes, you're married to him because talk about him, the intrusion into his life, has become impossible to deal with, so you're bound to hear all about that. Just please don't believe everything you hear. A lot of it is far from being fair."

Tess was a lot of things, but naive wasn't one of them. "I don't listen to what people say. I judge for myself. And I remind you that I now live with him in the same house, I'm bound to see for myself."

Muriel was beginning to see why Robert liked this woman. "You realize you're going to become a media persona yourself, right? In fact, you already are. Robert and Ian Blackwell Holdings' public relations department released the news yesterday. There is already a whole of lot of interest in Ian Blackwell's mystery wife."

Tess felt a tug of apprehension, which Muriel saw. "Don't worry," she said. "Ian will protect you. He protects his own. As for dealing with the attention you'll be getting when you're out there, just look at him, do as he does. He's very effective with them. With the serious media, that is. As for the others, just don't take notice of them. There's no dealing with that sort of people." She paused. "But you need to know that while the mystery will hold for a while, there will be speculations. No matter what Ian and Robert think they're doing here, the simple fact is that you and Ian are not in love, and ultimately that will show."

Tess contemplated her. "You're very open with me about this. And you don't seem to be judgmental, not at all."

"Look." Muriel leaned forward. "I don't know anything about you, or about why you're doing this. All I know is that you're now married to a man I care deeply about." She sighed. "And you know what, whatever this is, you're now in it, alone. And I'm thinking that you need to have someone you can trust, preferably a woman. And since my dear husband has had a decisive part in this absolutely crazy and unforgivable plan, I think I owe you that this someone would be me."

"You owe me nothing." Tess stood up.

"I'm sorry, that's not what I was . . ." Muriel gave herself a mental kick. "Look. I tend to be candid. Too forward sometimes, Robert says, but, you see, I grew up rich, spoiled, and surrounded by the kind of behavior that has made me rather averse to the games people play. I know you don't know me, and you certainly have no reason to trust me, but give me a chance."

Tess was considering her again, and Muriel quickly pressed on. "At least let me accompany you today, I promised Ian I would. And I really can help."

Muriel was assessing her again in the Bentley, but this time it was her clothes that were the target of the scrutiny. She was adamant to help, and Tess had to admit that she welcomed her company in this shopping trip she really didn't want to go on.

"You're a beautiful woman," Muriel said. "And you're also modest. And while you seem to prefer wearing simple clothes, clothes that I do not at all consider feminine, your choice is rather . . . no, not tasteful. Aware, I would say. Yes. You don't wear any makeup, but you do take care of yourself very well, don't you? That's a good start."

Tess chuckled. "Wow."

Muriel smiled, clearly enjoying herself. "I've always given quite a lot of attention to the way I look. I love clothes and I love buying them. And I love

Glimpse. That's the name the stylists we're meeting go by. They are two high-end designers who also act as exclusive personal stylists for the women they choose as their clients, and they do luxury, they do fashionable, and they do feminine. It will be quite a transition for you."

"I can do feminine and I know how to buy myself clothes." Tess stared out of the side window. She did, she just never wanted to. Did everything she could to avoid it, if she was honest with herself.

"You're about to go up many, many levels in the quality and diversity of what you wear," Muriel said.

"That will be new," Tess admitted after a pause.

"Ian has opened an account for you at Glimpse. It will remain open if you decide you like their choice of clothes."

"I have my own money." It came out more defensive than she'd meant it to. She wasn't about to let any man pay for her.

"This is quite a lot of money," Muriel said gently. "It's a completely new wardrobe for the wife of Ian Blackwell. And," she said, halting Tess's protest, "whatever money you have, and I'm sure Ian knows about it, he has still made sure you have an open account at Glimpse and he will continue to make sure you have everything you need, and I assure you he won't even feel it. The man could buy this city and not feel it."

Her attempt at lightheartedness failed, and she took again the no-nonsense tone the younger woman seemed more comfortable with. "Tess, he's not doing this because he thinks he owns you. He's doing it because he feels it's his responsibility. You're here for a purpose, his purpose, and he will provide all means for you to fulfill that purpose. And right now the means you need are clothes and shoes and purses and makeup and, well, more clothes. So let's go get them."

"I wonder that he didn't come with me himself." Tess had speculated about this since their conversation the previous evening.

"He thought you wouldn't feel comfortable with him doing so at such an early stage of your acquaintance. He will if he believes it's required later."

"He's a calculated man," Tess said quietly.

"You don't become what he is without being calculated. But that doesn't mean he's cold. And the ruthless in him extends only to business."

Tess wasn't anywhere near ready to believe that.

The Bentley slowed down, and Tess peeked out. They were in Nob Hill, Muriel told her, but that didn't mean anything to her, although she figured it would soon enough. Their destination appeared to be a three-story building just up ahead. While its ground level boasted a women's clothing store, made to look fancy and appealing, the second floor had a solid appearance more befitting an office building, and so did the third, except for its arched windows that, together with the entire building's light-colored plated stone cladding, gave it an old-world look. Jackson turned the car right, into a narrow driveway, and drove through to a private car park with an internal entrance to the store. Taking her cue from Muriel, Tess waited while he got out of the car, took a look around him, then opened the door on her side.

They entered a private hallway with an elevator up, and Tess walked over to a door in the corner and peeked through it into the store. It was huge, with a range of women's clothes that made her feel dizzy. A swirl of colors, low bodices, daring designs, flowing fabric, sheer, too sheer, she thought with apprehension, and turned away.

Muriel led her to the elevator, which took them two stories up and opened to reveal a vast space that would have looked more like a large living room, with the sofas and armchairs conveniently placed on the carpeted floor, if not for its numerous mirrors. There wasn't a piece of clothing in sight, though.

"This is where the real magic happens," Muriel explained. "Glimpse the store is the front that these designers use, but up here is the fashion house that caters to the privileged. Here is where they see their clients, work with them, see what fits them and what they want and need. And other fashion houses and designers can also be contacted from here if there's anything the clients want. And in the floor under us, immediately above the store, that's where the actual work is done, the preparation of their original designs or the fitting of ordered items. I've been with them for years, they're amazing. If you'll like them, they'll become your personal stylists, and everything you wear from now on, whether they make it themselves or send for someone else's designs because you happen to like them, will go through them."

Tess was listening with only half an ear. Her apprehension was growing. The clothes she had seen in the store downstairs were not at all her. They were much too revealing, not nearly what she would be comfortable in, what she could bear to wear. The resistance in her was higher than ever. She would not agree to this. She—

The big man who was coming toward them, half-walking, half-flowing, it looked like, in colorful robes and an equally colorful shock of hair, had her take a step back in surprise.

"Daaaaarling!" He swooned at Muriel and kissed both her cheeks in the air while he was still a good distance away. "Missed you. Miiiiissed you. And you" —he turned to Tess—"must be Mrs. Blackwell."

Tess was afraid he would swoop down on her, too, but he only stood back and scrutinized her. "Yes, yes. Very much so. I"—he pointed to himself with a flourish, his fingernails, Tess saw with surprise, as colorful as the rest of him—"am Juno. Amazingly creative, unequaled genius, and generally lovable."

"And a constant pain in the lower backside." The muttering had Tess turn her gaze to the man who followed the living rainbow. The complete opposite of Juno, the small man wore a chic but conservative white suit, a white shirt, a white tie. His hair was a shining white, too.

"And that is my ever cranky, loving husband, Hubi," Juno said with a wave of his hand.

"Hubert," the man corrected and rolled his eyes. "I am not cranky. You simply spread around enough headaches for both of us."

"Do not," Juno retorted.

"Do too." Hubert sighed.

"Do . . . Oh, never mind. We have guests!" Juno turned back to Tess, who was watching the two of them with curiosity. She had never anyone like them before.

"This is Mrs. Blackwell?" Hubert looked at her in surprise. "Really?" He turned to Muriel.

Muriel nodded her confirmation. "Tess Blackwell, meet Hubert and Juno Glimpse, geniuses extraordinaires," she made the introduction.

"I am. He not so much," Juno whispered in Tess's direction. Hubert rolled his eyes again and this time Tess couldn't stifle the smile.

"I expected her to be more . . . more . . ." Juno tried, "volupu . . . volupto . . . damn word. Vo-lup-tu-ous. Or modelly. Or both. Airhead. Oops, sorry, that's not always the case, is it? But those gold digger eyes, whatchamacallit, yes. A Blackwell-oriented chic. Dollar signs in the eyes. Maaany dollar signs."

"Juno!" Hubert actually raised his voice.

"Sorry sorry sorry. Still, you, you're a real beauty,

aren't you? Let's see. Slim. Wow. Nicely toned. You work out, don't you?"

Tess shrugged. She liked to keep her body in shape. Strong. She needed to, the reminder came, and she forced the unwanted thought away.

"Those clothes though! Oh my God. Why? Why, why why would a woman looking like that dress like . . . like . . . like thaaat?" Juno gave up his terminology struggles.

"Not bad color choices though." Hubert considered her with due seriousness.

"Yes but those clothes!"

"Modest, aren't you? Not one to flaunt around what nature has bestowed on you. Nowadays everyone seems to want to show skin, show everything they have. But you, you're a class act, aren't you? I like that."

"Yes but those clothes!"

"Juno!"

"Sorry, sorry, sorry, yes, classy, we can do classy. Classy do for a classy lady. Don't see much of those. Where have I seen one? Don't think I have. I love the hair. Let it down for me, come on, come on!"

Hubert rolled his eyes again but stopped when Tess let her hair down. Dark red, it's richness of color accentuated in the light she stood in. Hubert took several steps further into the floor and motioned her over, and she found herself standing in front of a line of mirrors, under a more complimentary light.

"It really is dark red," Hubert said in astonishment. "And naturally red. Look at that. You don't see that every day, either." It was thick and full and came down under her shoulders in long waves. Even though she'd had it up, it fell into place immediately, framing her face perfectly.

"You love your hair," he said, "don't you? You take care of it. Look at it, soft, perfect. Very well cut, too. I have the perfect hairdresser for you, don't worry. But we won't need that today. No. Perfect as it is." He sighed in content. "Beautiful. And those eyes. And look at that skin, fair, silky. Yes. Perfect."

"Easy." Juno swooned. "This is going to be so easy. Eaaasy. Measurements!" And he moved closer to Tess. She thought he was about to touch her, and her instincts kicked in. She stiffened.

But he only swirled away, not noticing. Neither did Hubert, who followed Juno with yet another sigh and a carefully controlled step as his partner flowed away. They were still talking about her, making plans. Making plans she wasn't sure she wanted to hear.

"They are very gay, very much in love, and you are for them a rare, exquisitely beautiful woman who is very much worthy of their attention. And they don't think that about just anyone. They choose who they work with."

Tess was still looking at the two men walking away.

"You're safe with them."

At that choice of words, Tess whirled around to

face Muriel.

"I'm not asking. I'm not passing this on, it will stay between us. I'm just letting you know that I saw. And that I'm here if you need me." The look in Tess's eyes made Muriel think about what Robert had said, that Tess was as inaccessible as Ian. She thought he was wrong. It was more than that. Tess was untouchable.

"Look, Tess," she said. "I'm Robert's wife. And I'm Ian's friend. But whatever is said between you and me will remain between us, I promise you that. You don't have to tell me anything you don't want to. You just need to know that no matter what you say, I won't betray your confidence. And that even if you choose to say nothing, that's fine too." The eyes that looked at Tess were somber.

Tess considered her. She could use a friend. She was alone here, far from everything and everyone she knew. Alone, and unsure of her footing in her new surroundings. But trust had to be earned, and while she would let Muriel—and Robert—remain close, as her husband's closest friends, she was not yet ready to make them hers. They both seemed nice, and unthreatening. But by her own account Muriel had led a safe life and was happily married, surrounded by people she loved and trusted. Tess didn't think she would understand and had no inclination to trust her with herself.

She had never trusted anyone with herself, and never would.

Still, she appreciated the honest, and seemingly unconditional, offer of friendship. She acknowledged the gesture with a smile. Then she turned away from Muriel and caught her own image in the full-body mirrors half-surrounding her, saw herself in a pair of jeans, a simple shirt in deep blue shades, comfortable shoes. She sighed inwardly. Right. She had made a deal, and she would stick to it. Muriel was right about that, she had to change her appearance. It wasn't as if she didn't know how to do this, she had tried femininity before and knew she had the natural tendency, the tastes that were hers. At least, she thought, this was different, this place was different. As Ian Blackwell's wife she would be safe.

She had to believe that.

She turned around as the two people who would help her determine what she would be wearing from here on returned, prepared for whatever it would take, her mind set on showing herself for the woman she was.

She ended up enjoying the day. Both she and Muriel did. They spent the entire day at Glimpse, where Juno and Hubert created for Tess a wardrobe from scratch. Once Tess learned that a lot of it involved three-dimensional computer simulations of herself with the various clothing rather than having to submit herself to physical measurements and trying on designs, and once she realized that what the two stylists had in mind for her was nothing like what she had seen in their store, and that it was important for them to understand what she was comfortable with and to know how she felt about their ideas, she relaxed. Later in the day the makeup arrived, some fancy brand she hadn't heard of, and both Hubert and Juno were elated—and relieved—to see that she knew what to do with the different items, and quite well. She had taken some courses a while back, she said, surprising them. Out of curiosity, she told them. She didn't tell them that it was when she had still thought there might be a chance for things to be different, before she realized there never would be.

No one was allowed up to the third floor of Glimpse while she was there. Not even the caterer who had come with their lunch, and who saw only Hubert and Jackson. And when Tess and Muriel finally left, it was straight into the Bentley again, with a stern Jackson making sure no one saw them.

Tess, Muriel decided, was an enigma. But she marveled at her, at the way she had handled herself at Glimpse. At her endless patience, at how Juno and Hubert came to adore her in no time—and Hubert didn't like anyone. It's such a shame this extraordinary woman isn't about to let anyone in, she thought with regret. In the short time she had spent with Tess, she had come to like her. But she wondered at the choice Robert had made. Ian always took care to keep a certain type of women around him. The type he could be sure would not remain in his life, the type he chose to satisfy his body, nothing else. Tess was quite obviously very different from that.

The problem was that she evidently was a lot more different than Robert thought.

Chapter Eight

Ian had thought the woman he had married would have more time to settle in, get used to her new surroundings—and to him—before she had to face the world that was lurking outside, waiting to see her. Unfortunately, that was not to be.

She had already received everything that Glimpse had either made or ordered for her. It arrived gradually in the days following her visit there with Muriel. He had seen it all and was pleased. He was surprised to learn that despite what she had chosen to wear in her life before she had married him, she had a good fashion sense. He knew she had played an active role in putting together her new wardrobe and could now see that her taste leaned toward the fine and the delicate.

Not only that. As soon as the clothes arrived she began to wear them, putting her own aside, as if determined to step into her new role as she had given her word she would do. And so even casual was no longer jeans and a simple shirt. Every outfit she wore was stylish—no dresses, though, he hadn't seen her with one yet although he knew she had them—and

befitting a woman of means, but not one who tended to flash her wealth around. Tasteful, understated,
complimenting, that was his immediate description
of the way she was dressed whenever he saw her
now. Which only raised the question yet again—why
hadn't she done this until now, dressed this way? She
was obviously aware of her looks and her femininity.
Why hide them so deliberately?

He was nowhere near answering this, or any other question he had about her. The mystery that was
his wife wasn't anywhere near being solved. Nor did
their relationship, if it could even be called that, thaw.
Their time together was limited, by mutual choice.
He made an effort to be at home at least part of the
time on weekends and on some evenings, as would
befit the fact that he was, outwardly, a happily married man, but even then he spent most of the time
in his den, his office away from Blackwell Tower. The
only time he spent with his wife was in that meal a
day together dictated by the terms of their arrangement. Still, at least the clashes ceased, and their
conversations—at the dinner table only, of course,
and in between long stretches of silence—became,
with time, somewhat less strained.

Although "conversations" was a loose term. They
consisted only of him telling her what she needed
to know about the business and social milieu he was
necessarily a part of and about the media's place in
his life and in his business, all the different facets of
it. He spoke, and she mostly just listened, although

he supposed she wouldn't know what to ask. And there was certainly nothing personal about these conversations, about their time together.

When he had conceived his plan, Ian had known he ran the risk of having to deal with a woman who would try to turn their arrangement into a more personal one, a woman who might only pretend to agree to the strict contract between them, thinking that proximity to Ian Blackwell would win her his heart, or at least his bed and therefore a more permanent place in his life. In fact, he had expected that. What he hadn't expected was the woman he had ended up marrying.

She kept strictly to the contract and to the rules it dictated. She did not betray anything of herself to him, and she kept her distance from him, and not just physically. That, he reminded himself, was what he had wanted. It was, in this sense, the perfect outcome of his plan. Except that she was not an open book to him as she was supposed to be. He was supposed to be in control of the situation. To know all there was to know about her, to be able to anticipate her without this being mutual. Instead, Tess Blackwell, his wife, was as much of a mystery to him as she was to all those waiting to meet her. He knew nothing personal about her, barely knew anything about her at all. And he couldn't begin to figure her out.

To be fair, they were both using the formality to maintain between them a solid wall meant to keep each other out. And it did the job. Neither of them, he realized, had even gone so far as to refer to the other by their first names. Not once. She never referred to him by anything other than Mr. Blackwell, the words controlled and with no endearment in them. As his were. And as his were, hers were meant to establish a cold fact, a constant reminder of the arrangement they had both agreed to.

Shaking his head, he stood up and walked over to the view of the city his office afforded, but it was more of a habitual move, born out of restlessness, out of the turmoil of his thoughts, the need to resolve the problem he was facing that had to do with her. Or rather, his current, and rather urgent, problem with her.

In the time since he had brought his wife to her new home, he had avoided any social functions that would logically have mandated her presence and that might therefore have led to questions had he attended them alone. He had wanted to give her time to get used to her new life, the non-public part of it, and she had spent most of that time in the house. She had met her stylists twice more, and Muriel had visited, befriending her, which Ian was glad about. But otherwise, she had spent her time alone in the house. Walking the grounds, running in the morning, he sometimes saw from his bedroom window. Using the gym, Graham let him know—she never did so when he was in it, of course. And at times, often in fact, she sat by the lake in the gradually warming days, deep in her own thoughts. Graham had told him that, too.

So far, the fact was that she had been isolated, and he had let it remain that way. Perhaps it was also because this was more convenient for him, because he'd been perfectly content to let them both continue getting used to this situation they were in. Or perhaps, he had to admit, it was simply because he wasn't at all sure about presenting her to the world, his world.

Either way, that made his situation on this specific day worse. Less than a month after marrying her, her isolation—or rather, *their* isolation as a married couple—was about to end. An invitation he had received could not be avoided. The CEO of one of his subsidiaries was retiring and leaving California with his wife to live closer to their daughter. His was one of the first companies Ian had taken over, right there in San Francisco, and he had kept Jonathan Barns as its CEO, never regretting the decision. But his retirement posed a problem. Not a business one, the new CEO was just as good. But the event itself was one that Ian Blackwell was expected to attend, and not alone.

Damn Robert and the choice he had made. Still, at least this wasn't a black-tie event, he reasoned, but more of an informal, semi-social, semi-corporate affair, which was why it wouldn't necessarily be the worst social function to start with—

Who was he kidding? This wasn't an office party.

It was taking place in a luxury venue, the sort of place he doubted she had ever been in, and the people attending it would be executives of his company and of other San Francisco companies, and socialites the retiring man knew—and he knew quite a few of them. And, he thought ruefully, anyone else who wanted to see the woman he had married would make sure to be there. Informal or not, the event was already widely publicized, to a large extent because of his marriage, and so when they would arrive at the venue the party would be taking place in, she was bound to be met by the kind of media he wanted to keep away from her. Perhaps, even, by Cecilia Heart, who had since recovered from her shock and was after him with a vengeance, already claiming that the Blackwell marriage was nothing but a business arrangement, a sham.

It would be far from low-key. Too many people at once would meet his wife. The same wife who was nothing like the woman he needed precisely for this purpose. And he had deferred the decision for too long, which was not at all like him, and that in itself said quite a bit. It also made things worse, since it meant he would have no time at all to prepare her for this.

Tess stared at the unbelievable amount of jewelry on the table. The woman who had brought it had arrived at the house with an escort of guards. They were outside now, while the woman, a representative of some jeweler Tess didn't catch the name of, was explaining to her about each of the pieces in their designated holders.

Tess had never worn jewelry, none but a simple pair of stud earrings she had worn for the Christmas parties at InSyn she had attended for just the polite duration, or for whatever other unwanted mandatory events had come her way. And she had never seen so many jewels in her life. True, they were all quite delicate and very beautiful. Nothing here was too extravagant, everything was something she could wear. But it was all so very much. Too much.

She let Lina take the woman upstairs to her room, where the jewelry she had no choice but to accept would be placed in the designated drawers set out for them in what she still thought of as her oversized closet. It was unbelievable, the clothes, the jewelry. Lina had been right—her closet was now filled with so many clothes, more than she could imagine she would ever need. Everything she had, everything around her was so different than what she was used to. Every need of hers was catered to almost before she managed to notice it, every request of hers was answered with a frenzy of action. Despite his obvious misgivings about her, it seemed her husband was making sure she was comfortable, and so were Lina and she thought that even Graham, who was still keeping a careful formality, was warming up to her, but it was all so much. Perhaps if it were real, this marriage. But it wasn't. It was a lie, a play in which she and Ian Blackwell had the lead roles.

Still, it was easier now than in the beginning. Then, she was constantly on guard. Not because she thought her husband might find out whom he had married, she knew he wouldn't, he hadn't before. But because of the mere fact that she lived with a man, a stranger. A womanizer, which was what even their contract spelled him out to be.

But the days went by and he had done nothing. He hadn't touched her. Not even by mistake, after that first dinner. In fact, he kept a marked physical distance from her. And so far he had abided by their arrangement in every way.

And it was more than that. She had expected him to not be there, in the house. To perhaps spend his nights elsewhere, with those women she had been told about, the women he was allowed to keep seeing under the contract. But he hadn't, or at least that was the way it looked. Not only that, it took her only a short time to realize just how busy his days were, and she understood that, just as Graham had told her, he really did work all the time, that his focus was his company, not playing around. While he was in the house, too, he was always in his den, although she thought this was partially due to the discomfort of having her in his home. Other than in their meals together, she barely saw him.

He was different than she had thought he would

be. She wasn't entirely sure what she had expected, but he wasn't it.

She was still sitting in the morning room, deep in thought, when she heard Graham open the front door and her husband ask where she was. A moment later he appeared in the doorway and remained standing there, contemplating her.

"The jewelry you bought has arrived," she said, a little disconcerted by him. This was a first. He had never come back this early, and whenever he came in he invariably went straight up to his bedroom first, then came downstairs either to his den or to have dinner with her.

"I saw the clothes, your tastes, the images were sent to me."

"Of course they were."

He didn't react to that. "I ordered some jewelry accordingly."

"Some?" She'd never seen so many in one place.

"It comes with the territory."

"Yes." She sighed inwardly. "I know."

"You can choose any of them you wish to wear on a daily basis, if at all. However, I will help you choose both your clothes and the jewelry that would fit them whenever there's a social function you need to attend. At least until you're capable of doing so yourself." He sounded colder than he'd meant to, and he waited for the objection. There was none. Good. What he was about to tell her was a problem as it was without her resisting him again. "In fact, I have already made the choice for tonight and have informed Lina. A dark green cocktail dress, I thought it might be comfortable for your first time, to get used to dressing that way. And fitting necklace and earrings, of course, Lina will show you. And you can pull your hair up or whatever, if you want, since you like that. We'll see how it looks."

"Tonight." She tried not to let the anxiety show. Or control her, for that matter. She had known this would come, she had just thought she would have more of an advance warning.

"An invitation I've decided to accept. Not too formal, but it does involve quite a few people I'd hoped you will meet only at a later stage. Still, it will allow me to see how you fare. After all, such social functions are an important part of this arrangement."

"You're in a bad mood," she said. He was no longer looking at her, instead busily straightening a cufflink.

"Analyzing me is not one of your roles as my wife." The way he said the last two words was too harsh. In fact, all the words were, and he regretted it immediately, but it was too late. The effect was clear in the eyes he now met. Angry at himself, but perfectly aware of why he was nervous, of the stakes involved, he continued. "I hadn't expected you to have to accompany me to a function of this scope this early, but it seems the decision has been made for us both. I suggest we do our best. I will guide you through the evening, naturally."

Saying nothing, she stood up and left to go up to her bedroom.

He cursed under his breath and went up to his.

By the time he was dressed for the evening—and he knew how he looked in the black suit he had chosen, replacing his customary black shirt with a white one and going with a tie this time—he thought he might just offer her the option to stay at home. It wasn't her fault that he had decided this late to attend the party. Or that this was happening, for that matter. She was in the middle of this because of his choice, his and Robert's, and if she needed more time, he would give it to her.

He made a business call to Tokyo in his den, and by the time he came out he had made the decision to suggest to her that she stay at home. He was even willing to apologize for having her go through the need to prepare for the evening. But then she might prefer it that way, not to join him. After all, there was no way she was ready, he was thinking as he reached the stairs and looked up.

He stared.

She was just coming to stand at the top of the stairs. She hadn't abided by his choices for what she should wear that evening, any of them. Instead, she had chosen a burgundy evening dress, a rich, dark shade chosen by the Glimpse stylists especially for her. Off the shoulders, the dress long, hugging her body perfectly, with a slit up its skirt, not too high, just right, and delicate heeled sandals. And her hair was not up, it fell long and wavy on bare shoulders. She had on none of the jewels he had chosen, either, only delicate, long earrings with stones matching the dress. Beauty, accentuated with natural elegance, on a woman that had both.

She took his breath away.

Realizing that she was watching him, and that he was gaping, he cleared his throat. "That will do, I suppose."

He turned and took several steps away before he realized there was no movement behind him. Turning back, he saw her exactly where she had been a moment before, looking at him, her head slightly tilted, those gold amber eyes quiet. Waiting.

A smile he had not expected crossed his lips and he walked back to the staircase and reached his hand out to her. "You will turn every head there tonight, Mrs. Blackwell, and you know it."

Her eyes, and the smile that now played on her own lips as she came down toward him and allowed him to take her arm, told him that she did.

The Bentley came to a stop in front of the entrance of the Ritz-Carlton hotel. Ian leaned back and let his wife see through the window on his side the place they would appear in for the first time in public as husband and wife. Reporters crowded the sidewalk and flanked the path the cars dropping off guests drove through, and cameras flashed at everyone who passed. Right now those cameras were aimed at their car, everyone wanting a first glimpse, a first photo, of her, of them together. Tess looked at them with some anxiety, knowing they couldn't see her through the car's tinted windows.

"You will learn to disregard them." Ian watched her, waiting patiently for her to be ready. "The business media, to them I do talk, but that's not them, not here. Most of those who are here I never talk to. They will throw questions at you. Don't answer, simply walk on. Some of what you hear might be meant to illicit a response from you. Don't worry about it. They have a job to do, and some of them have an agenda."

She looked at him.

"I won't leave your side," he said. She was clearly nervous. For him it was his first time out as a married man, and, yes, it was crucial for his plan. But for her this was her first time ever in such a milieu, and he was adamant to help her.

"This isn't easy for you, either," she said, a slight furrow in her brow.

The remark surprised him. "That's true," he said, glancing out. "But at least I'm used to the cameras outside, and to the people inside."

He turned his gaze back to her, meeting hers. Held it. "Mrs. Blackwell," he finally said, "when we go out there, I'm bound to touch you. Put my hand on your back, hold your hand, perhaps. Stand closer to you than I have until now."

"It's expected of us, I know." Her gaze did not waver. She smiled. To reassure him, and, no less, herself. "Don't worry, Mr. Blackwell."

He nodded, with no little astonishment at the woman who was his wife.

She looked outside again and took a settling breath in. "Right," she said. "Let's do this."

"Let's do this," he repeated the words and the sentiment, and motioned to Jackson who gave the go. The doorman opened the Bentley's back door, and Ian got out. Without giving the people around them so much as a glance, he reached his hand to his wife, who took it and came to stand beside him, her head held high.

The camera flashes intensified, and the questions came from all sides, all at once, the noise level overwhelming. But he never took his eyes off hers. She answered his reassuring gaze with one of her own. And when he put his hand on her back this time, his touch carefully gentle, and guided her inside, she was ready.

The evening was long enough to tax her as she played her designated role for the first time, but informal enough to allow her to find her way in it. Ian barely left her side. She was his focus that evening, and no one questioned it. Those present were skeptical, some. Disbelieving, some. But respectful, all.

And he himself was not propositioned, not once the entire evening. He was, after all, there with his wife.

And that wife was most unexpected, he had to admit. She seemed calm, and was graceful in every way. Any nervousness, the little of it that did show, could easily be attributed to her being new there, in that city, among these people who were familiar to her husband but not to her. Many reacted by introducing her to others, showing kindness, which Ian initially attributed to the simple fact that she was his wife. But before long he noted with astonishment that it wasn't only that. Most, if not all, had expected his wife to be different. Looks and little else, a prize more than anything. Proud, perhaps. Arrogant, certainly. Aware of who she was, whom she was married to. Savvy in the social game, game being the key word.

Instead she was open, honest. Nice. She smiled at them, spoke without self-consciousness or reservation. She conversed with casualness when needed, depth and intelligence when that was called for. They would eat her alive, he had told Robert. He'd been wrong. Toasting him from across the room, Robert showed him he was seeing as much.

She had them almost as soon as she began talking to them. By the end of the evening, although he knew his standing beside her gave her the confidence she needed, saw her eyes search for him whenever he ventured away for a moment, he knew that she would be able to handle them, handle them all.

She was more, so much more than he could ever have imagined.

"You were quite amazing tonight," he said, stopping at the bottom of the stairs, when they were safely back in the house.

"I was terrified," she admitted.

He knew, had felt the tension whenever he had put his hand on her, stood close to her. "And yet you hid it well."

She smiled at him. But she wanted to get away. This was getting too close, and tonight, being his wife for the first time, had been difficult in more ways than one.

"Good night," was all she chose to say.

He watched her as she went up the stairs. "Mrs. Blackwell," he called out, and she turned to him. "The woman I had with me tonight does not belong hidden away in a basement." It was a question, yet another question about her that was tugging at him, and while he did not expect one, for the first time since he had met her he wanted, needed an answer for himself.

He watched her as the veil fell over her eyes, as she took a mental step away from him, as she made sure the door between them was closed. Then she turned and walked away.

He remained where he was for a long time, his brow furrowed.

Chapter Nine

Ian chose to spend the next day, a Saturday, working from the house. He wanted to be there with his wife when the reactions to her came.

And they did, from every direction. By the end of the morning he had already received calls from a dozen of the people who had attended the party, all complimenting him about his lovely wife. Some, most in fact, tried to inquire about her, about them, about how he'd kept their relationship a secret, about the wedding that wasn't. He deflected all their questions. Let them wonder some more.

"You seem to have made quite an impression." He came to stand beside his wife in front of the television screen in the living room.

"It's unbelievable," she said, and changed channels to let him see. "We're everywhere. Even in the news! And on so many websites, I must have been photographed from every angle."

"You're famous now."

"Yeah, I noticed. I don't get it. Don't they have anything better to do?"

He chuckled softly. He imagined that any other

woman he might have married would have been ecstatic about her new fame. Yet this one was treating it as a minor inconvenience.

"You know, I understand quite a bit more now, I think, after actually seeing what it's like," Tess said thoughtfully, her eyes still on the images that showed her in the role that was now the life she lived, with the man whose life she was now publicly a part of.

"How so?" Ian's eyes were on her.

"Until now everything I knew was second hand. What you told me, and what Muriel and Robert have when I asked them." And what she'd read about him online, she didn't want to say. She had understood she would have to know it all, if not for herself then for the arrangement she had agreed to. And so by her first meeting with her husband's world she was already well aware of just how big Ian Blackwell Holdings was, how many companies existed worldwide that had IBH before their names, and how formidable the man who headed the company was. She knew he was respected, and that any item she would find about him in the business media would show that. She also knew he was envied and coveted, and that if she found an item about him in the society and gossip columns or blogs, that's what she would see.

"You checked me out?" Ian was dumbfounded. It never occurred to him that she might do that.

"Wouldn't you?" She glanced at him.

Yes, of course he had.

"And after last night it's no longer just words, things I heard. It has real context," she said. Speaking more to herself than to him, he thought. "I get what it's like now. But I need to know more. I need to know about the people I meet wherever we go, about their roles in your life, how to speak to them. What questions to answer and how, what I should or shouldn't say."

"You can ask me anything you want to know. I'll answer," he said, watching her with more than a little wonder.

She nodded. She knew he would, it was in his interest. But she wanted to be able to form her own opinion, decide on her own way in this life she now lived. And for that, she would also do some more studying about it, and about him, herself.

As always, her husband spent the rest of the day working in his den, then disappeared there again immediately after dinner. She had been in the den once. Just once, he had shown it to her when he had first shown her the house. In an effort, she supposed, to let her feel there were no restrictions, that this was her home now, that she should feel as free to move around in it as he was.

The den, a first-floor room that opened to the back of the house, was made up in the shades of a man, the dark mahogany desk and the similarly shaded wingback armchair standing against the opposite wall contrasting nicely with the lighter-shade floor carpeting and the white curtains that hung under heavier brown ones on the wide set of French doors that led outside. It was clearly his, meant only for him, and she had never gone in there since. He needed his corner of the house just as she did, and his hours there were, it seemed to her, his way to escape the company of a woman he hadn't wanted to marry.

She had her own quiet corner in this house, a place she felt comfortable in. The library, in the same part of the house where his den was, but a world away. She had instantly fallen in love with it, and it was where she spent most of her evenings. It was an old-fashioned library, a large space that didn't feel that way because of the sheer number of books in it. A circular staircase led up to a second floor, and antique rolling ladders were positioned against some of the shelves. All the walls were lined with bookshelves, except for a recess here and there where paintings hung, all by some known name or other, a few of whom she had heard of but even those she knew nothing about. Originals, she assumed. Ian Blackwell would have no less. The bookshelves were made of rich dark wood, which gave the room an ambience of comfort, supplemented by its specially designed recessed lights. A wide fireplace adorned the first floor, not far from it stood a sofa, and closer still stood a large overstuffed reading chair with a small round-top table beside it, a rustic table lamp on it. A comfortable reading spot on a cool evening, she could easily imagine. It was cozy and quaint and filled with the scent of books and she loved it.

The first time she had come in here, she had walked around endlessly. Finally, she had chosen a book and had curled up on the soft reading chair beside the dormant fireplace, reading for hours until she thought she just might sleep if she went to bed, not lay awake with unwanted thoughts plaguing her mind. The days were easier, and in them she preferred either to sit outside, down by the lake or among rustling trees, or in her room, on the comfortable armchair, her feet up on the ottoman, with fresh, calming breeze coming in through the open balcony doors. But the evenings, they were hard. And so she spent every evening she could here, in this peaceful hideaway in the home that wasn't hers.

But tonight she had come here with a different purpose in mind. She had her tablet with her and was here to do some more research about her husband. And she was engrossed in it when the library door opened, and he came in.

He took several steps inside before he saw her, sitting comfortably on the soft chair, her feet folded under her. She looked relaxed, he thought, but that was fast disappearing before his eyes.

She began to get up. "I'll leave you alone."

"No, please. Stay." He motioned her to sit back down. "I'm sorry, Graham did say you spend your evenings here." He didn't tell her that he had been inquiring about her these past days, weeks now, concerned that she might not feel comfortable in what should be her home. Nor did she know that the only reason he hadn't come in here since she had come to live in this house was that he himself had been unable to relax, to accept what he had done. To accept her. That the evening before was the first time he'd felt confident that at least the outwardly visible part of their arrangement might be what he had wanted, even though she herself was far more than he had bargained for. That he was finally able to let go, just a bit, and to come to this place that was, for him, his favorite room in his home.

That he had completely forgotten she might be here.

"It's peaceful here," she said. She was hesitant, and he realized this was the first time they had been together in the same place beside the instances mandated by their arrangement.

"It is," he said. "I had it designed like the old libraries, I saw one in an English mansion on one of my visits there and couldn't get it out of my mind. I also like to read here. To work here, sometimes." He wanted, needed, to make her feel at ease. "Do you mind if I stay?" he asked.

She was taken aback by the question, by the fact that he even asked. She tilted her head slightly, in that way he was learning was hers, contemplating him. Finally, she shook her head.

He walked deeper into the library and she heard him go up the narrow steps. A few moments later he came back and sat down, choosing one end of the sofa, the one farthest from her. She watched him for a bit and then returned to her tablet, and he could now raise his head, watch her freely. Even though she had chosen to stay, she was quite obviously aware of his presence there. She was all about wariness, and not at all about trust.

He lowered his gaze back to his book.

The next evening she found herself unsure whether she should go to the library. He was in the house, but while they'd had all of the day's meals together, they'd spent the entire day apart, and after dinner he'd withdrawn to his den once again. Finally she decided to go, needed that quiet corner, and ended up spending the evening there alone.

She wondered why.

The evening after that he was there when she came in, sitting in the same place he had sat in two evenings before, on the sofa, reading some papers. He had a glass of red wine beside him. She hesitated for only a brief moment, then came to sit in what she was already coming to think of as her chair. A moment later he got up and walked to the liquor cabinet in the corner, where he had a bottle of red wine open. He poured another glass of wine, came over to her and put it on the table beside her. Then he switched on the lamp, moving it to throw some light on the book she was reading this time in the dim lighting of the room, and returned to sit, saying nothing. When she raised her head to glance at him, he was already engrossed in his work.

It became a reprieve. Somehow, as the days went by, becoming weeks, their time together in the library became a reprieve. From this situation they were in, from their being complete strangers locked in an arrangement that provided strict rules designed to do just that, keep them safely apart, safely from each other. Outside the library were expectations. What the circumstances in which they had come to live together expected, what the rules their contract had set expected, what the world outside expected.

In here it was just them.

It became increasingly easier until it was finally comfortable for them to be there together, to sit in peaceful silence that evolved into a companionship of sorts, and eventually to talk. To ask how the day was, and to answer without reservation. To offer a glass of wine, and to accept. To check if the other was in the library, when they were both in the house, and if not to see why, and to invite. To suggest, discuss, debate a book. He saw her interest and taught her about the paintings he had chosen to collect, those he had scattered around the house and those he had designated specifically for the library.

"I read about them," she said one evening.

"Why?" He was curious.

"Some of them, when I look at them, they're a bit like books, aren't they? You can lose yourself in them."

That, he marveled, was precisely why he had bought them. Apart from their being valuable assets, of course.

"So I looked them up," she said. "To understand them better."

"Some things are meant to be experienced, not just read about," he said and motioned her to join him beside a painting that hung not far from them, which she did, no longer hesitating.

That evening he taught her to look at that painting, and then at another, and gradually, as the days went by, at them all, showing her how the way she looked at them could open her mind to a painting's heart, and how to recognize the differences between painters and styles. He then taught her about the wines he'd been placing by her side and choosing for their dinners, showing her his preferences among them and learning hers. He spoke of cuisines, having seen her appreciation of the nuances of food, and took her to places he thought she might enjoy. But unlike the various social functions they went to or instances when their dinner was with a business associate of his, these times they went out together were for her, and he invariably had a table set out for them in privacy and took care to heed no one and nothing around them, nothing but his time with her.

Her favorite place was an Italian restaurant called Antonio Torelli III, and so that's where he took her when he felt, thought he could recognize, that she was quieter, more withdrawn than usual. The restaurant offered a unique mix of old world and new world food by a chef who had never let go of his roots, and who had worked hard to revive a restaurant by a similar name that his grandfather had opened in Italy, and that his father had dreamed of opening again when the family had moved to the United States when he himself had been a child, but had never succeeded in doing so. Ian had chanced upon the place in its previous, shabby form several years earlier, and had gone in when he had seen from outside the three generations of Torellis working cheerily in the tiny open kitchen of the full restaurant. He ended up investing in it, the only restaurant he had ever invested in, and it was now a franchise of both luxury and family-frequented outlets. This allowed Antonio Torelli III himself to still be doing what he loved most, cook, in his favorite restaurant, the one they frequented.

He enjoyed this, giving her experiences he had no doubt she had never had before, constantly surprising her with yet something new. She was endlessly curious. And honest—nothing in her was assumed, nothing artificial, meant only to impress. There was simply no pretense in her. And for precious moments, though too few, she seemed to forget herself and simply let go, enjoy herself, the experience, with him. He found he craved these moments.

He wondered if she knew she was changing him.

Or that she was changing, too.

After Tess's first appearance in public, the invitations flowed in, with Ian choosing what to go to and what to disregard at this time when he needed to show his marriage outwardly but didn't want to overdo it in a way that would be too taxing for his wife, who was unfailingly there whenever he asked her to be. With time the flow of events tapered to a manageable stream, as the world he was a part of got to know, and accepted, his wife.

They always attended together, and he never ventured far away. The functions, the parties, the various events became easier as Tess gained experience and confidence. Keeping up the front she and her husband were putting up became easier, too. But then he wasn't a stranger anymore, this man she was getting to know, and who was nothing like she had thought he would be, especially in the privacy of his home or among the people he cared about, the rare few he considered his friends.

Or with her. Even though she no longer flinched at his touch, he never did more than place his hand on her back or lightly hold hers, and only in public. And as she got to know him, his body language, his own subtle reactions to her, she stopped being on guard, stopped expecting him to do more.

Their arrangement was still being strictly adhered to in every way but one—they were getting to know each other far more than was mandated by the contract they had signed. Nevertheless, it still afforded them both a sanctuary they needed from each other, keeping them within a comfort zone they were both still content to remain in.

Even now no one but the select few who had known from the beginning knew the truth, still only Robert and Muriel, now friends to both Blackwells, and Lina and Graham, the former having liked Mrs. Blackwell from the very beginning and the latter no longer trying not to, as he got to know her better, and as he saw a change he never thought he would in Mr. Blackwell. And Jackson, who was fiercely protective of the kind, quiet woman he felt responsible for whenever she was outside the house and in his care, since, it seemed to him, too many were trying to get to her.

As the weeks, then month, then another went by, the rumors waned, as did the type of attention that had originally led Ian to decide on the arrangement that was now their life together, but apart. Once again he faced—for the most part—only the attention he'd been used to before, that which he had learned to accept. There was no longer vicious gossip, him leading a seemingly stable married life ended all but the more persistent speculations, those he had expected to remain.

Even the lack of obvious affection between him and his wife worked out. At first enough people chalked it up to the new couple getting used to being together in public, not least of all Tess Blackwell who was new to them, to the life her husband had brought her into. And by the time the absence of closeness might have become too obvious, they were comfortable enough with each other for that to show, and the rest was perceived as being the need, which everyone knew about Ian Blackwell and had learned was also an inclination of his wife, to keep their personal life private.

And after their curiosity found nothing but a hard-working young woman who seemed to have met Ian Blackwell in a company he had eventually bought, without anyone being able to ascertain exactly when they had met, all those who had questions about Tess Blackwell left them behind and focused on trailing the couple when they ventured outside their exclusive estate, as was the case for every other rich and famous—and settled down—couple.

All but Cecilia Heart. The humiliation still stung. One minute the handsome, wealthy bachelor had rocketed to the top of what used to be her Pounce-For Bachelors list, bringing him unwanted attention but her an unlimited source of air and online time—and fame, and the next, without warning, she had to hear from everyone else that he was married, off the market and beyond her reach. She was the only one who still never received any press releases or advanced notices from Ian Blackwell Holdings' public relations department, and the only one who still never had any of her questions answered by it. No one would speak to her about Ian Blackwell or about his wife, not even her peers, who feared they too would be left out of the loop and denied all information related to them.

She had lost all her morning show appearances because of this, no late night shows ever called her again, and the magazine she had written for had made it clear it didn't want to hear from her again. She had lost all the readers of her blog, and the same people who had once followed her on social media now turned on her, leering at her shame. She was livid, and she was out for a vengeance. She was determined to prove that the marriage was a lie, and if on the way she could put Ian Blackwell's wife down, why not. The problem was that she didn't have a chance to do so. She could get nowhere near the woman and could find nothing about her that stuck. Her past was solid, her behavior was untainted, and she was well accepted and widely liked. She was gorgeous, intelligent, kind.

Cecilia Heart hated her.

Chapter Ten

Jeremy Alster was delaying. The extended delay had already brought him to the point of no return, Ian knew. The subsidiaries he had that were still viable were no longer getting new contracts, since customers and suppliers alike were aware of Alster Industries' uncertain future, and the company's already meager resources were now all but depleted. Yet he was still delaying.

And the vultures were circling. Most of the offers to buy the company were still on the table, but time had done its part and the other contenders for it were impatient. Talks of a hostile takeover, the kind that would end up crushing the company into a pulp, now prevailed, with everyone waiting to see who would be the first to make a move.

That was something Ian couldn't allow. He wasn't about to let what he wanted from Alster Industries fall into anyone else's hands. Which meant that he himself would have to make the move. He was stronger than the others, certainly stronger than Alster Industries, and could easily take over the company despite Alster's objection and do with it as he pleased.

He had done that enough times before.

The problem was that doing this and still sticking to the plan he had originally offered Jeremy Alster would cost more than he was prepared to invest in the failing company, in terms of both time and resources. No, in such a case it would make better business sense to forgo that plan and to simply tear Alster Industries apart. Not what he had originally intended to do, but he would never allow any risk to his own company, his own employees. His first responsibility was to them.

It looked like that would have to be his course of action, and the sooner the better. In the time that had passed, IBH Pythia Vision and what was now its subsidiary, IBH InSyn, had begun to work toward his intended goal for them, and he needed the Alster Industries subsidiary without further delay. Time was of an essence.

He wanted something, and he would get it. But that didn't mean he had to like the way he would go about doing it.

He was at Pythia Vision now, in its offices in Blackwell Tower, to hear about its progress in its work with InSyn—pending the assessment report about InSyn itself due later in the week—and any remaining issues that needed to be solved. He had thought he would finish here earlier, but he had asked the Overarching Projects Integration Team for operational assessments and financial estimates that would take into account the assimilation into Pythia

Vision of the third component of the venture, the patents and the development team of the Alster subsidiary he intended to have soon, and he would only make it back home to Woodside later in the night.

Mrs. Blackwell, he thought, would have to go by herself to the opening of the new gallery, here in San Francisco. He didn't even consider suggesting otherwise. By now she was certainly able to face an evening out without him. She was a natural, and no reporter or photographer ever managed to perturb her. She simply gave them her attention, if she wanted to, or disregarded them, where that was called for, but even then she managed not to offend them, and to gain a favorable word.

No, he wasn't at all concerned. And she wanted to go. She enjoyed art and loved paintings, and that evening's opening featured young, up-and-coming artists. New worlds, she called them.

He smiled to himself, his thoughts on her, even as the head of the team that was making sure all of Pythia Vision's projects were in synchrony was explaining what was to be expected once the piece of the puzzle Jeremy Alster still had in his hands would be where Ian intended it to be.

Tess was enjoying herself. The works were very good. The curator had chosen to intermix the different artists' paintings instead of giving them each a corner of the gallery, hoping to expose the visitors to all of them equally. At the same time, he had organized the intensity and the themes to create an atmosphere that changed smoothly through the gallery's two levels.

She was sorry her husband wasn't here. He had taught her how to look at art, how to have a feel for what she looked at in a way that enhanced her appreciation of it. She wished he could enjoy the exhibition with her. Standing before the paintings, she could imagine the two of them commenting, discussing, arguing even. There would be people around them, but he would pay no attention to them. When he was with her in the moments that were theirs, he seemed to be just that, with her.

With her thoughts on what she had seen, what had caught her eye most among the paintings, she descended the stairs to the gallery's lower level with a graceful step, smiling at a couple who passed by and looked at her with awed curiosity. She didn't mind it, didn't mind the people, the nice ones, and by now she was used to being recognized. And so far she'd enjoyed the opening undisturbed by the presence of anyone in any kind of media, since none of them were allowed into the gallery that night.

But when she had almost reached the bottom of the stairs, a woman rushed to her from below, thrusting a recorder at her. Tess stopped and looked at her, her gaze quiet. With everything she knew by now about the man she had married, she understood why he had chosen to marry in the first place.

When she had studied the life he lived, she had seen where and when the interest in him had suddenly peaked, when the attention became impossible to deal with, and she knew who was behind it, who had started it all and who had then made sure the unwanted attention wouldn't die down.

Cecilia Heart's eyes glinted. She had her. She'd never before managed to get this close to Tess Blackwell, that damn husband of hers always seemed to be there, hovering over her, keeping anyone unwanted away. But seeing her get out of that fancy car alone, Cecilia knew she had to find a way into the gallery, and she had. It took a bit of a bribe, a lot in fact, but it was worth it.

"Mrs. Blackwell, how are you enjoying the exhibition?" she asked, inching closer to the woman she finally had cornered.

"Very well," Tess Blackwell answered her. "These artists are all very talented, and I'm certain they have promising futures ahead of them."

Heart barely let her finish the sentence. Around them people turned to look. While the woman she was targeting spoke calmly, quietly, Heart's voice was a winning shrill. But she didn't notice. Nothing else mattered. "Interesting though, I see that you are here by yourself. Does Ian Blackwell not care enough to spend time with *his wife*?" She stressed the words cruelly.

Tess Blackwell looked down at her, slight amusement in her eyes, in the smile that played on her lips. "And you are?"

"I'm Cecilia Heart," Heart said, looking around her. She had her now, in front of all these people.

"Heart." Tess Blackwell contemplated her. "Heart. Didn't you used to be . . ." She paused for just the right length of time. "Used to be," she then said with a quiet finality, and continued down the stairs without giving her another look.

Heart paled and looked around her in embarrassment as the realization of what had just happened hit her. Tess Blackwell had just said it all without actually saying anything.

Jeremy Alster tried to keep his attention on the art, but that wasn't an easy thing to do. He didn't want to be here, he had only agreed to come to this exhibition for his wife. He would do anything for her, it was that simple. Nothing was more important than his marriage. For him, that was what love meant.

She was standing beside him now, speaking with one of the young artists who had their paintings on show, and Jeremy looked around him, distracted. This was an interesting building, built in a way that allowed anyone standing in any of the two levels to see into the other one and created the illusion of an open space that was bigger than the gallery actually was. He looked up, at the open spiral that made up the—

The identity of the woman coming down the stairs could not be mistaken. Tess Blackwell. His eyes searched around her. Was Ian Blackwell here? He didn't want to meet him. Blackwell was enough on his mind as it was, he wasn't ready to face him, not now. His conundrum as to what to do with his company, how to save his employees, was nowhere near diminished, even after all this time.

It was Blackwell's offer, his plan, that he wanted to go with, which was why he still hadn't sold Alster Industries to anyone else. Even after he had told Blackwell he couldn't imagine handing over his company to him, he couldn't get past the simple fact that the man's plan was the best one for it, that it was his employees' last chance. But no matter how much he tried to convince himself, he couldn't bring himself to trust the man. Yes, Blackwell was a brilliant businessman, Jeremy couldn't argue with that, and if he stood behind his offer Ian Blackwell Holdings would be a stable home to Alster Industries' businesses, and to its employees. But that exactly was the problem—would Blackwell keep his promise?

Jeremy knew he was thinking about it too emotionally, which was exactly what had brought his company to financial ruin in the first place, but for him there was simply no other way. He was thinking in terms of a home for his employees, with a home life Ian Blackwell would be responsible for. And Ian

Blackwell was a ruthless, driven man who took what he wanted and whose lifestyle Jeremy did not approve of. And that went a long way toward making him uneasy.

True, Blackwell had gotten married. And initially this had made Jeremy think he might have been wrong about the man. But he knew marriage, and he knew love. And from what he had seen—and he had taken care to look—there was nothing of the sort between that man and the woman he claimed was his wife, and that alone was enough to make Jeremy wonder if the rumors about the marriage were true. And if that was the case, how could he put his employees' lives in the hands of this man, a man whom he could not at all relate to, whose eyes never let on what was in the mind behind them. Who married, it seemed, to, what, manipulate public opinion? To get what he wanted? What kind of a man did that?

He sighed and touched his wife's arm, indicating, when she turned to him, the woman who was coming down the stairs. They shared a look.

Putting the encounter with Heart behind her, Tess walked over to a couple she recognized. Recognized, but had never personally met. All she knew about them was what her husband had told her in their library talks, once the trust between them had grown enough.

She came toward them with a smile. A genuine one, Jeremy thought. Funny, he wasn't expecting that from the woman who had married Ian Blackwell for God knows what reasons. Still, the easiness with which she had dealt with that pushy woman reminded him of the other Blackwell, her husband, and he was wary.

"You're Jeremy Alster," she stated, stopping before them, the smile still on her face, then turned her gaze to his wife. "And you must be Margaret."

"And you," Jeremy said, "are Ian Blackwell's wife."

"You handled that woman extremely well, Mrs. Blackwell," Margaret Alster said. "She was clearly trying to get a reaction for the crowd. A fight, I think."

"That is not who I am," Tess said simply. "And please, call me Tess. There's far too much formality around me as it is, and you, at least, I feel I know." She turned her gaze to Jeremy.

"Oh?" He was obviously suspicious, not forgetting even for a moment who she was. But he had to admit he was also intrigued.

"My husband has told me quite a bit about you."

He was taken aback by her frankness. "I assume he told you I'm a pain in his—"

"Jeremy!" His wife struck his arm lightly, appalled. "This is a young woman you're talking to! Behave."

Tess laughed softly. "As a matter of fact, he said you are a rare man. An honorable one."

Jeremy sighed. "I wish I could say the same about him."

"Jeremy Alster!" Margaret was flabbergasted. "You are talking about her husband!"

"Margaret, her husband is—"

"I know very well who her husband is," Margaret chided him, not without affection. "But she is no more at fault for who he is than I am at fault for who you are!"

Tess looked at Jeremy Alster with the slightest furrow in her brow. Her husband, when he had spoken of this man, had told her what he thought the problem was. It was true, he did tell her that Alster was a rare man, a man who cared more about his employees and their families than about success or money. He had also told her he thought Alster was comparing himself with him, that he was comparing his own home life, his marriage of decades out of love and with unfailing dedication, with theirs.

"If I may be forward, you've been married for a long time, happily so, haven't you?" she asked him. It was this man's heart that was making the decisions, and she would speak to him with hers.

Jeremy nodded, and Tess glanced at his wife. "And it seems to me, looking at the two of you, that you have learned to trust the judgment of a good woman."

"That I have," Jeremy said.

"Then trust the judgment of this good woman," Tess said, her eyes on his, her voice soft. "The man I married is a good man."

Jeremy was awed by this young woman, young enough to be his daughter. Awed that he believed her, completely and entirely so. "You are not quite what I expected," he said.

"Nor I," Margaret said, remembering everything her husband had told her. She put a hand on his arm. "Jeremy, I love you to bits, you know that. But I do believe you may have erred on the side of misconception."

Chapter Eleven

Ian was walking into the house after a day that had been far too long when his phone rang. Impatient, he pulled it out of his jacket pocket and looked at it. Jeremy Alster. He took the call.

"Alster Industries is yours," Jeremy Alster said without preamble.

Ian halted in the doorway.

"Your company, your plan for it. Forget the money, you're going to have to invest a whole lot in what I'm giving you, we both know it's a mess. And I have enough money to last my wife and me for what remains of our lives, and beyond, frankly. It was never about the money anyway."

"You're simply giving me Alster Industries? After all this time?"

"Nothing simple about it, there's much to be done there. But I have it on good authority that you are a man of your word and that you will take care of my people."

"I will. But they'll need you there too."

"I am also a man of my word," Jeremy Alster grumbled. "I will work with you on this, do all that is needed. One thing, though, Blackwell."

Here it comes, Ian sighed inwardly. There had to be something. This offer, this call, was, after all, an impossibility. These things never happened.

"You don't strike me as being a fool, Blackwell," Jeremy Alster was saying to him. "Whatever you're doing there, don't mess it up."

"I'm sorry?" Ian had no idea what Alster was talking about.

"That's one hell of a woman you've got. And if you don't, if they're right and you don't, then make sure you do."

Ian ended the call and stood rooted in place. He was completely and entirely at a loss.

He found his wife in the library's first floor, searching the section on painters and their art. She was still in the clothes she had worn to the gallery opening. She had opted for a pant set this time, with a lace knee-length open jacket that attempted, without quite succeeding, to lightly conceal just how perfectly the pants and top she was wearing hugged her body. Her hair was half pulled back, revealing a delicate pair of earrings, the only jewelry she wore. She was a picture of beauty and elegance, and he wondered if she knew it.

"Mrs. Blackwell."

She glanced at him and then turned back to the shelves, looking for a book about a painter one of the paintings she had seen that evening reminded her of. "Mr. Blackwell. How was your meeting?"

"What did you say to him?"

"To whom?"

"Jeremy Alster."

"Jeremy and Margaret? I met them at the gallery opening," she said. "We talked. They're nice, I like Margaret."

"Jeremy and Margaret?"

She nodded, her eyes still on the books.

"Mrs. Blackwell," he said again to focus her, and she finally turned to him. "Jeremy Alster just handed me his company. He just *gave* me Alster Industries."

"He did?" She smiled. "Nice."

"Nice?" Ian stared at her. "I've been trying to get Alster Industries since before you and I ever met. Before I even bought InSyn. And you got it for me after meeting Jeremy Alster once? At a gallery opening?"

"No, you got it. It was your proposal, your plan that he believed in. I just . . . sealed the deal, I guess." She shrugged.

"What the hell did you say to him?"

"I just told him the truth," she said and walked back to her reading chair.

He followed her, wanting to know more. But she wasn't about to give it to him, couldn't, found she was embarrassed to tell him what she had said to Jeremy Alster. "I met Cecilia Heart, by the way." She changed the subject.

"Yes, I know. I saw."

"You saw?" It was her turn to be surprised.

"Someone filmed it on his phone and posted it online. My public relations department sent it to me, Robert sent it to me, Muriel sent it to me, and Graham, of course, sent it to me. As did too many others to count."

He pulled a tablet out of his briefcase and turned it on, then brought up what he wanted to show her before handing it to her. The Art and Style magazine feature about the gallery opening was playing on it. He'd fast-forwarded the video to where she could see her encounter with Heart just before the Art and Style reporter spoke on screen.

"Well, Tess Blackwell certainly seems to have taken care of *that* once and for all," the reporter said while in the background the gossip blogger made a feeble attempt to regain her footing, with Tess already walking away, never once looking back.

"Impressive," Ian said, stopping the video. He really was impressed, and not for the first time. No matter what any of them did or said, the woman he had thought would be eaten alive by them simply would not be rattled. And this time, she'd finished what he'd started. She'd finished Cecilia Heart.

"I can't say I liked to belittle her that way."

"It was the best way to stop her. And I assure you she wouldn't think twice about doing the same to you, in fact she didn't." He contemplated her. "But then, that's why you are you and she's not."

After a bit of hesitation, she acknowledged the compliment with a nod.

"You're good with them. All of them. You always seem to know what to say."

"You were there in the beginning to give me the confidence," she said. "And you told me what I needed to know about them. The rest, I guess, comes from seeing or reading items about you. Business news, gossip. Lots of social media posts from before you and I were married. I probably read everything ever written about you and saw everything you've ever appeared in."

"Why?" He was nonplussed.

"To understand. I came here knowing nothing about you, about the life you lead, about the people around you or the ones who are watching you, media or otherwise. That first time we were out, remember?"

He certainly did.

"I told you then that it put things in a context I didn't have before, and that I needed to know more."

She had asked him, from that day on, every time they went out, about the people she would meet, about what would be expected of her. But he had no idea that she hadn't just asked him, no idea that she had gone as far as she had. "You're thorough."

"You need me to be."

"Still, I'm not sure how I feel about being studied that way." He said it with humor, but there was some truth in it. She had quite a unique mind.

"I'm not studying you," she said. "I'm studying them."

"Right. Well, just don't believe everything you've heard about me. Especially the gossip." He wasn't entirely sure why it mattered to him to say that. But it did.

"I don't automatically believe everything I hear." She looked at him quizzically. He was uncomfortable, she realized with astonishment. Embarrassed, even. Ian Blackwell, the man whose conglomerate had gotten from huge to huger just moments earlier, was embarrassed. "I like to check for myself. And I especially don't believe gossip. In fact, before you I never watched or read any." She smiled a little. "But I did hear a bit here and there from Jayden and his wife, they're avid gossip followers, they know everything about celebrities. Although you'd never get Jayden to admit it."

"Graham follows every single item about me, and that includes gossip, which I think he enjoys most."

"No way. Graham?"

"Yes, our Graham." He laughed. "If you're lucky, you might catch him shouting at the television because he doesn't like something he sees."

"Well, I can tell you that some of these items are quite . . . entertaining." She tapped her finger on the screen of his tablet, as if bringing up something on the browser, and turned away from him. "It does seem you've dated an impressive range of women."

"It's not as playboyish as they've made it out to be." He was surprised into defending himself. He began to walk toward her, to see what she was looking at. Then he stopped, getting it. "Wait, are you having fun with me, Mrs. Blackwell?" he asked, astonished.

"I do believe I am, Mr. Blackwell." She looked up at him, mischief in those beautiful eyes of hers.

Passing outside the library just then, Graham froze. It couldn't be. He inched closer and listened at the door. He was laughing. Mr. Blackwell was laughing. He walked away quietly, not wanting to interrupt.

"I imagine you studied me too, if you want to call it that," Tess was saying inside. It didn't matter now, after all this time.

"I read the report Robert put together about you, after he chose you," Ian conceded, trusting what was now between them. "I wanted to know something about you, that first day. I couldn't understand why someone like you would agree to enter into this arrangement. And even after we kept fighting. But that was the last time I checked about you."

She believed him. "Why?"

"It's not within my right to."

"We got married in a business arrangement."

"That doesn't give me the right to invade you in any way."

That, the choice of words, struck her, hitting an unseen wound. She hid it, but nowhere near fast enough. He knew her now, was far more sensitive to her than he had been, and he saw it. His own frown remained inward. He didn't want her to go, he wanted her to talk to him. To trust.

"The truth," he said, "is that I learned nothing from the report. Yes, I could have searched some more. But this was to be a long-term arrangement. I figured that anything I want to know, I will learn from you in time."

"Did you?" She was still trying to get a grip on herself.

"Yes. And you're not at all who I thought you would be. You're not . . . the wife I envisioned when I came up with this idea." He said it simply. And he said it allowing some affection into his tone, affection he never thought he would feel. Or consider expressing.

She nodded slowly, some hesitation in the nod. "You're not who I thought you would be either."

She handed him the tablet and turned to leave. He was getting too close, this was too close.

"Mrs. Blackwell."

She turned back to him.

"About my checking you out, I figure I owe you. Anything you ever want to ask me, I'll be glad if you do."

Too close, she thought again, her heartbeat quickening.

But he wasn't ready to let this end, let her leave. He wanted her here, with him, even if just for a moment longer before she would hide from him again. "So how was the exhibition at the opening?" he asked quickly.

"Very nice." She relaxed somewhat at the change of subject. "There were some good works there."

"Such as?" He was genuinely interested.

"Mostly contemporary work. Interesting diversity, each artist and his or her own angle, and very obviously so." Then she focused on something specific, and he saw the change before she began to speak again. "One of them painted a unique picture, a bit out of place among the other works there. An oil painting, which was also rather unique there. A landscape, looking out from a cliff to a gentle sea. After a storm, you can see that quite clearly. And he put two figures on the beach, in the distance. Hazy, you can't quite see them. He managed to catch something there, something dreamlike. A bit of magic, I thought."

She caught his eyes on her and shrugged, a little embarrassed, he thought. That she'd exposed something of herself to him?

"It was just a painting. He's a good artist, much of what he does is nice." She dismissed it and moved on, eager to steer his attention away from her. "By the way, Muriel has asked me to join her at the children's hospital tomorrow, for the collective birthday party she's throwing the inpatients there. She's short of volunteers, apparently everyone is coming down with that stomach virus. I'll probably be gone most of the day."

He watched her as she walked away from him again.

Tess was exhausted the next evening, but pleased. Even with the shortage of volunteers, the party, a huge birthday party for dozens of children, Muriel's idea to make them smile, even if wasn't really their birthday, was a success. She was also late, so that she didn't make it to dinner with her husband. He hadn't been there that morning, either, and so technically they did what they had never done until then when her husband wasn't away in one of his foreign subsidiaries—they missed a day in which they should have had a meal together as per their contract. But then things were different now, she mused as she let a hot shower wash the day away. *They* were different now.

And, she thought as she was coming down the stairs on her way to the library, the attorney who had drafted that contract, Robert, had been there in the second half of the day, having also been asked by Muriel to help. That had to count for something. She smiled to herself. Who knew she would rather have had dinner with the man she had married.

When she had returned, Graham had told her that Mr. Blackwell was in a conference call in his den, and when she found the library empty, she supposed that's where he still was. She entered the silent room and walked straight to her favorite reading chair, where the book she'd been reading lay. She sat down, her feet comfortably tucked under her, reached for the book on the table beside her.

And stopped.

On the wall she was facing, would always face sitting the way she always did, some bookshelves had been removed. In their place hung a painting, a dreamy oil painting of a cliff overlooking a gentle sea, with two hazy figures standing close together on the beach.

She stood up and walked over to it slowly.

"You bought it," she said, knowing he was there, had entered the library behind her.

"It's yours," he said. "I just thought this was the perfect place for it, for you."

Her eyes were glued to the painting. "Mine," she said, her voice barely audible.

A long moment passed without a reaction from her, and suddenly Ian felt like a damn fool. Theirs was a strict arrangement, his doing, and he had become slack in keeping to his own restrictions, his own rules on how to handle this, handle her. But she certainly hadn't, in fact she still kept her distance, had never stopped pushing him away. And yet here he was, giving her this painting just because of the way she had spoken about it, the emotion he had seen in her. He had wanted to give it to her, wanted to make her happy. Had expected, he supposed, a smile, excitement, whatever he had seen in women he had dated when he had chosen to give a gift, a jewel—that was always what they wanted. She was different, she would not go for such things and he wouldn't give them to her, not offhandedly, she was different for him, too. And so this opportunity, so rare, to know that he could give her something that would please her, was for him priceless.

And she wasn't even dignifying him with a word, a look. Anything. Uncertain of himself, surprised into protecting himself, into having to hide emotions he hadn't expected, he was about to speak, to tell her that if she did not wish to have the damn painting she could return it herself. That she need not worry, her discomfort with him was noted, the contract would be kept, he would not make the mistake of making such a gesture again, they would go back to the way things has been at the beginning. He would—

All thoughts and intentions disappeared, every notion he had of being able to even begin to anticipate her, use comparison to others he'd had in an attempt to figure her out, it all disappeared when she did turn to look at him.

Her eyes were full of bewilderment. And something else, something he couldn't quite put a finger on. When she spoke, he had the feeling she hadn't intended to say what she did, but her surprise, the emotion, had gotten the better of her.

"No one has given me a present since . . ." Her voice trailed off.

He made the connection immediately and spoke even as some, albeit too few of the pieces of the puzzle that was his wife fell into place. "Since your parents died."

The slightest hesitation, then finally she nodded. "I'm sorry," she said, "I just didn't expect this. Thank you."

"No, please, don't apologize. You're very welcome. I'm glad you like it." Glad couldn't even begin to describe what was going through him.

"I love it," she said softly, looking back at the painting. "And it's perfect where it is. You thought of that, too."

He himself was taken now, with the effect this was having on him. She, was having on him.

"May I ask you something?" His voice was soft.

She nodded, her eyes on the painting.

"You can easily afford this painting now. Why didn't you buy it for yourself?"

The eyes that turned to look at him were baffled.

"The possibility never occurred to you, did it?" he answered himself. "To buy this, to buy something for yourself." Something permanent, something to put in a home. Her home.

She turned away again but not before he saw the pain and knew he'd hit the mark. He didn't push further, not wanting her to back away, couldn't bear having her hiding from him again.

Couldn't bear to lose her.

Chapter Twelve

Tess didn't see her husband for much of the rest of the week, and when she did see him again, she was sitting in the library when he walked in. He'd obviously just arrived and had come straight there. He was still dressed in a suit, both it and his shirt looking as if he'd just put them on. Meticulous, but then everything Ian Blackwell wore was custom tailored.

Looking at him, at the way he held himself, the way he came to stand now, leaning on the back of the sofa he usually sat on when he was here with her, she could see why so many feared him. He was the formidable Ian Blackwell through and through, the man she had first met at InSyn.

And right now his eyes were as cool as they were the day they had first looked into hers.

"I have a . . . let's say, interesting problem," he said, contemplating her. His voice was low, and carefully controlled.

She put her book aside and waited. It hadn't been this way with him for quite a while now.

"InSyn's effectiveness is down seven percent."

She nodded. She now knew what this was about. "A further seven percent, you mean," she said. "Since I left, and despite your decision not to dissolve it but instead to have the new transition team help it stand on its feet again. A total of sixteen percent since you took it over."

"And you're not at all surprised. So you knew it would happen. Damn it, you knew." Ice-cold anger ruled the gray in his eyes.

Her first thought was to answer the accusation with a reminder that it was he who had told her that she was no longer an employee of InSyn and that she should stay away from it. But that wouldn't be right, not anymore. She knew now why InSyn was important to him, and the reason she knew was because so much had changed between them since that day.

And so instead she chose to take her place beside Ian Blackwell in one more way. "Are you talking to me as your wife now, or as a former employee of InSyn?" she asked evenly.

"I'm talking to the Tess Andrews who fought me in InSyn's basement that day," he retorted.

She nodded. That made it easier. "You only lost a further seven percent because you kept Jayden. What you failed to do was replace me."

"You."

"Yes."

She meant it. There was nothing arrogant, nothing condescending about what she was saying. She was simply stating a fact.

"Explain."

She disregarded the angered tone. The important thing was that he was finally ready to listen to what she had to say about InSyn, and that she could help him with it. "In the time Davis was the administrative head of the transition team, she made arbitrary changes in InSyn. She didn't care about the company, and she didn't bother to learn it. She was there to mold it into what she thought you wanted."

"That's not how I work."

"That's how she worked. Seeing her with you that day, she was obviously out to impress you."

"I know."

"Do you?"

"I don't sleep with my employees," he said, irritated.

"Who you sleep with is your business as long as you keep it discreet. That's what your contract says, remember?" It just came out. She didn't mean to say it, had no idea where it came from.

Yes, she did. She had wondered about it, more recently. Wondered with a pang she wasn't supposed to feel and that she had meant to keep to herself.

She missed the flicker of surprise in his eyes at what she'd said, and at the way she'd said it.

She breathed in. "I'm sorry," she said, raising her eyes to his. "That wasn't fair."

That surprise in his eyes she didn't miss. She hurried on, focusing on what she knew how to handle.

"Look, you didn't dissolve InSyn, you left it as is. And you replaced the administrative transition team with a good team, one that has improved InSyn's administrative side immensely. It wasn't that well run for a while before, we all knew that. And then you appointed the head of that team to InSyn's interim CEO until you see how things work out with it, which is perfectly understandable.

"InSyn's employees saw this. They also saw that their integration into Pythia Vision as its subsidiary, rather than just a part-time contractor, is giving them a new focus, practical applications to work on. An outlook InSyn had begun to lose simply because it was reaching a final milestone in its development of the algorithmic platform for the human-machine interface, one that the founders couldn't take them beyond—it's ready for the practical implementation, which you're giving them under Pythia Vision and the Alster virtual interface. So they're more confident now in their future."

"But?"

"Your second transition team didn't undo all of Davis's changes."

"Perhaps it agreed with some."

"It saw that InSyn was calming down. Cooperating. It didn't want to make more changes that might rock the boat again." She paused and considered him. "Okay. InSyn developed the ability for human intelligence and machine intelligence to work hand in hand. For that you basically need three things—the machine learning capabilities, the human reactions and practical responses, and the interaction between the two, which requires balancing assimilation and reaction times in order to facilitate the interaction of machine logic with human experience. These are InSyn's three main work teams, who have created three sets of algorithms that together form the platform, the theoretical interface.

"But InSyn also needs data experts. The people who in the beginning analyzed and modeled data, predicted from it, and prescribed situation-relevant impacts and responses—for the learning algorithms, and who later factored in the data related to the human operators working alongside the machine— for the balancing algorithms.

"In essence, they, the data function, they are the foundation of InSyn's work in that they've participated from the beginning in all aspects of the development, and have worked with all of InSyn's teams over time as these teams were formed and developed. But today they're also best positioned to look from above at the integration of the three parts of the theoretical interface."

"Jayden. You."

"Yes. Jayden taught me everything he knew, and later on he made sure I continued to progress with InSyn alongside him."

Ian nodded. What she was telling him was putting their first meeting in context. He understood more now. Not enough, but a bit more.

"The problem is that to an outsider who doesn't get the work behind InSyn, what we, the data function, did was less obvious. Davis saw the three teams working in their designated spaces on the upper floors, while we did most of our work apart from them, and she didn't understand that that's because by then we had our hand in everything. If on the day we met you saw Jayden sitting alone in the basement talking to a team on an upper floor, that meant there was a flaw in the interface—that day it was a mismatch in a balancing algorithm that meant the human operator couldn't 'talk' to the machine in a way that the machine could grasp it. You weren't there for the beginning of the conversation, when the human reactions team had been a part of it, too. Both teams knew to turn to him, they knew he would see the problem faster than they would because he sees it all, has seen it all from the beginning. He and I, we had eyes on everything. We could see flaws they didn't, help them fix them, run prescriptive analysis—suggest solutions and tell them their impact."

"You were both a fundamental and an integrative component."

"Yes."

"And then I took you out of InSyn."

"And Jayden alone isn't enough. Even together, he and I were no longer enough in the advanced stages InSyn's theoretical interface is in. And he certainly can't be enough with the work InSyn is now doing with Pythia Vision, moving into the interface implementation stage and gearing up toward the development of entirely new complex applications. He's been brainstorming with me ever since I came here," she finally told him. "But it's not nearly the same as being there, working with him full time."

"What do I do?"

She stood up and walked over to him, coming to stand on the other side of the sofa. "A few months after Pythia Vision gave InSyn its first project, I chose three people from across the company, one from each team. I trained them in a way that would ensure that together they could do what Jayden and I did, and work as efficiently as we did, under Jayden's guidance. I chose people who, with what Jayden and I would teach them, and with the know-how they've accumulated in their time at InSyn, would be able to both solve any type of problem with the algorithmic platform as it is implemented and to proactively suggest new ideas to improve the resulting interface, take it forward in the years ahead, and make it the most competitive, flexibly implementable interface there is."

He remembered the added workstations in the basement. "You essentially put together a forward-looking team that would accompany the integration of the theoretical interface's three components and its subsequent implementation as an actual interface in varied applications."

"Exactly. But Davis didn't get what we did. She

didn't expect the added team when she got to InSyn, and she refused to listen when we tried to explain to her its importance, that the change was needed now that Pythia Vision would need InSyn to help it build an adaptable, integrated interface. She sent the three people I'd chosen back to their original teams, and what we did fell apart. And so did the theoretical interface's integration."

"And the new transition team didn't restore them to the positions you'd created for them."

"That's right, they missed that. And later, when Jayden tried to talk to your interim CEO, he didn't listen either. InSyn was finally behaving better, and he thought that all its problems were fixed and that if Pythia Vision will need anything there to change, it will ask for it. But Pythia Vision is smart enough to give InSyn the freedom it needs."

"And you couldn't intervene, because you're Ian Blackwell's wife."

She nodded. "InSyn's strength is its people, and if you want it to succeed, you need to let them be. Let them do their work the way they know best."

He didn't tell her that this was exactly what the head of Pythia Vision's Overarching Projects Integration Team had told him after that last meeting they had. The man had also said that InSyn's people were worth every bit of trouble.

"Okay," he said. "What would you do if you were me?"

"Let Jayden put our team back together. And let

him know that you're not going to touch it again, or better, let me tell him. He'll believe me. And then just leave them all alone, let InSyn and Pythia Vision do the work, they'll be fine. If you do that, InSyn will know you're listening, it will trust you, and you won't have to worry about it again."

"And Jayden can deal with these three people of yours, work with this team like you both did?"

"He knows how to handle them."

"Like he handled you?"

"No one handles me." Her voice was quiet.

"Yes. I should know that by now." He considered her. "Mrs. Blackwell, why didn't you tell me?"

"I tried to. On the jet."

The day they got married. He remembered. They hadn't talked then, they had fought, and he'd had no inclination to listen to her. "I'm listening now."

"And you can turn InSyn around now. When you fix what was done to it, it will be the perfect component for the plan you have for it. It will be more, much more. I'll help."

He nodded, his gaze thoughtful. "At least now I finally understand what you did at InSyn."

"You do the same thing."

"Sorry?"

She smiled. "How did you choose InSyn?"

He shrugged. "It had vision. It saw what no one else did at the time and succeeded in developing it effectively."

"But when you started investing in it, its idea

wasn't anywhere near as advanced in its implementation as it is today. And there must have been other startups with similar concepts. How did you know InSyn was your bet?" She looked at him with a slight tilt of her head. "How do you choose all your companies? How did you become Ian Blackwell Holdings?"

No one had ever asked him that before. "I look at the company and I know. I see where it fits in, or where it will fit in if I guide it."

"And when InSyn was causing you trouble you went to see it and you knew how to fix it."

"Apparently not."

"What you missed was something only an insider would know. You knew enough to make the initial difference, calm it down. How?"

"I walked through it, saw the place, the people."

She nodded. "You look at the tangible components of the company on all levels, and you build a multi-dimensional picture in your mind where you see all of them and all the links between them. This combined fundamental and integrative view allows you to see what others don't."

He nodded. He'd never thought about it quite that way.

"That's exactly what I do with data."

He contemplated her thoughtfully. Finally, he decided to ask. "One thing I don't get. Why remain in the basement all this time?"

"My choice." She didn't elaborate, and he caught

something shift in her eyes.

He let it go. For now. Saying nothing, he turned to leave. Then he stopped and turned back to her as the realization hit.

"You trained people to replace you."

She looked at him in silence.

"That new team, you intended for it to stay under Jayden. Without you. You knew InSyn's situation, you saw that Pythia Vision was the only company it was working with, and you understood something was going on, even that far back. You figured InSyn will at some point be purchased by Pythia Vision's parent company and you made sure you could leave, didn't you? Without hurting who, InSyn? Jayden?" He considered her, going back in his mind. "Is that what I was? A way for you to leave?"

She almost said something. For the first time ever. To him, she almost did.

He saw it.

He turned away and went to the door, opened it, and then, as an afterthought, turned back to look at her. "Just so we're clear. Despite that clause in the contract, I haven't been with anyone since the day we got married."

And with that, he left.

The next evening he was in his den when she came in. He looked up from his laptop, and focused on her when he saw the expression on her face.

"You made Jayden the CEO of InSyn."

He'd surprised her, he realized, and found himself oddly pleased. "Joint CEO. He's helped build the company and he obviously knows the people and know-how better than anyone, but I need beside him someone who can actually run it. The interim CEO has agreed to stay permanently, and he thinks Jayden is a good idea."

He settled back in his chair, fully prepared to watch her squirm at the realization that she'd been wrong about him when it came to InSyn, that he was willing to listen and do what was needed. That he had thought one step ahead of her, by appointing Jayden as CEO.

"I did not see that coming," she said simply and walked out again, a smile on her face, leaving him gaping behind her.

It took him a while to focus back on his work.

Three weeks later he came into the library and handed her a report. Saying nothing, he took his jacket off and sat down on the sofa with a weary sigh. She put her book aside and read what he'd given her, noting the changes in InSyn, the improved numbers. Ian watched her with interest. He had certainly never done *this* with any woman he'd been with.

She was completely absorbed, and he could the wheels accelerating even before she looked at him. "And the cooperation with Pythia Vision and with the Alster virtual interface team?" The patents were in the process of being transferred to Pythia Vision, and the developer and the team he'd assembled were already working in its offices.

He got up, walked over to her, and handed her his tablet. She glanced at it, and then looked up at him. He'd just given her access to all the information about Pythia Vision and its projects, including confidential strategic information, such as his detailed plan for it. It had notes in it, his.

She read it. Even before she finished, she went to work. With what she knew, with her experience with InSyn and Pythia Vision's past work and her knowledge of their current cooperation, and with her knowledge about the Alster virtual interface and what her husband wanted, why he had started Pythia Vision and was buying specific knowledge for it, she could provide her own input. And she did. For the Ian Blackwell who she knew now, she did.

"Dinner time, Mrs. Blackwell."

His voice brought her out of her thoughts. She squinted at him. It had been almost two hours and she hadn't noticed he'd left and returned again.

"I'll eat later, I want to finish this," she said.

She turned her gaze back to her work, and so she didn't see the smile that crossed his lips. "We'll eat in the den," he said. "You can see what you're doing more clearly on the screens there, and you can work on my laptop if you want to."

She looked at him with that slight tilt of her head that told him she was thinking him through.

Finally, she nodded.

He'd had Graham prepare the ultimate dinner for the occasion. Pizza. And since he had no idea what she liked and had no hope of asking her now, while she was engrossed in taking his flag project apart and optimizing it, she came into the den to find the most varied assortment of pizzas she had ever seen.

She laughed in delight, and Ian was struck with the realization that the smallest gesture was more to her than all that the money and power he had could give her. And this was, he suddenly realized, quite romantic. Which was ironic, considering he wasn't allowed to be. Not with her.

As the night deepened she was standing in front of the screen that doubled as his television and work screen on the wall opposite his desk, crossing synergies. He walked over to her and put another slice of pizza in her hand, a choice of extra cheeses with tomatoes and onions. She looked at it.

"Eat," he instructed. She frowned but did, then frowned again when he put a glass of wine in her other hand.

"I need coffee, not wine."

"You need to sleep later, not lay awake. None of these companies are going anywhere, they're already IBH, and we already have what we need to move forward."

"Mmm," she said and turned back to the screen, sipping the wine.

He smiled.

It occurred to him later, as he went to bed, that he hadn't wanted the evening to end.

Chapter Thirteen

His den was arranged for one man, him. Where his office at Blackwell Tower was sprawling and as intimidating as him, designed to remind those who entered it whose domain they had walked into, this was his private workspace in his home. It was meant to accommodate no one but him, to allow him to work quietly, alone, and it was furnished that way.

And now he was sharing it with a woman. And this woman always came to sit in the same place, on the same armchair that she had moved closer to the doors that opened to the back of the house, where her thoughtful, contemplative gaze could rest on the skies up above or on the picturesque grounds stretching outside. As she did in the library, here too she would sit with her feet tucked under her when she worked or just sat deep in thought, lean her head on the back of the chair when weariness set in. He had initially thought he might place another desk here for her, but now, as he sat behind his desk, his eyes on the empty chair beside the doors that were open to let the evening air in, he was glad he hadn't. That wasn't her. This chair was.

He turned his eyes back to his laptop, a furrow appearing in his brow. Another month had gone by, InSyn's internal audit report finally came in, and he had left a message for her with Graham, to come see it. He had spent a large part of the day in his office, and had come home to find that she was out with Muriel. This wasn't disappointment he was feeling, he'd done his best to convince himself, just irritation that their work together would be delayed. But Graham's inquisitive look had told him otherwise.

He was engrossed in his work when she came into the den, looking, he couldn't help but notice, rather breathtaking in the white, delicately floral knee-length dress she wore on this uncharacteristically warm day. Absently, she shook down her hair, which she had pulled up. There was none of the hesitation that had been there at the beginning, not anymore, not with him.

"Hey," she said, slightly out of breath. "Graham told me, the InSyn report is here?"

He handed her the tablet and she took it and turned to her habitual place.

And stopped. His armchair, which she'd been sitting on whenever she'd worked in here, had been moved to the side. In its place, in the spot she liked to sit in, stood a copy of her softer, far more comfortable overstuffed chair from the library, made in a lighter shade more fitting her husband's den. She approached it tentatively and walked around it, her fingertips brushing its back.

His eyes followed her every move.

She raised her eyes and looked at him with that considering look of hers. Considering, but not guarded, not at all, he thought, and something new, something endlessly pleasant washed over him, although he did his best not to heed it. After all, it was, he made a final attempt to reason, simply a logical move to ensure that she could work comfortably here. It suited his purpose.

She sat down on the soft chair in that way of hers, her sandals fell on the carpet and she tucked her feet under her. A moment later she was leaning back comfortably, her eyes on the tablet screen she was holding.

His smile mirrored hers, and he made no effort at all to wish it away.

She finished reading the report and contemplated it. Inadvertently, her eyes turned to her husband. He was intent on his laptop and on the two external screens he had on his desk. The sleeves of his shirt were rolled up loosely and its top two buttons were open. She watched him, and had no idea that she smiled.

She turned her gaze away because she had to. It wasn't because she was attracted. It was because she was in love. That wasn't something she could miss, not even her. But he would not, could not, know, she would make sure of that. There was no other way. Not for her.

There was something in him for her, she knew him and so knew this even without the gestures he'd made these past weeks, like the new chair she was sitting on. But she couldn't allow herself to find out what. And not only because of her. The thing was that he was . . . the thing was that she had, as he had said it, studied him. And studying him meant that she saw the photos, and she saw the videos. She saw him at various social functions, much like the ones she accompanied him to these days, invariably with a woman. Saw the way he smiled, the attention he gave them. Yes, she had studied him, the man he was. And he was experienced. Very much so. He knew how to talk to women, how to be with them. How to get them.

And so the fact was that she simply didn't know what it meant, the way he was with her. It could be the natural closeness that had developed between them. They did live together, after all. She thought it might be more than that, but she wasn't at all sure. She had never let any man close enough to her to know. For all she knew he was just being . . . She had no idea. He hadn't behaved with her the way he had with those other women. She thought, it seemed to her, that with her he was different than he was with them, as a man, but . . . No, she had no idea at all. It was so much easier to see these things in others, and they seemed to be able to figure it out so much better than she could. She couldn't begin to figure out that part of it, of him. But then she couldn't begin to deal with that part of herself, either.

And anyway, it wasn't possible. She couldn't even imagine how it would be. Maybe if things were different, if she was different. Would it be possible then? The fact that she could even think about it, think about him this way, was inexplicable to her.

God, she was rambling on. And in her own mind. It was stupid, there wasn't anything between them and there wasn't ever going to be anything between them and that was that. They had gotten to know each other and had much more in common than they had thought, that was all, and it was good, it made things easier. And it was best that it remain that way.

So why did she know, quite painfully so, that if . . . no, *when* he would eventually choose to be with another woman, it would break her heart?

Okay. Enough. Enough, she chided herself. It wasn't to be, it was impossible, and she had pushed it away more than once already because it hurt. When it came to him, it hurt.

She pushed it away yet again. She had no other choice. Hiding was the only option.

Her eyes turned back to him of their own volition. His brow furrowed, and he shook his head. That made her focus.

"What's wrong?" she asked.

He looked at her. "Nothing, just something here." His eyes returned to his work and then immediately back to her. He considered her for a long time.

She waited.

"I see the workings of the tangible, you see the workings of data," he said thoughtfully.

She tilted her head in question.

"That's what you said when I brought you InSyn."

She remembered, of course.

He leaned back in his chair, still considering her. This wasn't about InSyn, she realized. He was considering whether to bring her in on something else. Something that required a hell of a lot of trust.

"I have a . . . suspicion, you could say," he finally said, slowly. "A gut feeling. It led me to watch Ian Blackwell Holdings more closely, but for now I'm doing this without the knowledge of anyone in it, not even Robert. I need this to remain that way until I know what I'm looking at." And if he was right, this coming out without him exposing it himself could have a reputational cost to the company. In the least. By sharing this with her, he would, in effect, be putting his life's work in her hands. If she accepted it.

He saw the understanding in her eyes. She put the tablet aside, the professional in her fully focused. "Let's do this," she repeated what she'd said to him in the car that first time they had gone out together as husband and wife. Shared fate.

He nodded. "Someone is making subtle changes in Ian Blackwell Holdings' numbers. As in across the entire company. Indiscriminate choice of figures—

it can be sales revenues, investments, current assets, pretty much anything. A number of subsidiaries and second-tier companies that I've seen, here or outside the United States, no obvious logic to it and not enough to identify a source. The changes are small enough and scattered enough to be chalked up to discrepancies resulting from human error if they are noticed. But I don't think they're meant to be noticed."

"How did you see it?"

He didn't hesitate. "From time to time, I look at the company from above."

"Ian Blackwell Holdings as a whole instead of any subsidiary or sector separately."

He nodded. "It allows me to see the entire picture, and to see things that I might otherwise miss. Anyway, no one knows I do this, not this way. No one except you."

"And no one will." The eyes that met his made him a promise he no longer needed.

He nodded. "I walk through everything, at every level of the company. Structure, supply chains, production and product rollout strategies, marketing strategies, investment strategies, human resources, finances of course, everything."

"Tangible and data, except that for you, the data immediately raises tangible links."

He wasn't surprised that he didn't have to explain it to her.

"So no one saw what you saw because no one

looks at your company the way you do. But then, no one else would feel the need to, certainly not for a company of this size, and whoever did it probably assumed that. Either that, or they simply made a mistake."

"Because they allowed a pattern to be created." He understood where she was going with this.

She nodded. "It didn't have to be something obvious. It just had to be enough for it to be a pattern you saw. Because of the timing of the changes, or because of a non-random dispersion of the discrepancies they created—some pattern that could only be discerned by someone who regularly looks at the company as a whole and who knows it as well as you do."

"It wasn't enough. I couldn't follow them. I can see the discrepancies in the figures that show me that changes have been made, but I can't anticipate where I'll find the next one, where the next change will be. I almost missed them myself even when I looked for them. In fact, I probably missed some."

"So we'll look together." Her eyes were on his, but she wasn't with him. She was thinking. He let her. Waited.

"Can you walk me through the entire company the way you do it, so that I'll see the changes that have been made in it?"

He was now talking to the data expert he'd first met at InSyn. "Where do you want to get to?"

"The bottom."

"You want the basement."

She smiled at the reference. "Yes. The underlying data only. But I don't know the company. Looking at it from top to bottom, with you showing me what you see, will give me enough of an understanding of it so that later I can work the data."

"That can't be enough."

"I don't need anything else, I have you for that. I just need to understand enough of the company's structure and content."

"You want to combine raw data analysis with tangible knowledge—me—that you can access whenever you need to."

She shrugged. "Under the circumstances, that's the best way to do this. And it's still going to take time. Think about the sheer amount of data for a company this size."

He frowned. "If I reschedule my days, work part of the time here or disappear completely so that I can be available to you the entire time, this will raise questions. With the Alster Industries integration into Ian Blackwell Holdings and the internal audits my subsidiaries are currently undergoing, it wouldn't be something I do."

"Do what you always do. If you give me an overview of the company in a way that later I can transition my thinking to its data, then, if you then give me access to whatever I need from the company itself, you I'll just need to fill in any gaps, answer questions when I have them."

"Give you the tangible," he said and brought up the structural layers of Ian Blackwell Holdings on the wall screen. "How do you want to do this?"

"Start as you normally do when you look at it, and I'll follow. When I can I'll start walking beside you."

"So, pretty much like the beginning of this marriage."

She laughed, nodding.

He remained seated in his chair, running his company on the screen as he had that first time he'd noticed the discrepancies, and in the times he'd looked for them since. She came to lean back on the other side of the desk, facing the screen. What he saw, she saw.

He was in it from the first image. She was seeing it for the first time, and looking at it his way, not hers. And so it took her more time, and she gave herself that time. She knew how her mind worked. With her experience after all the years at InSyn, she trusted it to keep everything she saw for later use when she would switch to working with the underlying data. She let the company schemes run, let the man who made this company what it was explain. After a while, it all began to make sense. And once it did, what she had seen until that point fell into place too.

He began slowly, for her, then accelerated to go at his usual pace. He couldn't see what was in her mind, had no idea what was happening there. All he saw was the focus set in, then intensify. From time to time she asked, and he answered. Whenever he reached a place where he had found a change that had been made, he dove down the layers and showed it to her. He noticed she wrote nothing down, made no notes. She didn't need to.

They covered it all, the way he did every time he looked at his company as a whole. When the company schemes stopped, Tess had a pretty good idea of what he had built. It was, to say the least, impressive.

She shook her head and looked at him. "All of that is yours?" Even when she had studied him, her search didn't see it all.

He smiled.

"What makes a man build that?" Nowhere, in everything she had read about him, was this question asked. Or answered.

"I guess we both have our pasts."

Her smile dimmed, and he regretted having said that. He moved on, not wanting her to distance herself from him again. "So now you need the underlying data."

"I'm going to start with the discrepancies you pointed out, within the companies you found them in, and see where it takes me."

"I'll give you access to everything, you can work in here. I'll try to have as many meetings as I can in my office, I won't fly anywhere unless I have to. Still, most of my meetings I can't cancel without eventually raising suspicion."

"There really is no need to. All I need is to be able to speak to you when I have questions, and as your wife I can do that without anyone wondering."

"How about we do more than that? Come with me to San Francisco tomorrow, work in my office. I'll conduct my meetings in the conference room. You should be close to me, at least in the first days, when you're bound to have most of the questions."

She thought about it.

"Those who need to know, know you've been involved in InSyn, the company you used to work in. That's what they'll think you're doing. And your working on it in Blackwell Tower wouldn't be that much of a surprise. Other subsidiary representatives will be in the building, too, working with the internal auditors. Your proximity to me is accepted because, as you yourself said, you're my wife. And you can work on your own laptop, as a standalone that isn't connected to the company's systems, so there will be no eyes on what you do. Just connect through the laptop I work with there, I'll leave it with you."

It made sense. "Well, I suppose it will mean no time will be wasted."

"That's settled then." He was pleased that she'd said yes.

Chapter Fourteen

This wasn't her first time in Blackwell Tower, or in her husband's office. She had made her way up to the top floor in his private elevator several times already. To see the place, as would be expected of her, and to get acquainted with some of the people who worked with him on this floor and on others in this impressive building that was Ian Blackwell Holdings' headquarters. She had also come here to meet him for a lunch or a dinner now and then, or for the occasional social function, if he couldn't make it home beforehand, although more recently it seemed to her that he'd begun to make the effort to do so.

And so she was familiar with the spacious sitting area, the offices of the administrative assistant's assistants—she was no longer surprised to hear a range of languages as she passed by them—the conference room, Becca's office, and finally Ian Blackwell's huge office beyond it.

She stood in the doorway of her husband's office, which was nothing like his den in the house. There, there was a coziness, a warmth that was absent here. Blackwell Tower was built by its owner just a few years back, it was new and modern. And so was this office. The wall to her right was floor-to-ceiling glass, with a tint that constantly shifted to allow just the right amount of light inside and that blended in with the room's colors, which were all in a play of the same dark shades—the dark brown, nearly black desk near the wall furthest from her, with the comfortable high-backed chair behind it, the just slightly lighter, textured wall behind them, with dark shelves on both sides, the sitting area to her right with its two sofas hugging the corner and the low glass-top table before them, the door far to the left of the desk that led to a private bathroom, the marble floor. Even the overhead lighting, built into the ceiling in a way that would throw light either separately on the desk or on the entire office, fit into the ambience.

This time she was here to work, and although it didn't show outwardly, her mind was already focused on what she had come here to do, processing what she had begun to work on with her husband the day before. She took a step in and looked at the sitting corner on her right, contemplating how to comfortably set it up for the hours of intensive work she needed.

"Take my chair." Ian indicated his desk. "See how you like it."

A step behind Tess, Becca started in surprise. Although she would never say anything—her loyalty to Ian Blackwell was heartfelt after all her years with him—she herself had wondered how real his marriage truly was. It lacked too much of what she should have been seeing in the conduct, the demeanor of her newlywed boss. And this was all too pronounced whenever she saw him together with what should have been the woman he was in love with. But this, Ian Blackwell offering his chair to his wife in this way, made her question what she had thought. This was a first for him. With anyone.

But then she hadn't seen Mrs. Blackwell for some weeks, and the two of them seemed different now together. Closer.

"You look good there," Ian teased, grinning, when his wife placed her laptop on his desk and sat behind it, on his chair. It was a good fit, she was only a few inches shorter than him.

"Go away," she said, smiling back at him, and he raised his hands in surrender and left for his first meeting. Becca followed him out, throwing another astonished glance at them both.

Tess worked both on her husband's laptop and on hers, which was not registered to the company she was looking into and was therefore suitable for her purpose. When her husband came back from his first meeting, she was intent on both. His was running data, hers was showing speculations.

"All yours," he said, settling down on a chair on the other side of his own desk and leaning back comfortably.

"Want your chair back?"

"No. I meant it, you look good there."

"I'd tell you to go away again but I need you."

He raised his eyebrows.

"Shut up," she said without looking up, but she was smiling, and he marveled at how far they had come.

And at the euphoric feeling that washed over him. He wondered what she would say if he asked her out on a date. A real date. It was time to find out, he thought, once they figured out what was going on in his company. He would take it slow, give her all the time she needed. And find a way to break through that impenetrable barrier around her.

She asked, and he answered. She had quite a few questions, many of them with regard to subsidiaries he himself hadn't yet found discrepancies in, he was concerned to hear. That meant that whatever was going on, it involved a greater part of his company than he'd thought.

They were engrossed in one of his foreign subsidiaries when Becca called to inform Ian it was time for his next meeting. When he opened the door to leave, Tess saw Brett outside. Brett Sevele was the chief technology officer and one of the founders of IBH Additive Manufacturing, a company Ian Blackwell Holdings had purchased three years earlier. She had met Brett in some of the social functions she had attended with her husband. He had seemed to be good with people around him, seemed to enjoy the company, the mingling. But she'd had a feeling that he was trying too hard to be near her husband and her. He seemed amiable enough, but she felt uneasy around him. At first she had accepted that she couldn't fully rely on her instincts in these surroundings she was still getting used to, but months later the uneasiness hadn't ebbed. Brett was around them a bit too much. He'd never been to the house, and this was only the second time she'd seen him here, on the top floor of Blackwell Tower, but still.

Anyone who came to meet Ian Blackwell was required to wait in the sitting area, everyone but his wife, who could go right into his office. But Brett had somehow gotten in, managing to pass Becca, and was now approaching the office, his hand extended to shake Ian's.

He caught a glimpse of Tess inside, sitting behind Ian's desk. "Is that Mrs. Blackwell there?" he asked Ian. "Well, isn't that nice. I should say hello."

"Maybe later," Ian said and led him away smoothly toward the conference room where the internal auditors assigned to Additive Manufacturing were waiting.

Brett let himself be led away, throwing a glance back at her, before Becca hurried to close the door.

Tess and Ian had lunch in the office, not wanting to stop their work, and when they finally returned home, late enough for Graham to complain that he understood they were busy but they really should call to inform him if they were going to be late for dinner, they still had no idea where the discrepancies they were finding throughout Ian Blackwell Holdings had come from.

Over the next days, Tess alternated her time between the Woodside house and her husband's San Francisco office, until finally the day came when she opted to stay in the house, spending the day in his den. By now she had some idea of what was going on, and she didn't like it one bit. She wanted to test her theory outside the company, and so she used Ian's personal system, which she had disconnected from Ian Blackwell Holdings to ensure the privacy of their work, and that was powerful enough to do what she needed it do.

When her husband returned home, as soon as his last meeting of the day was over, he found her sitting at his desk, both his laptop and hers working, as well as the external screens on the desk and the one on the wall. As soon as he walked into the den and closed the door behind him, she began to speak.

"Whoever is doing this, they're not trying to steal or anything like that. I think they're trying to take you down."

He focused instantly. "As in?"

"The discrepancies you've found, because of the changes these people are making in the company's figures, are interconnected, in effect creating threads.

That's what they—although it could be one person, I don't know yet—that's what they're doing, they are virtually weaving threads throughout a growing number of your subsidiaries. And every such thread is a computer code. The threads form webs that are each centered in a company or a part of it, depending on the company, its size, its structure, its position in Ian Blackwell Holdings' global structure, and so on. And these webs are also interconnected and are gradually forming a larger web that will eventually span Ian Blackwell Holdings. All of it. Wherever the point of origin of that encompassing web is, the place from which it started to form and where it's controlled from, when they pull at it, that is activate the threads that make up the overall algorithm, the company will crash. Financial systems, supply chains, production lines, human resources systems. You name it, it will come down."

"Will? So it can't crash now." Ian's tone of voice was factual, pragmatic.

"Whoever they are, they're not done. I don't know yet when they started, but I do know they need more time. These webs are still only in, I estimate, fifty-odd percent of Ian Blackwell Holdings' subsidiaries, and less than that in the parent company itself. It sounds a lot, hard to miss, but this web of webs is being constructed so delicately, with discrepancies that are negligible enough to indeed be chalked up to human error, so that no one would notice unless they knew the entire company, all of it, across and top to bottom, and actually tended to look at it as a whole. Like Ian Blackwell himself."

"Except no one knows I do that."

"Your company is huge. Who would imagine you still look at it now the way you might have when it was small? And even if someone thought you might, they would probably trace your movements in your office."

"While I do it here, in my home."

She nodded. "I know your company has good cybersecurity, I checked it out when I was in your office. But this, whoever they are, they're good. Smart, careful, and I'm betting this took some planning."

"How on earth did you figure it out?" He was impressed.

"I just . . . saw the threads." She shrugged. "See? You should have kept me as your employee."

"No," he said absently, his eyes on the layered scheme of his company she had put up on the wall screen. "I much prefer having you as my wife. What's that?" He pointed to a symbol on the top left of the scheme.

She was still reeling from his answer and it took her a moment to focus again. "That's a completion scale. I calculated the estimated worst-case scenario to completion."

He reached back to his laptop and clicked it. The scheme filled with fine threads, a timeline showing at the bottom.

"Are you sure?" This was bad.

"I think they've created a learning algorithm. Whenever they complete a part of the web at a strategic node, they can use it to reach out and initiate others around it, so that they're covering more ground over the same time span as they progress, and their work is less dependent on them and can continue without their being there. I can tell you they're not accelerating as much as I would expect them to, though. I ran a temporal scan to check that. I think they're progressing carefully. Which makes sense—the more threads they have, the more they run the risk of being discovered."

"So, one month."

"No."

He looked at her.

"We're going to stop him. Or them." Her tone of voice was determined. She wasn't going to let anyone hurt him.

He frowned. "You think it's one person, don't you?"

"I can't be sure, but yes. The pace the changes seem to have been made in at the beginning is too slow for this to be more than one person. And again, the fact that the independently forming parts of the web are forming slower than I'd expect despite the learning algorithm makes more sense if it's one person who understands he needs to watch what he's doing because there's no one to check that he—or she—hasn't made mistakes. One person can do it, it would simply take longer and require more focus."

"Could you do this?" He was genuinely curious. He was learning just that much more about who he had beside him all this time.

She shrugged. Yes, she could cause some damage. People who knew data also knew how to manipulate it. And data wasn't all she knew.

"I'm glad you're on my side," he said evenly.

"Point is, they don't know I am. Or, he doesn't know I am, if we do assume one person is doing this." She turned to him. "Mr. Blackwell, someone really hates you."

"You're me, you make some enemies over the years. Hell, nowadays I probably make enemies just by being Ian Blackwell."

Her brow furrowed. She'd never thought about it like that. She'd seen the money, the power, the freedom of it. She'd never considered there could be other sides to it. But then, wasn't his having to get married in the first place an example of that, albeit a negligible one compared to this?

Ian turned to look at the scheme again. "So now we find the point of origin and disarm it."

"Without him knowing. If he decides to trigger it even now, it'll still do some damage." She touched her laptop screen and the view on the wall screen changed. "I ran a trace that hit three pseudo-points of origin."

"Already?"

"It was easy to set up once I understood what

the threads were forming and had some webs to follow."

Easy, he thought. Right. "Why pseudo?"

"On the way to each of these three points, the trace encountered all the dead ends and snags I'd expect to see if it was intentionally made to seem difficult, to make me think someone is trying to prevent me finding them, that I'm on the right track. And by me I mean whoever might be looking. And every time I changed the search parameters, the trace found a different point of origin, in a different subsidiary, all three in Europe."

"Which ones?"

"It doesn't matter. None of them were it." She wasn't sure how to explain it.

"You're not sure how you knew. You just did."

It was her turn to be surprised that he got her. She nodded. "Something just wasn't right with them. It's like . . . when a piece of the puzzle looks perfect but when you try to push it into place you have to put some effort into it because it's actually not."

He wondered how many in his company could see what she could.

"I think it's a trap," she said. "You expose any of these points, or any of the other pseudo-points he's probably set up in other subsidiaries, and he knows you suspect something and triggers the real point of origin, crashing your company." She looked at him thoughtfully. "The thing is, I think the real point of origin isn't connected directly to the encompassing web, I think when he wants it activated he'll have to connect it."

He saw the frown. "That worries you."

She nodded. "This, what he's been doing, it's careful enough. From what I've seen, there's enough to throw off track anyone who might happen to notice what's happening. So why disconnect the origin? It's too risky. What if the reconnect fails at the crucial moment or takes too long?"

"You think you might be wrong about this?"

She shook her head. That was what worried her. That she was sure she was right about it. "But something is still off. I'm missing something."

He watched her. Trusted that she would figure it out. Trusted her. "What now?"

She touched her laptop touchscreen again and all the screens changed. He looked at them, gaping. They were all running data, dense data, as the algorithm she'd written did its job.

"We keep searching," she said.

Neither felt like going out. But there was nothing they could do now but wait for what the search Tess had set up would find, for the clues that would allow them to identify whoever was behind the damage being done to Ian Blackwell Holdings. And the facades they were putting up, the one of the past months and this new one they had devised together, had to continue.

Ian had agreed to participate in a panel on the first of a three-day young leaders conference in San Francisco, and Robert was waiting to accompany him there, and Muriel and Tess were due to participate in a girls' empowerment event in the city. Both had agreed to these events before they had begun to work on untangling what was happening to the company, and both agreed it should go on as planned.

Still, Ian was restless. He was due to leave for Tokyo the next morning, to meet with the representatives of the teams that would be auditing his regional subsidiaries, and, while he was there, to meet with the heads of these companies, too. He could, and already did, move up the meetings with the CEOs, thinking he would meet with them first and only then deal with all other matters, in case his wife discovered anything that would require his return. His audit teams knew their job and he had no real qualms about dealing with them from afar and meeting them later, if the need arose. What he really wanted to do was cancel the trip, but he couldn't risk questions being asked that could get to the wrong person. Not when he had no idea who wanted to hurt his company, and if his actions were being watched.

Tess had taken her smartphone with her, keeping it not in her purse this time but in an inner pocket in the jacket of the pantsuit she wore, so that she would know if the search found anything new.

She was using it now to look at the latest findings while they were in the back of the Bentley, on their way to their friends' home, where Ian would join Robert in a company limo while Tess would take Muriel with her.

"Here, look at this." She showed him the phone screen and he wondered if she noticed that she had slid closer to him on the seat, that their bodies were touching. He certainly did. Quite acutely, in fact.

"This is one mistake he's made in the earlier stages," she was saying. "Looks like here and there he made changes that didn't entirely fit in with what he wanted, but instead of restoring the original numbers and then making the changes he did want, he 'smoothed' the thread over the changes he'd already made, and the resulting thread is therefore just a bit skewed and so just that much visible. There's no way he expected someone to see what he's doing, at least back then, otherwise he wouldn't have risked it. There's ego there, and ego makes people make mistakes."

He looked at the screen, trying hard to disregard how close she was to him. She was wearing that delicate perfume of hers, the one she usually had on, the one she liked most, which told him just how much she had wanted to stay at home and work instead of going out. He had no doubt that she didn't know the effect she was having on him, had had for a while now. It had been easier for him to push away the physical attraction when they were strangers who followed a strict contract, but things were different now, quite significantly so. Certainly for him. And the physical was no longer as easy to control.

Just then, Tess raised her eyes to him, meaning to speak, and found her face, her mouth, near his, felt him, the proximity to him, in every inch of her body. She moved away, ending the touch, the closeness. But she did this without thinking. There was no fear, nor did she mind it, not at all. Her moving away from him was unintentional, old instinct more than anything. A well-learned, too well-learned, instinct.

Absorbed in her own reaction, she failed to see his. The flash of disappointment, the anger that followed, anger at himself. A fool, he thought. That's what I am.

Chapter Fifteen

Four hours later Ian was standing on the convention center's mezzanine level, around him the young and hopeful who vied for an informal word, some advice perhaps, from the participating business leaders. His mind was on none of them.

The panel discussion had gone well enough. In fact, he didn't regret attending it. These were talented, highly motivated minds who had come to hear him, the ones his company would be seeking not too long from now, and he had noted a couple of them he wanted to keep an eye on. And he had attracted their interest, too—once the panel was over he found himself surrounded by them, inundated with eager questions.

He had expected this. What he hadn't expected was to be propositioned by the panel's co-host. A good-looking woman, a mid-height blond, blue eyes, with a body it was somewhat difficult to disregard. But he couldn't care less. He had bluntly disregarded the attention she had already given him earlier, but that didn't stop her from pouncing on him the moment she saw him alone after the panel had ended.

Literally pouncing on him. She had crowded him behind the stage in the main hall and had pressed herself against him suggestively. He had pushed her away, politely but firmly. He was married, he had said. But it's not a true marriage, is it, she had answered, there have been rumors and they were true, weren't they, you haven't kissed you wife even once in public, you've barely touched her.

Robert, who had come to look for him, had seen what was happening and had intervened with an excuse that allowed Ian to escape. Ian had been through this before. And in the past, he would have reacted the exact same way to a woman who behaved that way. But that wasn't the point. The point was that she was too goddamn right. There wasn't anything behind his marriage, and there was nothing between him and his wife.

Even though he wanted there to be.

He'd been walking on eggshells for weeks. They'd been working together, spending more time together than ever before. And they were close now, he had never been this close to any woman, not like this. And yet she wasn't letting him near her. She wasn't allowing any kind of proximity, not even that which came inadvertently, as in the car earlier. She was deliberately keeping her distance from him and he was no closer to finding out why. He trusted her, and it seemed to him that she trusted him, too— but only to a point. Still, even now, only to a point.

Not a point. A bloody wall. She was resisting

what was happening between them with the same stubbornness he had felt from her in the beginning, when they were still only strangers. Every time he thought there was something between them, every time he believed his feelings for her might be reciprocated, every single time he ventured out, giving something of himself, letting her know while still not breaking their contract, she took a step away from him, hid behind that unseen wall, beyond his reach. Every time he tried to understand, to hint that he saw, that he wanted to know, every time he tried to get through to her, she turned away. She didn't let anyone near her, not just him, he already knew that. But this, them, that should have been different. Yet she was more guarded with him than with everyone else.

Damn her, he thought. This relationship had begun as strictly a business arrangement, and if that's what she wanted it to remain, then so be it. He was done. He had fallen for her, he knew that. He hadn't wanted to, hadn't expected it, hadn't thought it could be, and yet he had. For her, of all women. And there was nothing he could do about it, nothing he could use to break her hold on him by way of the pragmatism that had always guided him, the careful delimitation of the involvement he allowed himself when he was with a woman. He couldn't tell himself how inappropriate it was, that she was not the kind of woman he wanted, that he had no chance for happiness with her, that all she was after was what his name and status and money could give her. He could say nothing of what he could so easily say about all the others he'd been with. He couldn't, because none of those arguments stood.

She was, in every way, his match.

Rage flashed. He was angry and frustrated. Sexually frustrated, he admitted to himself, and feeling that woman against him hadn't help. The hell with it. He had the right to do this under the contract. Would the woman who was his wife even give a damn if he did?

He took the drink the waiter brought him and sipped it, scanning the room in leisure, the way he had done in the past. Before her. A speaker who had participated in an earlier session smiled at him from across the room, and two rather curvy women, employees of the convention center if to judge by their formal name tags, eyed him with interest and giggled at each other, too obviously trying to decide who would dare to approach him. Everything was as it had been before the marriage that these women certainly didn't appear to think stood in their way to him. Just like riding a bicycle, he thought ruefully. He looked at his choices. Who will I have tonight, he thought to himself, as he had countless times in the past. Who do I want?

He scanned the room again. The speaker, the giggling duo? Maybe he would give a call to that model who had just broken up with her boyfriend, she had sent him a message the week before to see if he wanted to hook up, out of everyone's sight, and she herself had an interest in keeping it a secret, which would adhere to the requirements of the contract. Yes. Maybe. So who did he want?

His wife, he realized with shocking clarity. No one else had even a remote chance of interesting him anymore.

He wanted, needed, his wife.

He handed his near-full drink to a waiter who passed him by and strode out of the building, leaving them all behind.

The house was quiet. He went straight to the stairs and walked up to the second floor, and turned toward his bedroom. But then, before the thought had fully crossed his mind, he changed direction and headed to her room, intending to straighten this out once and for all. If she reaffirmed her wish to remain within the strict boundaries of their arrangement, that would be it. He was perfectly capable of turning back the clock, he told himself. A contract relationship, perhaps still a work one, too, and that's all. But he had the right to know now.

He flung the door open.

And there she was. She herself must have returned not too long before and was changing her clothes. She was standing by the bed, undressed to her bra and panties, and she was so absolutely beautiful, he thought, staring, need, his need for her, threatening. And then her shock wore off and she moved to take her robe from where it lay at the edge of the bed, and this broke the spell he was under.

"God," he said, reality crashing into him in full force. "My God. I'm sorry. Tess, I'm so sorry." He shut the door clumsily and made his way down the stairs in a haze. In the living room, he grabbed the decanter and poured himself a drink, his hands unsteady for the first time in his life. He took a long sip and closed his eyes, breathed in deeply, tried to settle himself. Couldn't. He had never, ever done something like that. He wasn't sure what he had wanted to do tonight, he knew he had gone in there to talk to her, to get this thing that was or wasn't between them sorted out once and for all, but when he had seen her that way, standing there half-naked, his body had reacted and he had wanted . . .

He opened his eyes and caught his own reflection in the window. I've lost her, he thought. I've just lost her.

Tess grabbed her robe, put it on and tied it tightly around her. Her heart was racing, she was—

Not afraid, she realized with a start. At no point was she afraid that he would hurt her. She was, though, bewildered. And worried. She had seen his face when he had stood there. He had wanted to come in, had wanted her, *that* she couldn't have been mistaken about. But it was nothing like . . . she shook the thought off in determination. It was nothing like that, that was the thing. And then there was what she had seen in his eyes just as he had realized what he was doing, that split second before he had rushed back out.

She did what she never would have considered doing in the past. She went to look for him. And she found him in the living room, staring out of a window at the darkness outside. When she came in, he turned his head toward her, but then turned back to the window. Not looking at her.

"What I did is inexcusable." He played with the snifter, absently swirling the drink around. "That is not who I am."

She already knew that, beyond a doubt, which for her was a lot and which was why she was down here with him now, allowing them to be alone this way in the silent house.

"Why did you?" She surprised them both by simply asking.

"It doesn't matter. The point is that I did."

"You didn't. You never came into the room."

"I wanted to."

"The point is that you didn't," she used his own words. "The point is that you never would, not like that." Her absolute confidence in this astonished her even as she realized it was so very true, realized, from the pain in his eyes, that she now knew it better than he did. "What happened?"

He owed her that, at least. He risked it. "For a

moment there, earlier today, I regretted that our arrangement was just that."

She started at the admission and he chuckled mirthlessly.

"Yes, that was my reaction, too. I followed that with frustration and thought it would be a good time to exercise my right to . . . date, if you want to call it that."

She didn't expect the force of the pang in her heart. "And did you?"

"Pick up a woman at the convention? No, although I certainly had my choice. And it has been a while."

"So why didn't you?" She needed to know. More than anything right now, she needed to know.

"Because none of them was you." The admission to her, to himself, uttered aloud, brought it home sharply. "Look, Tess." He turned to her. "This has obviously gotten out of hand, and I accept full responsibility. If you wish to leave, don't let the contract get in your way. I will arrange everything with Robert—"

"It's okay," she said gently.

"It's not okay. It's not." His eyes met hers, angry at himself, at this. "It can't be okay because it's you. And because something happened to you, someone hurt you, that's what happened, isn't it? I see that every time I come near you, I feel it every time I touch you. And the fact that I made you feel anything less than safe with me—"

"That's enough."

She said it as she had that first day, and he stopped, startled. Then he laughed, and she smiled at him, and he felt something within him calm, a balance restored.

"Thank you," he finally said, and she surprised him, astonished him, by walking up to him and putting a soft hand on his cheek. He met those lovely eyes, the warm golden amber. Saw the trust. Needed to see it.

"You're tired, Ian. God knows you have enough reasons to be." Her voice was soft. "Let it go."

"This is the first time you've called me by my name," he said, and realized that that evening was the first time he'd called her by hers. He put the drink, undrunk, on the bar and turned to leave, not because he wanted to but because of what her touch, what was between them here, in this delicate moment, was doing to him. "Okay," he said, letting out a breath. "Okay. I'm flying out early in the morning, I won't see you tomorrow, then."

He was going to Tokyo, she recalled.

"I'll see you when I return?" he asked, softness in his voice.

"You will," she said.

"You're flying alone?" Robert was still at home, Ian saw on his phone screen. He himself was on his way to Tokyo by now, alone in the cabin of his jet.

"I have full days ahead of me, I imagine Mrs. Blackwell would be bored." He wasn't about to let on the truth. Both truths.

"Of course she would. In Tokyo, a city she's never been to, with a limo to take her anywhere she wants to go and people who would show her the city like only a Blackwell can see it."

"I might take her myself some other time." He would have liked to take her to places she had never been to. She would have enjoyed it. He would, too. If things were different.

If things could still be different.

On the screen, his friend watched him. He didn't think he was wrong. In fact, he was sure he wasn't. Damn, he thought. If I could only find a way to make this be.

"So, last night. What happened?" he asked.

"I got bored. I left." He raised an eyebrow. "Without telling you. I'm sorry."

"I don't care about that. I saw you leave."

Ian nodded.

"You were considering it." He knew Ian would know what he meant, what he had seen.

Ian said nothing, confirming what his friend had thought.

"Don't worry, no one else noticed. I know you better than most people do, Ian, I see what they don't. And frankly, despite those women there, most people don't expect you to do that any longer, so they wouldn't see the obvious."

Ian's eyes remained impassive.

"You didn't, though."

"Maybe I did." Ian was growing irritated.

"No, I think you didn't. I think you went home. Where your wife is."

"I think you think too much." Ian didn't want this line of discussion to continue.

"I think we've been friends for many years. And I think I've been privy to the truth of your marriage when it started, but that I'm no longer privy to the whole truth. Ian, you're in love with your wife, aren't you? You're in love with Tess."

"Let it go, Robert," Ian warned.

"It's a good thing, you know." And it was what Robert had hoped for from the moment he had seen his friend react to Tess Andrews as he had never reacted to anyone before.

"I have a meeting an hour after I land and too much work to do until then."

"You're a stubborn fool," Robert said in a rare show of frustration. "Fine, go work some more, buy another company. Whatever. I'm going to go say good morning to my wife and kids. See, I actually have a life." And he hung up.

Normally Ian might have been amused at that little outburst, but this time there was no humor in his eyes. He didn't need Robert to tell him how he felt about his wife. He'd known he loved her for quite some time now.

The problem was that, unlike Robert, he knew

there was a complication. Something was standing between Tess and him, and he still had no idea what it was.

The next incoming call had him raise his eyebrows again, irritated, until he saw who it was.

"Ian," was the name his wife used when she greeted him. There was something new in her eyes for him, something he hadn't seen in them before. Confidence, that was it. Confidence in him. Despite the events of the night before. Or perhaps because of them, he thought. He hadn't considered it, the possibility that what happened, or rather what didn't happen, and the truth he had told her, would be what would finally change things between them.

Whatever it was, he still had her. Nothing else mattered.

"Hi, Tess." Her name rolled easily off his tongue. "Good morning. I thought you might sleep in."

"There's something I want to do that I need to finish today, a simulation algorithm I want to build that might help us find that point of origin. I want to do it here, but then I'm considering going to your office, probably tomorrow, to run it directly from there."

He nodded, pleased. "Let me know if you do, I'll tell Becca to expect you. You should be able to work there undisturbed, since I'm not around."

"Yes, but I won't have my expert sidekick with me."

He laughed at that. "Call me directly whenever you want. Your calls I'll take."

She was smiling when the call ended.

So was he. And for the life of him, he hadn't thought that this morning he would.

Chapter Sixteen

She did end up going to his office the next day. And it wasn't just his office, the entire floor was quiet. Ian Blackwell wasn't there, and so the only people around were Becca and her administrative assistants, all working in their offices. The floor was hushed.

By now Tess was used to being here in this capacity, and Becca had expected her, receiving her with a genuine smile and making sure she had everything she needed before leaving her alone in her husband's office. Tess went right to work. She had a lot to do. This time she wanted to use the algorithm she had prepared the day before to simulate the continued formation of the individual webs within Ian Blackwell Holdings' subsidiaries, which would give her a wider platform for generating specific location identifiers, markers that she could use to go backward and pinpoint where in the huge company the encompassing web the individual webs made up had originated and when it was first created, when whoever was doing this had started.

And this was the best place to get whatever

supplementary data she would need for her simulation while she was running it, here in Ian's office, where she could access everything without any delays. She worked on her laptop, but connected to the company through his, the one he kept here. This way she could use his authorizations to easily access and walk through the data she needed, and still hide what she was doing. She had to be careful, those pseudo-origin points had shown her just how vigilant whoever was behind the web was.

Darkness ruled the sky outside by the time she had what she wanted. She shut down both her laptop and Ian's, her brow furrowed. She didn't send him a message, although she wanted to. It was the middle of the day in Tokyo and he would be in meetings now, and there was nothing urgent here, by now she knew more than enough about Ian Blackwell Holdings to continue their work without him. She would go back to his den and incorporate what she'd found into what she had there, and speak to him later.

She was disappointed that he wouldn't be in the house when she got there, she realized. It had been almost two days since he'd left, and she missed him. This made her shake her head incredulously. She still couldn't believe it, how much she'd changed. Trusting him. Wanting, needing him to be around.

Loving him, this still wasn't easy to admit.

She put her laptop in her bag and stood up, preparing to leave.

"Well, well. Sitting in Ian Blackwell's chair, behind Ian Blackwell's desk, in Ian Blackwell's office. I suppose that says it all."

Her eyes snapped to the man standing at the door. No one was supposed to be on this floor this time of night. Even Becca had already gone home, having been prodded to do so by Tess, and after making sure Tess had a fresh cup of coffee beside her. And yet there he was. It was just Brett Sevele, but her instincts had already kicked in and she didn't let her guard down. She remained where she was. Waited.

The tone of his voice was the first thing that alerted her something was off. His eyes as he came closer, close enough for her to see them clearly, were the second. There was something new there. Brett had always been all charm, with an almost perpetual smile on his face whenever she saw him, no matter whom he was speaking to. Including her. But there was no charm now, no smile. If she wasn't mistaken, that was a hostile tone in his voice and resentment, even hatred in his eyes.

"Good evening, Brett," she said, her voice carefully controlled. "What are you doing here this time of night?" And how did you even get up here, she didn't ask. This floor should have been off limits, with no elevator or stair access. Once Becca left every day, no one was authorized up here but her husband, her, and the building's security guards.

"But then I already knew you have his ear, this

has become quite obvious," Brett continued, not answering her. "You've been checking Ian Blackwell Holdings for him, haven't you, his little data expert? Isn't that why he 'married' you, brought you here?" Brett's eyes flickered to her bag on the desk, with the laptop inside it. "I checked you out. Someone in your caliber could find things." He turned his eyes back to her. "That's why the added scrutiny of my company, isn't it? Everyone else is just being audited. Additive Manufacturing's audit should have been over by now, but no. He's still looking at it, still asking questions. He knows, doesn't he? It's not just the company he's looking at, it's me, isn't it? See, good thing I came along the other day. I wasn't supposed to, you know, he wanted only finance and operations. But I thought I'd better come myself, make sure nothing's up I should know about. And then I see you working in here."

"Brett, what are you doing?" He had to know that his behavior was odd. Alarming even. So why was he behaving this way? And why was he here, had he hoped to find Ian here alone, to face him? Of course, he couldn't have known Ian wasn't here, there was no reason for him to. And what did he mean by—

The realization dawned on her. He *had* known Ian wouldn't be there. And to know that, he'd need to get into Becca's computer. And he knew *she* was there. Alone. So he had to have known who was coming and going. And he had managed to get into this floor, and security wasn't there to stop him, so he'd found a way to evade them, too.

One person, wasn't that what she had told Ian? One person who was patient enough, smart enough, and with the right knowledge could be behind what was being done to Ian Blackwell Holdings. One person who was the chief technology officer of one of its subsidiaries and who therefore had more access than someone on the outside. Who knew the head of that company and seemed just a little too interested in that man, his company, his life. Her.

A person who could easily just happen to have been at Blackwell Tower the same day she had been there, and who would immediately connect her being there with something he himself had done that he feared would be discovered. A coincidence that had set him thinking in the wrong direction, leading him to expose his actions.

She thought hard. The only people who knew she was here were the building security and Jackson, whom she had called earlier to let him know she would be done here soon, and who was probably already waiting for her in front of the building. Obviously neither knew Brett was there.

"He knows, doesn't he, Blackwell knows. Damn him," Brett threw his hands up in anger. "Damn him and damn you. I'll have to—"

"He doesn't." Fear gripped her, fear for Ian. "He just thinks someone may be using an enterprise-wide system glitch to embezzle money, and he's looking for where that glitch might have hit. Only I know, I just understood, today," she lied, praying he would believe her, knowing she had to make him lock on her, steer him away from Ian.

"Oh no. No. And you didn't know it was me, did you? How much did you know? Damn, damn it to hell, I went and told you now, didn't I? Yes, see, but it's all his fault for bringing someone like you here. It got me all paranoid and now I've gone and made a mistake." He was pacing across the office, ranting. Abruptly, he stopped and looked at her. "I can't let you get in my way."

She took a step back, bumping into the chair, and he raised a hand. "Oh, no, no, don't worry, it's nothing like that. I won't kill you, that would just start an investigation and attract too much attention to him, to his company. To what you were doing here. And I am not a killer. I believe in more . . . elegant methods."

She relaxed a little and assessed her position in the large room. Moving unobtrusively, she hoped, from behind the desk and toward the door, she asked, hoping to keep him busy, "Brett, what are you talking about? You don't have to do anything."

He wasn't listening. "All I need to do is make sure you won't say anything, that you won't tell that husband of yours what you know. Or about this conversation, for that matter. That you will keep your pretty mouth shut and let me go on with what I want to do. That's it. Oh, that will be so perfect." Even as he spoke, he moved to position himself between her and the door, seeing what she was trying to do.

She froze in place.

"But then, that shouldn't really be difficult to do, should it? I mean, he is not really your husband, or you his wife. It's an arranged thing, isn't it? I figured it all out, you see, as soon as I saw you working here the other day. He brought you in on his company. And Ian Blackwell would never do that. He never brings anyone in, not this way." He uttered a short laugh. "And you are not with him, after all. You're in his office, alone, while he's away in Tokyo. If you were really his wife, you'd be with him. Or at home. Not here, working here this way. Smart man, that Blackwell. What, he had you working hidden away until now, in his house, right? Where you're staying with him? Is there even a marriage or are you still Tess Andrews? A powerful man like him, he could make things look like he wants them to."

"How do you know where he is?" She had to keep him talking, had to find a way to get away from him.

"You know how. Don't tell me *you* don't know what I can do."

She didn't know. She knew what the capabilities were of whoever was tampering with her husband's company, but she couldn't connect that to Brett.

She thought fast. This was a good opportunity to get him to tell her how he was able to do what he had done, it could help toward stopping him. "No, I don't know," she said. "I didn't know it was you, remember?"

"Right, right. Might as well tell you. But only juuuust a little." He brought his thumb and finger together, squinting at them.

She moved a little to the left and he moved with her, blocking her way.

"No no, we're not done. See, I know my stuff. Like you know yours. I used to hack, as a kid. I was bored, you know. Got in trouble for it, but, see, I was able to get my record expunged because I did what I did when I was a minor. Not that it mattered, what kids do is forgiven. But, see, I'm not allowed to hack. Of course I did, I do, just learned to be clever about it. And at the same time, I made sure I would be a model citizen. Went to college. Got interested in three-dimensional printing when it was just starting. And got asked to help set up Additive Manufacturing. Fascinating company, I have to say. At least I wasn't bored."

Her mind was working. She didn't care about his background. Except for one thing there.

"But I've always been a hacker. A closet hacker. See? I just thought of that one. Closet hacker. Yes. Accurate, too. I do it from my house. And you know what I did there? I watched Blackwell. And then I started watching his company. Ah, the things I could do. The things I did. You saw what I did, you know. Yes, slowly. But not slow enough, not careful enough, was it? He saw something? What was it? He saw something too soon, far too soon, and then he brought you here. No. How could he see?" He was speaking to himself now more than to her.

"Why would you do this? To hurt him?"

He nodded. "But not quite the way you think."

She opened her mouth to ask more, get more information, but he cut her off. "No, no more questions from you. You. Yes. Your looking into Additive Manufacturing, the way you can do, I checked what you did at InSyn, see. I spoke to that loser who had lost it to Blackwell. And you're good. You go straight to the core, you find the right data, you see where it goes, where it's wrong, you see what others don't. Yes, you did that, didn't you, and you traced it to the initial attempts I made to change Additive Manufacturing's numbers to perfect how it should be done, right? Back when I started this? And I never even knew you were looking. But you must have, or Blackwell wouldn't have initiated that check, it was camouflaged as an audit, right? Yes. So lucky I was here that day, saw you here. Yes, lucky. I knew immediately. And I knew if you found it was me, I'd have to stop you. Yes, I knew." His eyes glimmered. "Clever, huh?" He pointed to his right temple. "See, so I prepared evidence."

"Evidence." His ranting was erratic. He was obviously quite brilliant, but Tess wasn't sure he was all there.

"Yes, you know, items implicating you in . . . certain matters. Proof."

"You mean, in what you're doing?" She asked. He wasn't making sense.

"No, that again would mean an investigation that might uncover what I did. And I still need that, I'm not done. And in any case, you haven't been here long enough to do this, what I'm doing took much longer than that to plan, to try, to see that no one saw it. No," he was angry now. "I told you I was clever, weren't you listening? No, what I did goes straight to Blackwell's weakness. You are his wife. The woman whom he married so suddenly when no one even knew you had a thing going between you two, the woman to replace all those pretty women he's had." He said that in a way that made Tess realize he was jealous of Ian. "No, see, there are things someone like me can do that would be so much more fun—for me, of course, not him, or you—and that could be used so much better for leverage. People can pretend to be so much, they can mislead so easily if they want to, and I can do so much with that. And Sex," he finally said. "Sex always does the work."

"Brett, what did you do?" She couldn't breathe.

"I created infidelities. You, fooling around with other men. Yes, I prepared hotel records, photos. Videos, that one was fun. So much you can do nowadays. Well, so much I can do, obviously."

"But there was nothing. Ever." She was horrified.

"So? By the time it's proven it would be over. The doubt would remain, people aren't exactly fair, are they? The stain on you would never go away. And as for Blackwell, the damage would be done, he would be a laughing stock. Finally he gets married, and it's to someone like that, she fooled him and he didn't even know."

Tess's anger mounted. Brett was closer to the mark than he knew, this would cause considerable damage. And it would undo everything she and Ian had achieved since they had gotten married.

It would hurt Ian. That, she couldn't stand the thought of.

"So you be a nice wifey, keep quiet, and I won't do anything. You know what, I promise I won't even continue what I'm doing, how's that? I'll back off. Do we have an understanding?"

He was lying. That kind of obsession didn't simply stop, she had no doubt he would continue. Now that he thought he had neutralized her, there was no reason for him to stop.

He took a step closer to her, enjoying this. "And if you think you can tell him what you know, or about this little talk of ours, for that matter, don't think that'll work. I have all that 'proof'. You have nothing. And when he comes to me, asks me, I'll know you talked. And then I'll give him that proof of mine, enough to destroy you. And who do you think he'll believe? He's known me longer, I've always been reliable, always that nice person around him. I'll convince him, you'll see. And then I'll resume what I started and destroy him."

"Why would you do that? You've known him for years, you're his friend."

"We were never friends," Brett said bitterly. "Business associates, yes, but never friends. No, I'm not good enough to be a friend of Ian Blackwell, the handsome billionaire, owner of one of the most powerful companies in the world."

"This is all about envy? You're jealous of him so this is what you do?"

And that's when the fury came. "Why wouldn't I be jealous? He has everything! I've been watching him since he bought Additive Manufacturing and he just keeps doing it, he keeps growing! Me, I'm smarter than him, I'm a bloody genius and I'm still in that crappy little company while he's doubled, tripled his since then and they're all after him, all the news and cameras and fame and women, and we're the same age, you know!"

His voice was shrill now, hate taking over any coherent thought left. "And then he brings you, his clever little . . . You're a real looker, a sexy thing, aren't you? Taking you to all these parties, showing you around like you're his prize, throwing it in my face, another woman, he always has one, always some hottie he takes home and fucks in that mansion of his!"

Tess looked at him in horror, at the fury on his face. He was out of control.

Fear gripped her.

"See, I've been watching you. Interesting woman. Intelligent, oh, I know that. But beautiful, so beautiful, too, I wouldn't mind you being mine." He gave her a suggestive look that went down her body, then up again, lingering on her chest. She shuddered in revulsion. "Does he even touch you? Has he had you? Haven't been any new tarts around him lately, only you. But a man like him, he can hide it. Does he? Or is it all you now, is your body his? If I have it, will I be sharing something of his, taking something of his?"

She realized too late what he was up to. He grabbed at her. She didn't have a chance to scream, but then no one would have heard her on the empty top floor of Blackwell Tower anyway. He gripped her upper arms, tried to pull her to him, but she fought him, she was strong and she pushed at him but he only he gripped her harder, crazed lust giving him an edge she had no hope against. He tried to pull open the jacket of the pantsuit she wore and tore off a button, then ripped at the delicate lace of the top she wore under it, and her panic peaked at his touch on bare skin. She managed to push his hand aside and he growled in anger, grabbed her waist and pushed her hard enough for her to lose her balance and fall back, and he fell on top of her. Victorious, he grabbed at her hair, tried to kiss her but she turned her head and he slapped her. Shocked, she stopped fighting for just enough time

She had fought hard. Her body was bruised so badly he wanted nothing more than to take her to the hospital, have her thoroughly checked. But that would make it worse for her, he knew. He would take care of her himself, he finally decided, and see in the morning if it was enough. She didn't need hospitals and doctors prodding her. She needed peace and quiet.

She needed love. His. And he had every intention of giving it to her.

He put the kit back on the nightstand and handed her the tea. As she drank, he raised a hand to her hair and moved it back from her face. She didn't move away, not at all, but something appeared in her eyes. An awareness. Wariness, even.

Like an abused child, he thought, being offered shelter, safety, love, and not knowing what to do with it, how to even begin to dare trust. That was it, he realized, putting together what little he knew about her. All her instinctive responses spoke of embedded fear. And what he was doing, what he was offering her, giving her, she had never had that before. She had undoubtedly seen others who had, like her friend Jayden and his wife, and Muriel and Robert, but she had no idea what it was like to have anything like that for herself. And now she'd been attacked, shown the terrible opposite.

But she had fought, and she had gotten away. And yet she was damn near broken. Something was terribly wrong here.

to allow him to undo the remaining buttons of her jacket and try to open her pants. She fought him, and his hand grabbed her thigh, his fingers digging into it through the fabric, hard enough for her to cry out in pain.

"Don't fight me, don't dare fight me or I will show him what I have, I will—" he panted, wild eyed, even as he tore at her clothes, his hand grabbing the top of her pants, frantically pulling at them, touching skin again.

She closed her legs tight, not letting him get to her. Still fighting with her pants he raised his body over hers, his legs on both sides of her.

She stopped fighting.

"That's a good bitch," he said, leering, and balanced himself over her with a hand on one side, his other roaming her chest, taking his time, thinking she had given up.

She kicked him, kicked him with her knee so hard that he fell off her, doubled over with pain. She scrambled aside and when he reached to grab her she kicked back with her shoe, the heel catching him in the shoulder. He lost his balance and fell back again, and she was free. She scrambled up, ran to the door and opened it. Only then did she dare turn around, panting in exertion.

He was still squirming on the carpet.

"Remember what will happen if you tell him, remember," he managed to growl at her, vivid hate in his eyes.

"I won't let you hurt him. I won't let you. You just try, and I swear to God I will get you," she said, her voice low, threatening enough for him to stare at her in surprise.

She turned and left, walking, not even running, and fear took him over. She was supposed to succumb to him. Ian Blackwell's wife was supposed to be at his mercy, his at will.

He could still see her eyes, staring into his with vengeance.

Chapter Seventeen

She didn't stop, didn't look back until she reached the private elevator and got in. But Brett was in no shape to follow her. As the doors closed she turned around and saw herself in the mirror spanning the elevator, and that's when the shock set in. Her cheek was red where he'd slapped her, and her hair, which she had pulled up, was in disarray. Her top was torn, and the top button of her jacket was hanging by a thread. As she was, the thought pushed itself into her mind, and she forced it away. She made an effort to straighten her clothes and her hair, and kept her head averted from the security cameras.

"Please," she kept saying to herself, "please don't let security see this, don't let anyone see me."

They didn't. No one was watching the CCTV screens in the control room, and the night guards in the lobby barely looked up when she came out. They all knew she was in the building, and she was, after all, Ian Blackwell's wife, she could do what she wanted.

She walked out of the building and got into the Bentley, and Jackson, who held the door open for her, frowned. But she looked away, and he took that as a sign not to ask. The drive back to the house took forever, and when the car finally stopped she didn't wait, not for Jackson to open the door for her or for Graham who barely had time to open the front door before she passed by him quickly, saying nothing.

She was, Graham noted with apprehension, terribly pale, shaken, he thought, although she walked with her customary stature, tried, he could tell, to look her normal self. But she had looked away from him, which she'd never done, and he saw the button that was hanging loosely in place, as if she had tried to fix it. She was, in fact, uncharacteristically disheveled, and unless he was mistaken, and as someone who had seen her when she had left the house that morning, he could tell that her top was torn under that jacket.

He followed her with his eyes, a frown on his face, as she walked up the stairs, stumbled on a step and grabbed the railing so as not to fall, then hurried on. Then he went out to speak to Jackson who was still standing beside the car, a not so different expression on his own face.

Tess managed to get to her room, close the door behind her, lock it, and make sure she locked it, before she collapsed on the carpet. No tears, there were none. There should be, a small voice in her mind said, but she was numb, just numb. Think, she said to herself, you've got to think. You know what to do, how to deal with this. You know.

She didn't. This was different, she was different. She had been safe, had begun to feel safe, and nothing, *nothing* had prepared her for what happened that night. And it was too much, oh God it was too much, nothing had healed, it was all simply covered with layer upon layer of hiding and time and more hiding.

No. No, she had to get herself under control, had to think.

Brett had an interest here. He wouldn't want anyone, least of all Ian, to know about him having attacked her, this was, in the least, a criminal matter. And he had a clear notion in his mind of what he thought was going on, what he thought Ian knew, what she knew, and a vested interest in not giving her a reason to give Ian the information he thought she had about what he was doing to her husband's company. And he had seemed sure that he had enough to secure her silence, enough to be able to convincingly threaten her that he could turn things against her, that so-called proof he had prepared that would make her look bad to Ian and that he could go public with if he wanted.

Which would hurt Ian. God, he would hurt Ian. She couldn't bear that, would never allow it.

Her eyes, dark, no gold in them anymore, were determined. She would contain this and find a way to stop Brett without Ian being hurt, use the fact that she now knew who was behind what was happening to Ian Blackwell Holdings to stop him before he could do anything. Use the time she just might have, assuming he would in fact choose to continue with his original plan thinking she would say nothing about what had happened that night.

She had no choice but to contain it.

She didn't want to. She wanted to tell Ian, wanted so much for him to know. Wanted to trust him to help her. Would he? She remembered what Brett had said. Who would Ian choose to believe? Her, his contract wife of just months, or the man he'd known for years, whom he trusted to hold an important position in one of his subsidiaries? *Would* Ian trust her? He cared about her, and he'd trusted her with his company. But, faced with the convincing proof that the man who was smart enough to do what he was doing to Ian Blackwell Holdings had deliberately prepared, with only her word against his, would it matter? She lowered her head. It didn't matter. All that was needed was for Brett to think that she had told Ian what she knew, or what he had done to her, and he would destroy her husband. And if Ian did care as much as she hoped he did, his first reaction just might be to go straight to Brett, to confront him.

All roads led to Ian being hurt.

Enough, she told herself. Enough. She knew she would never allow harm to come to him. This was not who she was. This was not who she was, and he mattered. God, he mattered so much. No one else had ever mattered to her this way, no one had even come close. And so all she could do was try to figure this out on her own.

And keep Brett away from her in the process.

Her mind was in turmoil, trying to think about everything but his attack on her, his hands on her, the fact that he had almost . . . She shuddered and pressed her hands to her mouth, stifled the sob. No, she couldn't do that, couldn't go there, couldn't even begin to deal with it, with what happened, with what it was doing to her.

She got up and walked to her bathroom in a daze, turned the water on hot in the shower, took off her torn clothes and threw them into a corner. Then she got into the shower and scrubbed herself, tried to scrub herself clean.

An hour later found her huddled on the shower stall floor, her face buried in her arms.

She felt so alone.

That night she woke up in sweat as the dreams returned. She pressed her face into the pillow, stifling the scream. Tears followed but she fought them.

Don't cry, you can't cry.

He can't know.

Graham went into Mr. Blackwell's den, closed the door behind him, and locked it before he turned on the lights. He walked around the large desk and squatted on its right side, then touched his index finger to the bottom drawer. The reader recognized his print and it opened. He took out a small console and skirted the desk again, coming to stand before the wall screen as it turned on. He then used the console to choose the day and the hour range.

The footage began running on the screen. Only video. That was all he had.

He stood there for a long time, watching. Fast forwarding most of it. Until that evening. There he stopped fast-forwarding and resumed watching, a frown on his face.

Then he blanched and took a step toward the screen, then another, as if trying to get in, to be there. To do something, anything.

The console fell from his hands on the desk with a loud thud, and he fumbled, cursed, and finally found his phone in his pocket. His personal phone, not the house line. He made a call. It was rejected.

He dialed again.

This time the call was answered, and the impatient face of Mr. Blackwell appeared on the phone's screen.

"I'm in a meeting—" Ian fell silent, seeing the loyal house manager's face. "Will you excuse me for a moment," he said to the people sitting around the conference table, and took the phone to the adjoining private office. Graham waited until he looked at the phone again and nodded for him to speak.

Graham didn't say anything. He just sent him the footage on their secure connection. He knew that the software in Mr. Blackwell's phone allowed him also to hear, not just see.

When Ian's Tokyo-based assistant walked into the conference room to apologize to the internal auditors for his having to adjourn the meeting, Ian was already in the car, making arrangements for his jet to be prepared.

Back in the house, Graham walked quietly to Mrs. Blackwell's room and listened at the door. The silence was deafening.

Tess didn't want to come out of her room the next day. She didn't want to eat, nor did she want anyone around her. She was hurting, in more ways than one. She had feigned feeling ill throughout the day and had refused when Lina had tried to convince her to eat something, or perhaps see a doctor, and when Graham himself had called, asking if he could get her anything, trying in vain to hide a worried expression. She had told them all she needed was some rest, and they had finally let her be.

But she had made a decision to continue as if

nothing happened, and that was how it would be. And so in the afternoon, much later than was usual for her, she mustered the strength and came down the stairs, wearing slacks, a simple top, and a long sleeve open front cardigan that she wrapped tightly around herself. No makeup, she'd considered putting on some, but Brett's slap left only residual redness, and thankfully not a bruise, not there. At least, she thought, Ian wasn't due back for a few more days, more if business warranted it. That would give her the time to settle herself, to try to deal with—

She came to an abrupt stop, her heart missing a beat, then took an involuntary step backward. Brett Sevele was coming out of the living room, Ian following him. Her eyes remained glued to her assailant, who was with his back to her husband. Ian didn't see the fleeting leer, the look Brett sent her. I win, it said.

"We will speak more of this soon," Ian stepped around Brett, positioning himself between Tess and him and steering him to the front door. "Privately, of course."

"Yes, we most certainly will," Brett said, a hint of smugness in his voice, the look he threw behind his shoulder meant for Tess.

She was still standing there, rooted in place, when Ian returned, having escorted Brett out himself. He stopped and looked at her. She looked pale, dark circles under her eyes, and she wasn't looking at him. She was staring in the direction he had just taken Brett in. His eyes flickered to the sweater. It was a warm day, as this entire week had been. She could have done with just a light top, certainly inside the house. Not this long sweater that covered her.

"Are you feeling okay? You look a little pale," he said.

She finally raised her eyes to him and forced a small smile. "Yes, sorry. I'm fine, just a bit tired."

He contemplated her quietly and she braced herself. Too late. Brett was bolder than she had thought he would be, he had done it. He had gone directly to her husband, her fighting back and her threat to him must have convinced him he couldn't trust her to obey him. Is it over? she thought with a pang of pain. Is it already over before I even had a chance to fight back?

"Come into the den, will you?" Ian said, and she did. He followed her inside and closed the door behind him.

"You're back early." Her voice was quiet, hesitant, her movements slow.

"I came back a few hours ago, Brett called me while I was on my way and I told him I've finished my business early and that he could meet me here. I was hoping to see my wife earlier, but it seemed you weren't about to come out of your room today." He watched her carefully. Gave her a chance to speak. To tell him. To say something, anything.

"I'm sorry, I didn't hear you come in, if I had

known you were here . . ." Her tone was subdued. There was nothing of the liveliness, of the way she would have answered him normally.

"Brett had some interesting . . . observations," he tried.

She said nothing, just leaned back on his desk. But not as she usually did. This time it was as if she needed the support. He had expected her to react, wanted her to defend herself. But the woman before him was, simply, defenseless.

"Aren't you interested in hearing them?" he tried again.

"It is what it is," she said, weariness in her voice, in her stance.

He'd never seen her this way. But then he had never seen her look as she did now, never seen her so pale. So pained, he thought.

He took a step closer to her, fear closing its icy fingers around his heart. "No, that's not you, Tess, you're a fighter. You're fire and strength welded together into a powerhouse. You would fight. So why aren't you? Why aren't you talking to me?"

Because this will hurt you. He will hurt you, and I couldn't bear that, even at the price of losing you. She couldn't say this. Couldn't speak.

He saw and understood. He wouldn't have, if he didn't know her. And if he didn't know what had happened.

But he did. And she needed to know that, needed to know that she could trust him, that she could turn to him no matter what.

That no one came before her.

He nodded to himself. Time to do this. "I had a break-in to my office at Blackwell Tower, oh, about two years ago. Which was quite inconvenient, to say the least. It was," he said conversationally, going to the other side of his desk, "fortunate that security noticed in time and caught the thieves, so that nothing was stolen. However, following that unfortunate incident I had a surveillance system installed inside the office, unbeknownst to anyone. *Anyone*," he emphasized. "It sends its video and audio directly here. The audio can only be accessed by me, but the video is periodically skimmed over by Graham—even if seemingly nothing happened—since I don't have the time to monitor it all."

Her eyes were still lowered but he saw the furrow form in her brow.

"Last night my wife returned home late. Graham knew she had been in my office, so he wasn't worried, but when he saw her, he thought something was wrong. He can be very perceptive, Graham. So he asked Jackson, who confirmed that he had taken her from Blackwell Tower directly here. And then Graham came into this room and viewed the video for the duration she'd been there. And what he saw was enough for him to become very much unsettled. Graham, if you haven't noticed, is never unsettled. Yet this had him calling me while I was in a meeting—which he has never ever done before—and having me watch it." Ian paused. "And what I saw made me come home."

Her eyes closed, and he saw her fingers tighten on her arms.

He turned on the wall screen, and then came back around the desk and stood beside her. Close, but not quite touching. She didn't move, but he felt her tense up. The storm inside him threatened, but he did nothing but stand and look at the screen.

She didn't look. She never once looked up, never moved but to flinch, tighten her arms around herself at the sounds when the attack on her came, right there on the screen in this room with her.

He stopped the video and turned off the screen. His teeth were clenched. He'd already seen this and even that once was too much.

And she had been through it.

In the terrible silence that ensued she suddenly moved, moved to run away from him, from here, to escape, to escape this, him, what was happening inside her, unable to deal, unable to contain it now that it was out, that he knew, that she knew he did, that he saw what was done to her, that it happened, oh God it happened—

She didn't make it very far. Before she realized what was happening he was in her way and she was in his arms, wrapped tight, his embrace minding the places where he knew she must be bruised. The bruises that would make themselves visible, must already have, not the ones in her soul. Those, he knew, would take so much more care to heal.

She fought him, and not because she was afraid of him, she didn't even remember to panic with his touch. Much stronger than her and driven by everything that was for her in him, he would not let her go. "Don't," he murmured, "Don't. Let me hold you, let me counter his touch with mine." And he stood there, wrapping her, shielding her, murmuring to her, until she stopped, until she collapsed to the floor, held firmly in his arms, sobbing, finally allowing herself to feel the horror of the past day.

"I'm sorry, I'm so sorry that this happened, and that you had to deal with it alone." His voice was soft. "I'm sorry I didn't protect you."

As the sobs finally subsided, she shook her head weakly, exhausted. "You just did," she said in a shuddering whisper.

"Too little, too late," he said, angry at himself. One thing he could not get past. Even after Brett had attacked her, even as she was escaping, hurt, it was him she had thought about, him she had threatened her assailant not to hurt. And even here, facing him, knowing that Brett must be using his plan against her, she still hadn't defended herself. Instead she had chosen to protect him. He, who had put her in this position, in this danger, in the first place.

He forced himself under control. She needed him, and she was far more important to him than anyone, anything else.

He picked her up. She resisted, just a bit, but he

stood there, holding her, his lips against her hair, calming her. When she finally relaxed in his arms, he took her out of the den. Graham was just outside, pacing nervously, helplessly. Ian indicated the kitchen, mouthing an order, and Graham rushed off, happy to have something useful to do.

Ian entered his wife's bedroom for the first time since she'd arrived at their home. He sat her carefully on the edge of the bed. Then he kneeled down before her and waited until she looked at him and he felt that she was able to grasp what he was saying. Exhausted, and obviously in pain, but alert.

"Will you let me call for a doctor? Mine, he's extremely good. Or I can have him call his partner, a woman."

She shook her head. "No, please. I don't need a doctor. I don't want anyone . . ."

"To touch you," he said softly, and was worried that she had let him. It showed him more than anything just how much this had hit her, the attack that had taken the life out of those beautiful eyes. "All right then," he said. "Do something for me?"

She was surprised at that. Hesitantly, she nodded.

"Get into bed, I want you to be comfortable."

She nodded again. There was nothing left in her that could resist.

"Good. I'll be back in a minute." He stood up and left, closing the door behind him. Outside, he leaned on it and rubbed his face. He felt helpless. He had done this. He had allowed this to happen to her. To his Tess.

My Tess, he thought, and now, finally, knew that he would not, could not let it be any other way. He would no longer be held back.

She undressed slowly, with some difficulty. The bruises hurt. Her entire body ached with them, and with the strain of the day. She put on a pair of shorts and a simple top, not even realizing she'd gone back to what she used to wear to bed before she came here, before she became Ian's wife.

She pulled the blanket on herself and lay back, turned to lay on her left and sat right up again when the pain seared through her. She remained seated, hugged her knees and lowered her head onto her arms.

And raised it again when someone knocked on the door. Ian had said he was coming back, she remembered hazily and called out for him to come in. As he did, she pulled the blanket up on her shoulders, hiding without thinking about it.

He came in, carrying two mugs. Seeing that she was in bed, he smiled, and came to sit on it beside her. "Drink this," he said, offering her one of the mugs. "Sweet potato soup. Graham says you haven't eaten all day."

"I'm not hungry."

"That's why it's soup and why it's your favorite one. Drink."

She took the hot mug from him and drank, her

258

hands shaking so hard that he reached out to steady them. The soup was rich, tasty. Lina's. She must have prepared this earlier, Tess thought, and then realized that Graham had known since the night before what had happened to her.

She drank some of the soup, enough for Ian to be pleased that she had. He put the mug aside. "Good," he said. "Now this." He handed her the other mug.

She squinted inside. "What's that?"

"Sweet tea with a bit of whiskey in it."

She made a face.

"Drink. It will help, you're in shock. It will also help you sleep."

"I'm not in shock."

"Mrs. Blackwell," he said softly in a way that made her look at him without any objection, no ability whatsoever to resist. "You are. Now drink or I'll just sit here and stare at you until you do."

That made her smile a little, as he had wanted it to. She drank a bit. Then a bit more.

"Will you allow me to do something?" he asked, his voice tender.

She met his eyes, saw them flicker to where the blanket covered her arms. He had seen, she realized, remembering. He had seen it all.

She lowered her gaze, and he took the tea from her and put it on the nightstand. He reached out and pulled the blanket away as gently as he could.

And had to take in a deep breath, had to fight

the emotion. "I'm going to kill him," he said, his voice low, rage dominating.

She finally looked up at him and he was surprised when she put her hand on his. "No, don't do anything that would come back to hurt you. I couldn't bear that." She sighed, tired. "Please, Ian."

"It's okay, I won't. I promise I won't do anything without telling you first," he said, and stroke her cheek, his thumb gentle on the trace of redness still there. He was worrying her, and that wasn't what he wanted. Needing a moment, needing to handle this, to get a grip on himself, he got up and walked out again, saying nothing, leaving the door open this time. She watched him leave, and the fleeting thought crossed her mind that this, she, had disrupted his day, his life. She let her head drop back on her arms, the tears threatening again.

When he returned he was holding a small kit. He put it on the nightstand beside her, then stood and assessed her. No, not her, she realized dimly. The bed. He left again and returned moments later carrying a tower of pillows, bed pillows in an assortment of colors. He must have taken them from all the guest rooms in the house, she thought with wonder. Saying nothing, he organized them around her, then had her move and completed the mosaic of pillows that now made up her mattress.

"That should help you sleep," he said, thoughtfully assessing his handiwork.

She didn't know what to say, wasn't expecting

this, the way he was with her. She smiled a little, but the smile disappeared when he sat beside her again and took the kit. Opening it, he took out a small cream tube and some soft cotton pads.

"No," she said, inching back a little.

"It will numb the pain," he said gently, and proceeded despite her protest. There would be no pain for her in the coming hours, at least not a physical one.

He dubbed the cool cream on her bruises. His touch was gentle and so very careful, and still it hurt. Every time he touched her she flinched, and every time she did he hurt with her. When he was done with her arms, and with the back of a shoulder, where she had hit the floor hardest when she fell back, his gaze flickered down. He knew there were more.

She moved the blanket with some hesitation, and he saw the angry bruises on her left thigh just below her shorts, the imprint of fingers on soft skin. He took care of these too, and then of the ones under her undershirt, which she had pulled up a little, enough for him to see the bruising on both her sides, where her assailant had grabbed her, hurting her. The bruises were large, but he didn't see any significant bruising on the ribs. With a breath of relief, he treated these, too, then moved back, aware of how close he was to her and wary of making her uncomfortable in the vulnerable state she was in.

It was time he knew.

"Tess."

She raised her eyes to his.

He asked, not saying a word.

She nodded slightly. Trust, she thought, had to go both ways. He deserved to know, and she was finally ready to trust him with that part of herself.

Chapter Eighteen

"When I was fourteen and eight months old, my parents were killed in a car accident."

She saw the surprise on Ian's face. That wasn't what the report he'd read about her said. She nodded slightly to confirm. That hadn't been the truth. This was.

"We used to live here in California, in Palo Alto. My parents were both information security analysts there. My mom became pregnant, my parents didn't think that would happen again and were so happy about it. They thought it was a good time for a change, a quieter life, less intensive, and they decided to move to Southeast Texas. To Montaville, a town north of Houston. It looked like a nice place. Friendly, I remember that that's what I thought. Good for families, for kids. Lots of schools and parks. I didn't want to move, and it was worse because we moved at winter break, in the middle of the school year, because my parents wanted to get settled before the new baby was born. But I knew it wasn't an easy decision for them, to do things that way, and I knew they cared about me, that they were trying to make things better for me, too. They kept talking about this place, how much better it would be for us as a family, the school they found for me, how nice it would be to go house hunting together—they'd rented a place at first because they wanted to find the perfect home for us when we got there. And once we got there, they looked happy, more relaxed than I'd seen them for a long time. There wasn't that tension anymore, you know, they'd worked such long hours before, barely had any time off, and now my dad had a less intensive job waiting for him in Houston, and my mom wanted to find something maybe in Montaville itself. They wanted to be able to spend more time with me and with my . . . who- ever it would have been who would have been born if . . ."

She stopped. Needed a moment to push it away with everything she had, the thought of the life, the family she might still have had if things had been different. "Anyway, we had just moved to Montaville two weeks earlier, two weeks before they died, so I didn't know anyone there and no one knew me. I didn't even go to school there yet, and if you'd asked me the name of the street where we lived, I probably would have fumbled it." She lowered her eyes, hugged her knees.

Trying to contain the memories, Ian thought.

"I had no one, no other family. I was in the acci- dent, but I wasn't hurt, nothing but some scratches and bruises." Her eyes came to rest on a bruise on her left arm and she averted her eyes. "The police-woman who took my statement took me from the hospital to child protective services. I was a late bloomer, young looking. Sweet, gentle. Naive, my parents were very protective. Looking back that must have been what attracted him to me. That and the fact that no one cared if I lived or died. Not any-more. He, the social worker assigned to me, did what it was he was apparently too easily authorized to do in that town, maybe because it was a small place and everyone knew everyone, I don't know and I don't care. All I know is that by that night he had custody of me. He and his wife. They already had two foster kids, Justine, eighteen at the time, who had left for college just a few months earlier, and Maddy, twelve, and it must have made sense for whoever was in charge there to approve their taking me, and so immediately. And he was, after all, one of them. He joked with everyone there, everyone seemed to like him. And he was nice, he said it was going to be okay, that I'll like Maddy, that I can stay in Justine's room, they'll figure it out when she comes home for the holidays. I thought I could trust him. I thought I was safe."

She spoke quietly, tiredly. Ian wanted desperately to hold her, to have her tell her story while she was safely wrapped in his arms. But he knew he couldn't, shouldn't, move any closer. She needed to do this her way.

"Montaville had a number of neighborhoods, and

they lived in the northeast one, an older, less dense area. Houses that were far apart, not big houses, just an older neighborhood with more wooded land around it, some fields here and there. Far enough from the town center and schools not to attract attention. I don't know. I tried to understand more about it later, tried to understand how they'd managed to keep anyone from knowing for so long. Anyway, my parents had their eye on a house on the western side, in a newer neighborhood with more children in it, so that was the only place I knew, it and the town center and the place we rented not far from it.

"All I know is that when I saw the house, when he brought me there, it looked normal. Two stories, well kept on the outside. A big back yard, a white fence around the front yard. No neighbors nearby, although the house was near a road and I could hear cars go by now and then. It was just . . . normal. His wife met me at the door and welcomed me to their home, and she introduced to me to Maddy, who was standing beside her. Maddy said nothing, just looked at me. I didn't see anything on her, I didn't know about any of that yet. I was exhausted, my family had just died, and I was lost. I remember the pain, the grief. But at least I thought I was safe.

"There was a small room for Maddy and a small room for me, both upstairs, with a door connecting them. The rooms were identical, no personal signs of . . . anything. Memories, hobbies, personality. Nothing. The room I was to stay in wasn't really Justine's, because Justine was already dead. She wasn't in college, he'd forged all the necessary documents that showed she was away. But it didn't matter, no one cared because she was eighteen. I was her replacement. He'd thought to take someone younger, but I was a windfall, that's what he'd told me later."

She stopped for a long time. "He didn't start with me that night. I woke up when he opened the door between my room and Maddy's, to make sure I knew what he was doing. When she screamed, I ran over and jumped on him, attacked. His wife was the one who pulled me away and beat me up. She was big, fat, strong. And she was a horrible abuser with no conscience whatsoever. When she finished with me I couldn't do anything but lie on the floor and bleed, while Maddy was screaming in the bed not far from where I lay."

Her voice was hollow. She raised her eyes to his for just a moment and saw the horror in his eyes. She continued. She wanted him to know. God, she needed him to know. She needed it because it was important that he wouldn't be this way with her and that he wouldn't love her. He mustn't because she was so damaged.

It was bad enough that she would have to live with loving him.

"The next morning the two of them came to my room with Maddy. She could barely walk, and she wasn't dressed this time, so I could see the bruises, the old ones and the new ones. But she was silent. No speaking, no crying, no living was allowed in that house unless permission was given. They took me to the corner of the back yard where Justine was buried, so that I would know what happens to those who do not obey. Then they laid down the ground rules. Basically, from now on you do not exist. No one looks for kids like you, kids disappear all the time and no one ever finds them, no one cares, we can do whatever we want. No one will help me, that's why they said, because as a social worker he could easily cover their tracks.

"He gave me a few days to heal. Wanted me to be pretty again the first time he raped me. And he didn't stop. For days later, weeks. I was his new toy. I fought. He beat me. His wife beat me. And still I fought. I fought when he raped me, I fought when he raped Maddy again because she was docile and I was trouble. I fought and I never stopped fighting and I have no idea how, or why I didn't just curl up and die. I just fought."

She had closed her eyes and now she stopped speaking, and he saw the struggle for control. Then she opened her eyes again and saw his hand on the bed, clenched into a fist. She didn't have to look up to see the anger, the rage, it flowed from him in waves. She reached out and touched his fist tentatively, then drew her hand back again. Suddenly he knew what she was thinking. A fist, his, not there to hurt her. There to protect her. Still, he didn't want her to even remotely equate him with what she was remembering, and so he willed himself to relax his hand.

Even though he really wanted to kill someone right then. Two people, in fact.

"Maddy would come to me, after. When it was clear that he was finished with me for the time being. She would hug me hard and then go back quickly, just in case. After a while I did the same. The rapes, the beatings, the starving to try to make me obey, the . . . everything, it continued for an endless year. And no one from child protection services ever came to check up on me. Maddy said no one would, she'd been there much longer and no one ever came for her. He filed the required reports regularly, and had his boss sign them. No one had any reason to suspect. And no one cared. I was nothing. We were both nothing. We were two of countless kids in an understaffed, overworked system. Whatever. No excuses. They didn't care.

"I thought about trying to get out, to run, or at least to find someone, get some help. But I didn't manage to. Until once, just that once I thought I might succeed. We were always locked in our rooms, and our windows were locked, too. But there was a lower roof under my window, so I worked on it gradually, over time, and one night I managed to pry it open, and I climbed down. Maddy said she was scared, so I promised I would come back for her, I figured maybe I could get to another house, or to the police. To someone, anyone.

"I made it to the ground, just that. He was waiting for me, he'd known all along what I was doing. He punched me, pulled me by my hair to the middle of the back yard, and raped me right there. Just to show me he could do whatever he wanted and no one would know, no one would stop him."

She fell into pained silence. After a while, she spoke again. "You know, that one time, when I lay there, after, just before he dragged me back inside, I thought about it. It hadn't occurred to me until that moment. This wasn't a completely faraway place, people have gone by there. How could it be that no one ever heard me? That night and all those months and months of nights and days and hell, how could it be that no one ever heard me scream?"

Ian's heart broke.

"And then Maddy fell ill. It was the dead of winter, and cold, starvation, torture, they did their thing. She died a week later. I don't know what was wrong with her, but I know she didn't mind dying. She told me so." She raised her eyes to his again. "She was the last person I ever hugged, you know? Who hugged me. I haven't willingly touched anyone since, let alone hug."

Ian couldn't bear this. In his mind he could see it, see her as a young girl, huddled in the corner, cold, starving, alone. Knowing she will be hurt again. Knowing there was no one to help her.

With all his money, all his power, he couldn't go back in time and save her.

"They buried her in the back yard, near Justine. When they came back into the house, they were arguing. They forgot to lock Maddy's door after they took her out, and the door between her room and mine was always unlocked, so I went outside to the corridor and eavesdropped. There was nothing they could to me that they hadn't done already, so I risked it. And I heard them say that I was trouble. A year on and I was still fighting. I wasn't broken, docile like they wanted me to be. He wanted another girl. Another victim. But bringing another, that's not good when there's such a troublemaker in the house, his wife said. And I was older, it was difficult to control me. That's why they killed Justine. And anyway, he wanted a younger girl, one he could keep longer. Maybe one no one would know about, this time."

She wrapped her arms tighter around herself, trying to escape. To hide. When Ian moved, she jumped, but all he did was reach out and wrap the blanket around her, tuck it close so she wouldn't be cold. She hadn't realized she was shivering badly in the comfortably warm room. The gesture made emotion erupt and she struggled, fought to keep the tears back.

"I thought that was it, that I was dead. But they made two mistakes. The first one was not killing me that night. She wanted to, but he refused. He needed someone to . . . use until he found a new girl. The second I learned about a few weeks later. You see, when we moved to Montaville, my parents had my school transcripts sent to the high school I was transferring to—something he didn't know about. But I never showed up. I don't know what happened the year before, maybe because I was supposed to arrive after winter break, the middle of the year, they forgot about me, or maybe they were told what happened and thought I was taken away by family or something. I have no idea. What I do know, what I heard there, in that house, what he told her after he returned one day, was that when winter break approached again my name came up with that of another new student who was transferring there just then, and the school realized that my school records were still there, that no one had called for them, no other school or anyone else. The school district then checked and discovered that I was in foster care, still in Montaville, and asked the monster who had taken me what happened, why I hadn't attended school.

"He said he told them that I was being home-schooled, that it was best after the trauma I'd been through. And he thought they believed him, he told her that they'd just raised the concern that they hadn't gotten any information about my schooling and that he'd promised to provide it to them immediately. He intended to forge some records, school works, exams, things he had from other kids, he was a social worker after all. He hadn't had the same problem with Justine. And with Maddy, well, no one asked about her. It was that specific school I was supposed to be in, they were the ones that raised the issue, and they just happened to approach the one school official who decided to make an issue out of it. But after all, I was just an unwanted kid, they won't care enough to follow up, that's what she kept saying, and he said that she must be right, that they must have believed him.

"I mean, finally, after all that time, someone actually remembered that I existed, and here he had managed to deflect them again. I had no idea what that meant for me, if they would decide to get rid of me after all and make up some story to explain it, because they couldn't risk anyone finding me. I do, though, remember what it meant for me that night. They were both angry, both worried, and I was right there for them to take it out on." She shook her head wearily.

"But as it turned out, his story wasn't that believable. And he didn't expect that, or that the reaction would come so soon. The very next day, just before noon, he got a call telling him that a school district supervisor was coming by for a visit. To see me. In a panic, he left his wife to meet the guy by herself and took me out of the house. On the way he got a call to report to an emergency social workers' meeting because some kid committed suicide in the next town and the media was all over them. He needed to do something with me, so he threatened to kill me if I didn't do as he said, and he made me put on his coat, and I was wearing an old hoodie underneath so he made me put its hood on and behave as if I had a cold and just wanted to wrap myself up, so no one would see how bad I looked. It was January, so it was a plausible excuse. Not that it mattered, because he managed to get me into his office unseen."

She raised her eyes to Ian's and there was something else in them now, whatever it was that had awakened in her back then. "My luck that day was that he thought he had no choice but to leave me there, and that he thought my being alone with him after Maddy's death had finally broken me and he had no idea I knew I was the next to die. And then there was the duration of his absence. He got held up long enough, you see. Just long enough. And what you need to know is, I learned a whole lot from my parents, I grew up around work discussions and if I ever came near one of their computers at home, they would let me sit with them and they would answer every question I asked with all the patience in the world."

This time, a tear escaped. And then another.

She cleared her throat, breathed. "And whatever happened to me since they died, some things you never forget, especially when your life depends on it. You see, for the first time in more than a year I found myself in front of a computer. Social services there still worked mainly with paper, and he didn't have a workstation. But he did have his own laptop, one of those heavier ones of back then, which he always had with him when he left the house, and that he left right there beside me, thinking I had no idea what to do with it. Except I did.

"I knew what the laptop was for. That when he was at work, he wanted to be able to see us, his toys, as he called us, in our prison cells whenever he wanted to. I knew because he told us, because he would give orders sometimes, or have that monster of a wife of his punish us when there was something he didn't like. So I looked for the way he did it, and found them, his webcams, the way he was streaming their feed. I figured a sick man like him, he would like images, videos, whatever, and I found them, too, I found where he'd hidden them, the remote file storage he used.

"I opened an account in a free file storage service, and I copied everything he had on his laptop and in his remote stash. What he had about us, the links he used to see us at the house, more links and videos I found that showed he liked to browse online for the . . . the things he'd later do to us. What was on his laptop, I copied as much of it as I could. The rest, in the remote storage, would take too long, but it was online, account to account, so I set it up to continue to back up to my choice location even when I'm not there to watch it. I simply copied his storage to mine, making sure as best as I could in the little time I had that what I did couldn't be traced." Her eyes were closed as she remembered, retraced her steps.

"Apparently the risk of someone looking in his laptop, or the risk of being hacked, hadn't occurred to him. Or maybe he just got used to not getting caught. Either way, it made what I did easier, and I managed to get most of what I wanted. Most, but not all, I didn't dare stay too long. As soon as I was done, I got out of there. I picked the lock on the door, I knew how to do that from all the times I tried to unlock the door of my room at the house. His laptop I left there, exactly where he'd put it, I didn't want him to even suspect what I'd done.

"No one saw me, they were talking somewhere not far away, arguing about something, I remember the voices, someone was shouting. No one was there to stop me when I left. I have no idea when he got back or what happened, I just walked out of the building and kept walking. I did take the money he had in his wallet, but I didn't dare go on a bus, I needed not to be seen. I'd left his coat, I was scared someone would recognize it as his and remember seeing me with it, so I just left it there, but I had my hoodie on, and I covered my head. I stayed away from people, walked through alleys until I got to some woods, that entire area is heavily forested so I could move through it basically unseen, and I did, I just walked, and then I ran, and then

I walked some more, I didn't dare stop. I tried to stay low, and I just continued in what I thought was the opposite direction to that house, as far as I could away from it. And then it was night, but I didn't stop. I figured he wouldn't call the police, but he could look for me himself and so could she and I had no intention of dying that day."

Ian flinched, and she surprised him by putting her hand on his. He held it, needing to hold it, but then she pulled it away, with some hesitation, he noticed, and he wondered if maybe she had wanted to keep the touch.

She kept her eyes down, not looking at him, and continued to speak. She wanted him to know it all, to judge for himself. "When I got to the next town I chose a house—it was night, everyone was asleep —and I stole some vegetables from their garden because I was so hungry. It was raining, and I was soaking wet, freezing, so I also stole some clothes. A teenager's clothes, a boy. And a backpack that sat on the porch, because I thought it would look less odd if I walked around with it." She raised her eyes and met his. "I had the money I stole from him, I could have bought something, some food, at a gas station down the road. But there was a man minding that station and I knew what men do."

His gaze didn't waver and something in hers did, and for a moment there she thought those stubborn tears would finally come.

They didn't. And she was determined to finish

her story. "I continued that way for a long time, hiding during the days and walking at night, when it was dark and there was no one around. It wasn't just them I was scared of, I was afraid of meeting anyone. Anyone who might ask questions. Any man who might figure out I was a girl walking alone. My hair was chopped short, it's easier to maintain it that way when you're keeping a girl prisoner. And I was thin, underdeveloped, starving. So with the clothes I was wearing, and it being winter, and with my head down, I could easily pass for a boy. But there was no way I wasn't going to be as careful as I could.

"I ate what I found in some greenhouses and in storage sheds on the way, took a little with me for when I would walk where no one lived, and I walked on. It took me a while, I wasn't strong. But I survived, I survived all that way, in the winter. Until today I've no idea why, what made me fight that way, to live. But I did. Once, in a city along the way, I went into an internet café at night and checked my storage account. Everything had downloaded to it, it was all there. As far as I could see no one had tried to touch the account, but then they never would have thought I would have done anything like that. Didn't know I could. I transferred everything to another storage account and closed the original one I'd used, to cover my tracks, and then I left. I kept moving this way for a while longer, but the fact was that no one was coming after me, as far as I could see I wasn't on the news, nothing."

She paused. "Finally, I understood I couldn't continue that way forever. I had to risk it. And so, at some point, with every step I took further away, I made a small change, to look more normal. I got some clothes at a thrift store. I had my hair cut properly in some town, so it wouldn't look so strange—I still wore that hoodie, I'd kept it, I still wanted to be seen as a boy on the road, but I knew that at some point that would have to change. The hairdresser asked questions, and I gave her a name, made up a story. It worked, she believed it. So I figured I could do that again, tell whatever story I chose to.

"Those weeks when no one had caught up with me, the fear turned into thinking. I knew I had to disappear forever. To become someone else. I was in Denver when I decided that, and that's where I made my mind to stay."

"You walked all the way from Southeast Texas to Denver, Colorado?" Ian gaped.

"For about . . . a month. Four weeks. At some point I couldn't, I barely had any strength left and I wasn't making enough of a headway. So far I'd pushed forward on adrenaline, all I wanted was to get away, get as far away from them, from him, as I could. But it wasn't enough, I just couldn't feel that I was far enough from him. So eventually I sneaked into the back of a pickup truck. The driver was a woman, I was passing by a gas station and I heard her say she needs to make it to Denver by morning. I didn't want to talk to her, I was afraid she'll tell someone or even just remember that she saw me, if anyone asked later, so I sneaked in and got off as soon as she slowed down at a traffic light when she entered the city. That's why I got to Denver in the first place, it wasn't as if I was planning to get there. I had no idea what direction I was going in."

"God, Tess." He couldn't imagine it, her making all that way alone, in the winter, in the condition she was in. Afraid to meet anyone, not knowing who she could turn to for help.

"I had no money left, but I managed to check into a tiny motel managed by an old woman, a nice one. You kind of learn, you know, to tell the good ones from the bad. Anyway, I gave her some story, and she let me stay there and pay after a few days. I'm not sure she actually thought I would pay, but she let me stay. She even gave me some change for the vending machine. I didn't ask for it, she just gave it to me. Anyway, I spent the first couple of days there creating a story, a new background for myself, and when I was ready, I went to look for a job. I needed money, and I needed to start my new life somewhere.

"I didn't know Denver, and I got lost. And then I chanced upon a small company, a startup that was just setting up shop in a building of its own. They had actually stuck a handwritten note on the wall near the entrance, saying that they were looking for a couple of people without any experience, just to help set up, move stuff around, clean, you know. They were just moving there that day, there were boxes all over.

I thought maybe I could get some work there and went inside, but then I got scared, there were too many people around there for me, mostly men, and I tried to get out and took a wrong turn and ended up in the basement. And there was this guy there, this big guy, older—mid-forties looked old to me then—and I remember he was muttering to himself, he was trying to set up a computer, a desktop tower, under a desk, and I wanted to go, I thought I could leave unnoticed. But then he tried to get off the floor, and he bumped his head on the table and cursed, and then he saw me. And stared. And then he just called me over, in a kind of distracted way, asked me to help him set up the computer. And I did. To this day I don't know why. Why I went to him instead of running. Maybe because of the way he looked. Even then." She shrugged. "Later he told me I looked lost and neglected and hurt and he had a feeling he shouldn't just let me disappear."

"Jayden," Ian said.

She nodded. "By the end of the day he'd figured out I knew something about computers. He asked me to come back the next day, help him some more, there was still the server to finish setting up. He said that none of the hotshot developers upstairs would bother being there, in the basement, even though this system was the heart of the company, the core of what they did. Of course, I found out later that they would have loved to help, everyone did everything at that early stage of the company and they all certainly wanted the computer systems to work, but he wouldn't let anyone near what was then the only server, his baby." She smiled and shook her head.

"He let you near it."

"Yes. At the end of the next day he asked me if I wanted to stay, as his assistant, to continue helping him set up the equipment, maybe see what he does. He explained that he was actually the company's data analyst and suggested that maybe I could learn from him. If my parents didn't mind. I told him the story I made up, the one you know. He said fine, just give me your full name, address, social security number, let's get you all settled. I looked at him and he looked at me and he knew. I was about a second from bolting, disappearing again, but then he said something. He asked me, will they hurt you if they find you? Just that, not who, not why. And I don't know why I didn't run, why I answered. Looking back, I guess he was kind to me, didn't try to . . . do anything. There just wasn't anything like that, anything bad at all, around him. He was such a good person and I was just a kid, and I was terrified someone will find me and send me back and I knew what that would mean, and I was just so alone and I had nowhere to go. I had run half the country and I just didn't have anywhere to go but run some more."

Ian's fingers flexed. He had wondered, but he'd never imagined it was as bad as this, what happened to her. He wanted to touch her, let her feel he was there. She saw this, looked at him in wonder, wonder at him, at the strength he was giving her, the ability to speak, to finally tell her story. To continue.

"I said yes, and he just said, right. Just that, right, and then he took a piece of paper out of the drawer, grabbed a pen and motioned me to sit down. Let's get the story straight so I can do something with it, he said. Just like that. He wrote down my name, the name I chose from a couple of books I saw in a store somewhere on the way, a place I went into to get warm. Tess Andrews. A birth date. A birth place, I said it was Denver, but he must have known it wasn't true. Was there a family that would be looking for me, he asked, and I said I had no one.

"That was the last time he asked me about myself. He said they'll fill in the rest, didn't say who, but a few years later I found out he'd used some people a friend of a friend of his knew to buy me an identity. A few days later I had a social security number, a birth certificate, papers to back up my background story."

"That couldn't have been enough to hide, certainly not for so long."

"The beginning was the hardest. I was trying to pass for seventeen, and I wasn't even sixteen yet. And I certainly didn't look seventeen, not then. But

I needed to pass for that age because then I could claim I graduated high school, and with that, with no family, and with a job and a place to live, I would be left alone, could be considered independent. And it worked. I kept to myself, stayed out of people's way for a while, and nothing happened, no one came after me. And it got easier with time.

"Jayden had a lot to do with it. What he did, helping me get an identity and covering for me, gave me enough time to think about what I needed to do to build for myself a story no one could see through for the years ahead, and to learn how to put it in place, back it up with records. And during that time, I got to know Denver and could build a real, credible story. Once that story was in place, time was all that was needed to cement it. I was betting that no one would have any interest in going back to the schools I supposedly went to, to see if I was really there years earlier, or ask supposed neighbors if they remembered me. And every year that went by made it more plausible for me to be able to say that there were many kids in the schools I'd gone to, that I moved around a lot, and anyway Denver is a big city, why would anyone remember me. Anyway, I'd set it up so that I knew if anyone searched for information about Tess Andrews. No one ever did."

It sounded logical. Cut and dry. Ian couldn't even begin to imagine the reality behind it, long years during which she had looked over her shoulder, afraid she would be found. Scared she would have to run again.

"Anyway, the day I got my new identity, Jayden hired me officially. By then I'd already moved into the apartment on top of his garage, the one he had built for his son, when he went to college—he'd moved away by then—and he and his wife are the only friends I've had since. They never asked, I never offered any information. And they've never betrayed my trust."

She looked at him. "InSyn was perfect. I couldn't go to college, I never finished high school. And it was too risky, anyway. I kept thinking someone will find out I wasn't who I said I was, or maybe he'll find me, and I'll have to run again. But Jayden taught me everything he knew, and I developed alongside InSyn, the work it's done over the years. And it sent me to courses. I didn't need any formal education for these, my experience and InSyn's backing were enough to get me accepted to them. It was a good place for me, a small, development-oriented company that kept to itself.

"And living at that apartment at Jayden's house, it was perfect for me, too. It's in Greenwood Village, you know, in a quiet spot without many people. It's not a big city like Denver, and it was easy to keep to myself there. And Jayden and his wife have lived there for a long time, they told everyone I was a family friend so it was easy for people around there to accept me without too many questions."

"So you remained in hiding in the basement, in all manners of speaking."

"Yes. I preferred . . . not to be seen. It was easier." She lowered her eyes. "After a while, I wasn't a scrawny kid anymore."

"You grew up into a beautiful woman." He understood so much now. The simple clothes, the hair pulled up in a ponytail. The lack of makeup or any adornments.

She nodded. "I knew what to do, how to take care of myself, how to look. I grew up in a normal home until I was almost fifteen, after all, and also, it's easy to learn these things. And there was a time, a short time a few years ago, when I tried to be . . . a woman. But I kept getting hit on and too many times guys got pushy, and I couldn't be touched, and I figured that that part wasn't there for me anymore, that monster had destroyed it, and I just wanted to be left alone. So I went back to being . . . what you saw. And it all worked out for quite a few years. And then earlier this year a conglomerate named Ian Blackwell Holdings goes and buys InSyn. A few months later, Ian Blackwell Holdings' owner decides to visit his new acquisition, has a run-in with my friend Jayden and pisses me off in the process."

"And the next thing you know you're married to him."

She nodded.

"Why did you accept Robert's offer?"

"I didn't know it was you."

At that, he laughed. "Still, why?"

She shrugged. "You purchased InSyn, and a new ownership meant my uncertainty as to what would happen with it increased, and the way your people were meddling in it only made it worse. But if that wasn't bad enough, the morning before we met I was called to see your transition team's human resources rep and told that you've decided to dissolve InSyn, to merge it into Pythia Vision and reorganize its specialty functions. I was told that I will be one of the employees relocated, that as one of its young talents I should expect to be invested in and promoted within the merged entity, which would require an in-depth background check and security vetting because of my expected exposure to Pythia Vision's projects and its future plans. Later in the day I received an email telling me that that process was to begin the following Monday, less than four days later. So I knew I had to leave. But if I simply left, there would be questions, and Jayden would be in trouble if the truth ever came out and what he did for me was ever discovered."

"He lied to InSyn, to everyone, to help you, and he kept up that lie for years." Ian wondered if there was a way he could ever repay the man for what he had done for her, for the girl who had survived to become the woman who was now his wife.

She nodded. "I thought that run-in I had with you would do the job, but instead you prevented my getting fired." She stopped. "I still don't know why."

"Because you were right. And because of the way you protected Jayden."

There was wonder in her eyes when she looked at him. It took her a moment to continue. "Anyway, when Robert called I was in my apartment, trying to figure out a way to disappear without hurting Jayden."

"And Robert gave you a way to disappear in plain sight, such that no one would dare ask too many questions." He contemplated her. "That's quite a price to pay to protect a friend. And an impossible price for you to pay if I had been a different kind of man."

"I owe him. And you kept your word."

"So did you."

"I always do."

"And as far as you were concerned, there was no hope or chance for a life anyway. Love, a relationship. Life," he said evenly.

"I never thought . . ." She frowned. "It was impossible. That much I knew."

"You grew up, and there's no arguing who you became, your looks. Was there never anyone?"

She shook her head, unable to meet his eyes. "And with time I learned that it's not that difficult to keep men away from you if you really want to." She raised her eyes to him. "We live together, and I still managed to keep you away."

"No, you haven't," he said conversationally. "But I don't force myself on women. As things changed between us I might have considered making advances toward you, but we're under a contract, which I would never break unless you wanted me to. And it was clear to me there was something there, something wrong."

"And it would be complicated, because we live together, as Robert has made clear."

"That's no longer an issue for me." He had no intention of holding back anymore. Now that he understood his wife, that he knew it all, that he had almost lost her, he would no longer hold back.

He saw the surprise, saw she had no idea how to react, before she lowered her eyes again. He went in a different direction. He would take it slow. She was vulnerable now, so very exposed, and them, him, what he was hoping would be, would be a first for her. He wanted her to fully understand, to be able to fully accept what she was for him, to know beyond doubt that he would go through all walls, all worlds, to truly have her as his.

"What ever happened to them?"

He didn't have to say who he meant. "As soon as I thought I was hidden well enough," she said, "once I was safely Tess Andrews, I sent all the information I'd collected to the Houston district attorney's office. I thought Houston was big enough, major enough, that if they became aware of what happened they wouldn't let it go. And they didn't.

I sent them everything I took, everything I knew. About the two of them, about Justine, about Maddy. About another girl who was in the videos he had, while Justine was still there but before Maddy. It was more than enough proof to start an investigation. It put the two of them in prison, and the social services department in Montaville was dismantled because of what it had allowed to happen. She died in prison four years later. He tried to kill an inmate and was transferred to another prison, and was killed by another inmate last year."

"You were in that information, too," he said quietly.

"And there was a formal record of my having been in their care. Yes. And I couldn't remove myself from all the images, the videos, without damaging the evidence, possibly invalidating it. So I didn't. But I had, effectively, disappeared, after all. I followed up on the investigation, the trial. The indictments included me as a victim who had been killed by them, burial place unknown. There was, of course, the question of who sent Houston the information, but I don't know if anyone even dwelled on that, I wouldn't be the first anonymous source. And since I was listed as a deceased victim, it didn't matter to me."

"You never stopped being afraid."

"Before I reported them, they looked for me. At least he did. I suppose he couldn't report me as a missing person because if I was found I could talk, and"—she hesitated—"it was . . . easy to physically prove what was done to me back then. So he used the social services network and his own connections to see if I turned up somewhere. He also contacted certain . . . bad elements, sex offenders mostly, in the surrounding states. Offered to buy information. Offered me to the finder."

He didn't ask her how she knew this. By now he knew what she could do. But his face must have shown something, because she shrugged and said, "Because I'd already been in it once, I could get into his laptop easily, remotely, but he didn't know that, so he used it freely.

"Anyway, after he was arrested I had no doubt he would know it was because of me. The authorities might have thought I was dead, but I figured he and I both knew the two things that would convince him I was the one responsible for him getting caught. That he hadn't killed me, and that I fight back. So I continued to follow what he was doing, using . . . other ways, since he no longer had his laptop. That's how I knew that once he was imprisoned he kept, for a while, getting people on the outside to try to find me. I guess he made some friends in prison who helped him with that. Eventually he stopped trying, and, yes, logically I knew that he had no idea who I was now, and that he probably wouldn't recognize me if he saw me. But still, I never stopped expecting someone to find me. I couldn't know if anyone outside might have been paid by him to continue doing so, or maybe just developed some interest in finding me."

He frowned. "So even after he died you couldn't assume your former identity again. But then it was impossible by then anyway, wasn't it?"

"And there was nothing to go back to, don't you see? Nothing. I was dead. The girl I used to be, they killed her. That part of me died there along with Justine and Maddy and that other girl. And even when I knew he couldn't . . . couldn't hurt me anymore, the memories, the feelings, those horrible sensations, they stayed. Yes, I was living a lie, but that lie had become my life, and I couldn't go back, I couldn't be her anymore, it was better if she stayed dead." The words flowed, full of pain.

He desperately wanted to hold her. To make her feel safe. To make sure she knew she was safe, with him. Had she looked at him, she would have seen this, would have seen her, in his eyes.

She fell quiet, took the time, all the time it took for her to force back the pain that welled up. And then she braced herself for what she was about to do. Or at least tried to, as best as she could. This had to be done.

She looked at him. "Under the circumstances, I'd understand if you decide to terminate the contract. I could disappear for a while, for as long you need me to until you can dissolve this marriage or create whatever story you'd like. I won't contest it."

"You'd go into hiding again," he said.

It would be harder now to go back to some obscure basement, she realized. The life she'd lived these past months, what had been the closest to a life she'd had in a long time, she would miss it.

She would miss him.

"You're a powerful man," she said. "Do whatever you need to do to make sure no one will look for me, tell them you didn't want me anymore or something. I know how to disappear. And they're not likely to find anything about me, I made sure of that over the years. I had the means, the time, to foolproof myself, and obviously no one had found anything, not even Robert, that report he gave you about me. That's why when he approached me despite running his own check, I knew I could do this. I just never thought . . ."

"That you would ever decide to tell anyone the truth. That you would trust me."

His voice was soft, and it hurt. God, it hurt so much. "I'm sorry, I really didn't mean to make you a part of this, a part of my life. I'm sorry." She lowered her head.

"You should be," he said, his voice gentle. "I was looking for a superficial, easily controllable woman who would provide for me the semblance of my wife, represent what I needed without causing me any grief and stay out of my way. Instead I got a woman with a mind of her own, generous to a fault, caring, smart, interesting. And frankly, I think everybody likes you better than they do me."

294

She was trying hard to hold on now. "Graham doesn't," she said in a shaky voice.

"I'm not so sure about that," he said with a deep sigh, and it warmed his heart to see her smile, even if for too brief a moment. "I *am* a part of your life," he said to her. "A willing one. And now that I know, that I finally know everything, I will watch out for you. You don't have to do this alone anymore."

She closed her eyes, hoping the tears would stay back, but they didn't. She opened her eyes again when he finally wrapped his arms around her, and for the first time allowed herself to be pulled to him, held by him, without resisting.

He stayed close to her even when he had eased away, asked her to drink some more of the tea. He then tucked her in, wanting her to sleep. She was pale, so pale now. This day, and the night it had brought with it, had been too much of an effort.

"You didn't ask me." She was lying on her side, facing him, on the soft pillows he'd arranged around her. Cried out, exhausted. Still unable to grasp that she no longer had to run.

Sitting on the armchair, which he'd pulled closer to the bed, he looked at her in question.

"My name." Her voice was slurred with sleep.

"Your name is Tess Blackwell. My wife," he said softly, then hurried to her when the tears returned. When he let go of her again, she was deeply asleep.

He sat on the bed and stroke her hair, then touched his lips to a tear-streaked cheek, lingering.

Then he went back to the chair and settled back to watch over her.

She slept the healing sleep that comes with finally letting go of hell, finally letting someone in on a secret kept hidden for almost half her life. When she opened her eyes to a sunny autumn morning, Ian was sleeping on the chair beside her, his feet on the bed, his hands folded across his chest. She stayed still, watching him, bewildered. She had told him what she had never told anyone, never thought she would. She had slept while he was here, in her bedroom, and woke up with him still here beside her. And it was right. It felt safe, and right. But what would happen now? she wondered with a tug of sadness. He knew now what she had done, and what had been done to her. Would this mar what had been growing between them, what had started to take its rightful place in both their lives? Would he look at her differently now, was it lost forever? She wasn't sure anymore that she could bear that. She couldn't—

His eyes opened, meeting hers. And they had everything in them for her.

Chapter Nineteen

Ian went to his own bedroom in the morning, but not before he treated Tess's bruises again. He took a hot shower, to take the kinks out of his muscles that ached after he had fallen asleep on the chair the way he had, dressed and returned to find that Tess had put on a dress, one that would hide the bruises but that was still part of that elegant, compliment-ing wardrobe the woman she had become would wear. It was a good sign, but too much about her was still not her usual self.

"My laptop, it's still in your office," she said ab-sently, stopping on the way down the stairs. "I left it there. But he could never hope to turn it on or take it apart without wiping everything on it."

"He didn't take it, he scrambled out of there as soon as you left," Ian said. "It's in the den, with your bag. I had Jackson bring it here yesterday."

She nodded, still distracted.

He watched her with concern. She had none of her characteristic alertness about her. "Tess, you need to rest. Please go back to bed."

She shook her head.

"I'm staying at home today, I'll work here so that you won't be alone. I'll work in your room if you want me too."

She looked at him in surprise that turned to wonder, but at least now he knew why. She shook her head again. "I want to help."

He looked at her in question.

"I want to take him down." Her voice was low. And determined.

He considered her. She was fighting back. Good. He would have liked her to rest, recuperate under his watch, allow him to envelope her with his protection, his care. His love. But perhaps right now fighting back against the man who did this to her, and who was still doing it to them, was the best thing for her.

"All right," he said. "But we do this here, at home, and you don't push it. First order of the day," he interjected again when she started protesting, "is breakfast. You've barely eaten anything yesterday."

Her eyes, raised in objection, met his. His were a warm gray that would not be argued with, not when it came to her wellbeing. You're far too important to me, they said, and she was lost in them, in this care she was not used to.

Breakfast was eggs, scrambled the way she liked them, and warm, soft rolls, her favorite sweet ones that Lina had made especially. Followed by pancakes this morning, made by Graham. No one could do them as well as he could.

"Pancakes," Tess mused and poured a generous amount of maple syrup on the ones on her plate.

"Food for the body followed by food for the soul," Ian remarked.

"Philosophic," she said.

"Tasty." He put sugar powder and berries on his. She concurred.

She went straight to her bag, which sat on his desk, took out her laptop and turned it on.

"He didn't go anywhere near it," Ian told her. "I think the way you stood up to him after what he did to you surprised him."

She shuddered at the reminder of what had happened, of what had almost happened, and Ian moved closer to her, let her feel that he was there. She relaxed again, visibly so, and managed to think. Analyze. "That's why he came to speak to you despite what he said to me. He couldn't trust that I would remain silent."

"You were supposed to be his victim, but instead you are a threat. Or were, as far as he's concerned his talk with me took care of that."

She turned to look at him.

"Before he came here, he sent me an email with that proof he threatened you with. It's on my laptop if you want to see it."

She didn't, not in the least. He didn't think she would. He hadn't either, hadn't needed to, and he said so now. "He asked to speak to me in confidence, and came posing as a concerned friend who wants to protect me from the embarrassment that the woman I married could potentially cause me with her outrageous behavior if anyone found out. He actually apologized to me for having to do that, to cause me such grief, that's how he said it. Luckily, I was prepared to act suitably. All shocked and enraged."

"I'm just glad you knew it wasn't true."

"You thought I would believe it? Tess, we've been together for more than five months now. I know you. I'm just sorry I didn't do enough to let you know that, to give you the confidence to come to me. It hurt you."

"It's all right now," she said, still too quiet.

"It will be," he said softly, and she breathed in, tried to draw a bit of confidence from him.

"What does he think you're going to do?" she asked. "It has to be something he would be sure would neutralize me while allowing him to continue with his original plan."

"He thinks I'm sending you away."

She tilted her head, just the slightest.

He shrugged. "I feigned anger, a bit of a tantrum. My wife, my own wife! If this ever gets out I'll be a laughing stock, it will be an absolute disaster."

She had to smile at the way he was playing it. It was easy, knowing that he knew the truth. Easy, except for the fact that the man who was doing this, who had hurt her and was hurting her husband, was still free to do what he wanted.

"So," Ian continued, "he suggested that perhaps I should send you away for a while, and I jumped at the idea and said that I would much rather send you away for good. That I couldn't bear to look at you after what he's told me you've done. And after all, someone like me could make sure of that, make sure you wouldn't return, wouldn't go anywhere near me or mine or there would be consequences." He spread his palms. "He bought it."

"So he expects me to be gone."

"I said I would do it yesterday. You're supposed to be gone from my life for good by now. If he sees that, he'll think you're no longer an immediate threat."

"And you'll be safe."

"I was thinking more along the lines of you being safe," he said gently. "I already knew what happened when I spoke to him, remember?"

She did, too acutely. "So how do we do this?"

"We already are. You can't go anywhere outside the house, or the grounds immediately around it at the most. This property is big enough and the house is positioned in a way that the hills around it prevent anyone seeing it, and the airspace above it is closed, I made sure of that when I moved here. Also, no one will come here in the coming days, and Graham will make sure anyone who happens to ask will think you've gone away for a while. To visit friends, whatever. If Brett happens to hear that, he'll think I'm trying to hide what happened. That should give us some time."

"So I'm grounded," she mused, and he laughed. "Well," she said thoughtfully, "at least now that we know it's him, we've got more to work on. I'll start looking into him, see if there's anything he did in the past or something in the way he thinks that will help me refine the location identifiers I've already prepared, and maybe also help uncover flaws, patterns, or access points in what he's doing to Ian Blackwell Holdings." Much like she'd done at InSyn, in the part of the work required to analyze the human element of the theoretical interface.

"Can you dig into him without him knowing?"

"Yes. Because he believes I'm out of his way. Normally I'd think he might consider me a greater threat now because I might be out on a vengeance, but you've made it clear to him that you've sent me away, and someone like you could easily make sure I won't contact anyone, so that should be enough. Still, I'll be careful." Her eyes narrowed. "I'm going to get to him, and I'm going to disarm him."

Ian nodded. No fire there yet, but she was fighting what she could, in the way she knew best. He hoped that taking Brett down would go some way toward her healing. "I can help you get started," he said and went over to his laptop. "I can get you all the information I have about him as well as about Additive Manufacturing. Including"—he was already preoccupied with accessing the information—"everything since its inception and until I purchased it, so mainly concept development and preliminary technology implementation. Since he's on the company's technological side, it could help, right?"

"Very. It'll show me how he thinks," she said.

And it did. Over the next hours she studied Brett using what Ian gave her and what he told her about him. Not about Brett as she herself had seen him before the day of his attack on her, the man she had met in social functions, but what Ian had seen when he had met Brett back when he'd first taken interest in purchasing Additive Manufacturing, and the professional side of Brett he had seen and heard in product meetings since the company became one of his.

By nightfall, she had enough to integrate into her search additional parameters that would help her trace when and where Brett had begun to build his web. This would, she hoped, reduce the number of Ian Blackwell Holdings subsidiaries in which what she was looking for possibly was, the origin of Brett's work, the point from where he could bring down her husband's company.

The intercom sounded a soft chime, and Ian, who for the past couple of hours had been sitting in his armchair watching her while she worked behind his desk, completely engrossed in her work, got up to answer it.

"Mr. Blackwell," Graham said impassively, "*Mr. Sevele* is at the gate."

"Let him in," Ian said, glancing at Tess. "Show him to the living room." He stepped behind his desk and activated the wall screen. Several clicks and a split view showed the main door of the house and the way to the living room and the room itself, for her to see and hear. "He must be here to make sure I did as he suggested," he said. "You'd better stay in the den."

Brett already felt at home here. It would be different now, Blackwell owed him for saving him. Or so Blackwell thought. Their conversation the day before had gone well, and he had obviously succeeded in speaking to Blackwell before *she* did. It was pure luck that Blackwell had been on that fancy jet of his back overnight, pure luck that he'd already completed his business and had decided to return to San Francisco immediately to be present for the remaining subsidiary audits, he'd said. Yes, luck was certainly on Brett's side, as it should well be. And apparently Blackwell was more preoccupied with his company than with his wife, so that Brett had met him before he had a chance to speak to her. He did say she was feeling ill. And he had said that rather dismissively, and so Brett understood that he'd been right, that Blackwell did not care much about his wife.

Nice one, though, Tess Blackwell, he thought, for

keeping away from her husband. Probably trying to think what to do, and obviously she was not about to tell Blackwell what he had done to her. Excellent, she was obeying him. Still, it worried him, the way she had fought him instead of simply succumbing to him. One never knew with women, it paid to be careful. And he had gone too far, he hadn't meant to. Well, maybe he had, he'd had his eye on her, on having Ian Blackwell's wife, since the day he first saw her. But he should have done it later, when she was too entangled in his plan to have any other option but to let him have what he wanted, and certainly in more appropriate settings. For him, of course. What had happened, it had gotten out of hand, he had lost control. But then he had not expected her to be so feisty. Or to be so protective of Blackwell, he had certainly underestimated how much she cared about him.

No matter. Blackwell didn't care about her, and if he had in fact done what they had talked about the day before, Brett was free to continue what he'd been doing, to destroy Blackwell as he wanted.

Blackwell came toward him now, a somber look on his face, and dismissed that butler guy who had remained with him in the room. Not wanting anyone to know, Brett thought. So he had him, he had Ian Blackwell right where he wanted him. And *she* was indeed gone, Blackwell then told him. She had denied, he said, but he had shown her the proof, the implicating images he now thanked Brett for again, and she'd been shocked into silence, no longer try-ing to deny. He had sent her off to one his more isolated properties the night before, threatening her not to speak to anyone until he finalized all the nec-essary arrangements, and she had not objected, she had wanted nothing but to leave.

So maybe he was wrong, Brett thought. Maybe he had scared her more than he'd thought. Or may-be she simply understood that leaving was the way to protect Blackwell, women were like that. Either way, she was gone. He assured Blackwell that the matter would remain between the two of them, and, yes, of course, an attorney, he understood that one must be employed to help deal with getting rid of her and ending the marriage.

It worked, he thought with glee as Blackwell him-self walked him to the door. The only person who could stop him was out of the way, and he was free to do whatever he wanted.

Ian returned to his office, allowing the ice back into his eyes. Tess was sitting behind his desk.

"Looks like he believed it," she said quietly.

"Just as long as you didn't."

She smiled a little, her eyes on the screens of both their laptops.

He came up behind her to see what she was do-ing and leaned over her shoulder, his hand on the back of the chair. He was close, but she didn't mind.

He wasn't touching her, though, not like he had the day before, and she wondered fleetingly if he was avoiding touching her on purpose.

And then he did. As he leaned closer to the screens, he put his hand on her waist, and immediately moved it away with an abruptness that for her could only mean that he'd had time to digest what she had told him, what was done to her, and was repulsed by it.

She wasn't prepared for the force of the stab of pain she felt. She struggled to contain the emotions, to hide them from him, but it was different now, so much more difficult to do that. Her eyes remained glued to the screens as she finished setting up the refined search, and as soon as she could she excused herself, saying she wanted a bit of rest, which Ian accepted.

She was sure he would leave her alone, and that's what she wanted now. She was still raw from what had happened to her, still hurting, still trying to come to grips with it. And after the previous evening, having told Ian the truth, what she had never told anyone before, what she had never uttered out loud, and reliving the horrific memories in the process, she was now far too vulnerable. Not in the least because the entire ordeal had also shown him how much she cared about him, and that too she had no idea how to deal with. She felt exposed, and entirely uncertain as to how to tread in this new territory for her.

With the storm of emotions raging inside her, she had no idea what would happen once she was alone in her room, the room he'd been in with her the night before.

She had no idea she wouldn't be able to keep the tears back.

Ian knocked on the door and came in. "Tess, I asked Graham to serve dinner in the den, looks like your search turned up—"

She had no time to turn her back to him. Her eyes were red, and he saw it and covered the distance to her in two steps. "Tess, what's wrong?"

"Nothing." She tried to sound as if nothing happened, but she'd been caught unprepared. "I'm just a bit tired."

"No, that's not it," he said slowly, racking his brain, trying to understand what was going on.

She breathed in, trying to steady herself. "You know, I can handle the search by myself," she said. "There's no need for you to be here. Why don't you take my place at the Corwell banquet in the meantime?" She was originally supposed to attend the charity event herself while he was in Tokyo, but obviously couldn't, not now, and it had slipped her mind. She hadn't told them she wasn't going to be there after all.

"I can't. Brett is going to be there. Thinking I had sent you away, he would expect me to behave as if I'm no longer married, maybe even leave with a woman by my side."

"Maybe you should," she said, her voice quiet. "I would understand."

"Would you? It would be okay with you if I was with another woman?"

"It will happen at some point. And you've . . ." It was difficult for her to say this, excruciating. "You've made it clear that . . ."

"Clear? How the hell did I do that?" He was truly absolutely confused.

"You moved away, earlier. It's the one thing I recognize well, isn't it what I've been doing to you all this time? Look, now we both know that it's not . . . that I'm damaged, okay?" She found the strength to say it as it was. "So there's no need to continue—"

He took a step toward her, finally understanding. Frustration flared. At her, for thinking this. At himself, for letting her think this. At this goddamn situation that was preventing him from touching the woman he loved like a man should. "Is that what you think? I moved away, so you think, what, that I don't want to touch you?"

She turned away from him and he did something he had never dared do before. He caught her hand and pulled her back to face him. Her eyes opened in surprise, then anger. Good, he thought with relief. There was that spirit he'd been waiting to see again.

"You were raped," he threw at her.

At the words, her eyes closed and she pulled away, but he held on to her. He had to do this. To say this. For her.

"You were violated when you were a young girl," he said, "so you think I wouldn't want to touch you? That this, us, would have been different if I had known from the start? Is that how much you trust me? That's who you think I am, what you are to me?"

Raging, anger flowing from him in waves, he turned and walked out, the door slamming behind him. She stumbled back, finding purchase against the wall.

And straightened up in surprise when, no more than two minutes later, the door was flung open again, slamming into the wall, and he strode back in, holding papers in his hand. He raised them. "My copy of the contract. Where's yours?"

She stared. She had never seen him lose control this way, never seen him turn into raging fire.

"Where the hell is it?" He was, just now, dangerous. And he didn't care.

She walked over to a drawer, opened it and took the copy out.

He snatched it from her hand, and, putting the two copies together, tore them into pieces, letting them fall to the floor.

"Now we can speak freely. Ever since you first set foot in this house, every single thing we've said or done has been bound by the strict limits of this damn thing. Well, that's over, we've been through too much together for that, and we certainly care about each other too much for that. From now on we say what we want and do what we want. And let's start with this. The only reason I'm not touching you is because you're so terribly bruised and I don't want to hurt you, I don't want you to even remotely associate my touch with pain. And I want to make sure that when I do touch you, you're not as vulnerable as you are now, so that you will know, really know, that I mean it, and how I mean it. It's certainly not because I'm put off by what happened to you or because I think you're damaged."

She shook her head and he surprised her by taking her hand again and pulling her to the full-size mirror on the other side of the room. Making her face it, he stood behind her, his hands firmly on her shoulders. "Look at yourself. Just look, damn it," he said, and she did. She saw herself, and she saw him, the rage in his eyes, boring into hers in her image. "You were hurt by a degenerate bastard I really wish I could kill with my bare hands. But you fought back, and you made sure he doesn't do that to anyone else, and then you fought some more and grew up into a remarkable, not to mention gorgeous and damn desirable woman. And let's get one thing straight—I wanted you before, and I damn well want you now. The only thing that's changed is my understanding of why you are as you are and how things need to be done for me to get you. Which I will, let's get that straight, too. And one more thing. I understand now just how inexperienced you are. So just to make it clear. I *am* going to touch you again, and we are now dating."

His hands dropped to his sides. "Now let's go see what the search found. Your laptop is beeping like crazy in the den and Graham is complaining the fish needs to be taken out of the oven or it'll dry, and you know how he gets when he doesn't get his way."

She nodded, still shocked.

"I'll see you downstairs." He turned and strode out again, leaving the floor strewn with the torn contracts. As he reached the stairs, he breathed in deeply. There. Now she knew. He descended the stairs, hoping to God he'll see her again.

When she joined him in the den, after minutes that to him seemed like an eternity later, the light was back in her eyes and she looked better. Much better, in fact.

"The results of the search don't make sense," he tried. "I'm not sure what it found."

She deliberated him for a long moment, then came to stand beside him before the wall screen. Relief passed through him like a fresh breeze. She was still here, still with him, more than ever with him.

She saw immediately what the search results were indicating. It wasn't that they didn't make sense, they

simply needed to be looked at from a different per-
spective. She took a confident step toward the screen.
"Command," she said, surprising Ian, and her laptop
indicated it was now in listening mode. "View level
one sub-search."

The figures on the screen changed. Ian looked
at her. Her eyes were focused. He couldn't see what
she was seeing, but trusted her to do her thing.

"No," she said to herself. "View level two sub-
search."

"No," she said again after viewing the result.
"Switch to temporal." And she started calling out
dates. At some point she backtracked, then reorga-
nized the data, then pulled up the connections to the
tangible for him, going back up several levels in the
schemes of his company to simplify the image. And
now he could see it.

"Son of a . . ." he said. "How did I not catch it?"

"He's good, and he started it gradually, constantly testing himself on the way, making sure he won't
get caught. You can see the temporal pauses. God,
he's been implementing his plan since . . ."

"Since that first time you and I went out, to the
retirement party. He was there, that's when he first
saw us together," he said.

"And his jealousy of you finally drove him over
the edge."

"The irony." Ian shook his head.

Tess looked at him in question.

"I've decided to expand Additive Manufacturing's

operation. Substantially so. As CTO, his importance would have increased accordingly."

"I don't think . . . I think what he wanted was to be you. Nothing else would have been enough."

"I really don't know why I bother." Graham came in muttering, pushing a serving cart with their dinner on it.

"Sorry, Graham. We were having a fight," Ian said with some amusement.

"Yes, I know, and I understand that a good fight is conducive toward a healthy relationship. But, fish, I'm just saying."

"Sorry, Graham," Tess added, stifling a laugh, and Ian put his hand lightly on her lower back, warning her not to laugh a split second before he himself did. The instinctive touch, the way it felt this time, made her look at him, made him glance at her with something new in both their eyes.

He slid his hand around her and held her close to him.

"Don't blame me if the fish is dry. Really, I don't know how I put up with you two." Graham left the room, indignant, and so very happy to see them together.

"Told you." Ian was still laughing when they sat down to dinner.

Not only did the search results tell them when Brett had started making the changes in Ian Blackwell Holdings' numbers, creating his web of algorithmic discrepancies, they also narrowed the range of relevant data, pointing Tess, after further reorganization, to subsidiaries where the point of origin possibly was. And so midnight found them treading through these subsidiaries, the company's non-profit ones, which it had in a number of locations worldwide. Wherever the origin was, it was in one of them.

"Smart. And cold," Ian said. "The way he placed the discrepancies, if anyone would have found them, they were more likely to see them in one of the profit subsidiaries, think someone was embezzling money there and launch an investigation that would have alerted him, and he would have had enough time to trigger the point of origin hidden in a non-profit no one would look at in this way."

"Yes," Tess said thoughtfully, her eyes on him.

"What's bothering you?"

"I don't know," she said.

"Sleep on it," he said. "I'm not doing anything with any of this anyway until we have it all and we can get him."

"I'll probably wake up with it at two in the morning," she mused.

In fact, it was half past two when she did, waking up with a start not too long after she had fallen asleep. She sat up in her bed. No, she thought as fear wrapped itself around her heart, but was immediately washed away by her anger and resolve. Damn you, I won't let you do this, I won't let you hurt him, was what went through her mind.

Moments later she was sitting in her robe behind Ian's desk, searching. A little over two hours later she strode into his bedroom, turning on the lights as she did. As she approached the bed he sat up, surprised. She'd never come in here before.

"Tess? Are you okay?"

"You're Ian Blackwell." She stopped at the foot of the bed. He looked at her in question.

"You're Ian Blackwell, the man who built a huge multinational company and is busy running it, but still flew half the country to check out a small company named InSyn even though he could decide what to do with it from afar and get his people to do the work. You're hands on, and guess what, he knows it. He must have studied you more closely than we thought, and longer than we thought, even if he started on what he's doing only after you got married."

He was now completely awake. "What did he do?" He got out of bed and she realized fleetingly that this was the first time she'd seen her husband half-naked. He grabbed his robe and followed her to the den.

"When he talked to me, he said something about misleading," she explained to him on the way. "He said that people can pretend to be so much, mislead so easily if they wanted to. I thought he was talking only about me, about what he intended his proof to show. But then he also told me that he was going to hurt you, but not in the way I think. That's what got me thinking. See, he did know that you look at everything, and that there was therefore a chance you'd see something. He was just worried that you'd see it too soon. And he was certainly worried that you have once he found out who you married. So he lined up everything, *everything*, to be traced back to you, implicating you." All the screens in the den were on, and she directed him to the ones on his desk, showing him what she'd found. He sat down and listened to her.

"His point of origin is, in fact, in one of the non-profits, I found it. But remember I told you that it was disconnected from the web of webs that will eventually encompass the entire company and I didn't know why? It's because he never intended for it to directly activate that web. Once his web was advanced enough, he disconnected the point of origin from it. He then created another point of origin in Ian Blackwell Holdings, the parent company. And it's one that is built as if *you* created it, and as if only *you* can trigger it. He's not going to activate the web spanning your company. He's going to trigger his point of origin, but instead of it activating the web, it will trigger your point of origin, and it will be your point of origin that will activate the web, crashing the entire company. It will look like you did it. It will mislead everyone to think you're to blame." She was angry. "And that's another reason he used a non-profit. The data densities there will enable him to destroy all tracks from the web and from your point of origin to it—and to his— more quickly and more efficiently. It will be as if that specific subsidiary was never part of the web, and as if his point of origin never existed."

He was quiet, his eyes on her.

"No," she said.

"No what?"

"You're considering what to do with him. But it's too early. I still need to deal with his main point of origin, which is the only place from where, if I can interfere with it, I can unravel his plan in a way that will destroy him and protect you." Her tone was thoughtful, and he realized she probably had no idea what she'd said. That she was protecting him.

"What do you need?" he asked.

"That location where the origin is, is also the most protected one. That's why, while I know where it is, I can't touch it remotely. I need to be there, to dig directly all the way down to it in a way that he won't know I'm there. He would never expect anyone to do that."

He nodded, understanding. "Where is it?"

"Sydney. The point of origin is in IBH Ivory."

He stood up. "Get dressed."

Chapter Twenty

He watched her. She was deep in thought, her eyes on the clouds outside, the soft white blanket they were flying through light enough for the flight to be smooth.

"Coming to live with me, in my house, it must have been so much more difficult that I'd initially thought."

Her eyes remained on the hushed sky outside as she laughed softly. "When I understood it was you, I was . . . alarmed, to say the least. The powerful and ruthless Blackwell. The womanizer Blackwell, which is what your own contract *and* your attorney clearly implied."

"I'm not a womanizer."

At that, she turned her eyes to him, amusement clear in them.

"Well, yes. I guess I was."

Her brow furrowed slightly at the past tense, but he had no intention of correcting himself. Instead he held her gaze. "You stayed."

She contemplated him. "I don't just back out of my promises because of fear."

"No, you wouldn't." A smile passed his lips.

"And . . ."

"And?" He wanted to know.

"Remember the day you first brought me to the house?"

"Of course."

"When you showed me my room, you made sure I knew no one would come into it except for Lina. You specifically said that *you* will not come into my bedroom, that I was safe from you." She shrugged. "No one has ever done that before, taken such care to try to make me feel safe."

He remembered. "I'm glad you stayed."

She turned back to the window. "So do I."

She woke up to find herself covered with a blanket, her seat comfortably reclined. She straightened up, confused. "When did this happen?"

"About an hour ago," Ian, in the seat opposite hers, said. "You couldn't have gotten much sleep last night."

"Neither did you," she remarked.

"I slept more than you did. Why don't you go back to sleep? There's a comfortable bedroom here." The last time—the only time—she'd been in this jet was on the day they were married, and neither of them had wanted her in it. They had spent that entire flight sitting in the same places they were sitting in this time. How different things were between them now, Ian mused.

"A bedroom. Right, very funny." Tess laughed and shook her head. "I'm okay. I'd love to freshen up, though."

Ian smiled and pointed to the back of the jet. "All the way back there. I'll order us some coffee, something to eat maybe?"

Tess nodded and got up. She peeked curiously through the next divider, and smiled at the sight of Graham, who had fallen asleep on a divan that stood along the sidewall on the right, apparently while watching a movie on the big screen television on the other side of the aisle. The wireless headphones were still on his head.

She walked on through the next divider and then stopped, her jaw dropping. When she continued to the bathroom in the back, she did so slowly, looking around her in astonishment.

The astonishment was still on her face when she returned to her seat. "You have a bedroom. With a double bed and shelves and books and . . . I think that was a closet. Was it? And there's a real bathroom back there. Shower and everything."

Ian smiled.

"This is . . . it's like a house. An apartment. I don't know. This thing is big."

He nodded. "There are also crew quarters up front, and a fully equipped kitchen. That was the whole idea, a jet for longer flights—we're flying from San Francisco to Sydney without needing to refuel on the way. And it allows me to rest if I haven't had time to sleep, or to fly wherever I need to and back without staying there overnight."

"I've never seen anything like it." The first time she had been on this jet, she hadn't noticed anything about it. But this time she saw it all. The dark wood of the tables and cabinets, the same as in his Blackwell Tower office. The warm vanilla seats that fit in perfectly with the light creamy sidewall and darker carpet. The bathroom she had just been to, the bedroom. That media corner Graham was still deeply asleep in. All that on a jet. It was incredible.

Ian watched her, enjoying her awe. Enjoying the fact that after all she'd seen in her time so far with him, he could still surprise her. "It's a Bombardier jet. I've worked with them through my company for years, and I finally decided to go with this new model of theirs for my personal use, too. It was actually delivered to me just a month, I think, before you and I met."

"Seriously, is there anything you don't have?"

His answer was a smile, and something in his gaze that made her heart beat pleasantly faster.

She lowered her eyes, unable to meet his. Found herself wondering at this, at traveling with him, at flying with him halfway across the world—

"Wait," she said, the realization dawning on her. "What if someone at IBH Ivory talks to your San Francisco office and Brett finds out I'm with you?" They had made the decision and had left so quickly that she hadn't had a chance to think it through.

"It's okay," Ian said. "Only Becca knows where we are, and I made sure she doesn't note it anywhere on her computer this time. And I'd like to see someone try to get that information directly from her. She knows to alert Robert if Brett shows up, and I told Brett I would be involving Robert in my plans for you since, as he knows, Robert is also my personal attorney. As for Ivory, they think I'm dropping by for a visit since I'll be in Australia with my wife, on our way to the honeymoon we never had, and they understand my need for privacy."

"Aren't you at all concerned about the media?"

"You'd be surprised how many times I'm somewhere and no one knows. Ira makes the necessary arrangements for me wherever I go. In Sydney, too, the driver who will be driving us around is one of his men, and he's made sure we have everything we need to limit our visibility there."

She shook her head. "Still, maybe this is too much of a risk, maybe I should go somewhere else, see if I can guide you how to do what's needed, the direct access part of it at least." She tried to think how else she could do this without exposing him. "If he realizes what we're doing and that I'm still with you, he can hurt you before I can do anything."

"I want you with me," he said softly. "I need you with me."

She couldn't say no to him.

The car, not a limo but a sedan with tinted windows to attract less attention, took them directly from Sydney Airport to IBH Ivory. Tess looked curiously out at the city, lively in the comfortably warm spring day, high-rise buildings shining in the early afternoon sun. Ian couldn't stop watching her, thinking about all the places he wanted to take her to when this was over.

They drove through the city until they reached streets lined with commercial buildings alongside hotels, tall buildings among lower, older ones—Tess thought she saw a harbor in the distance, to her left, but she wasn't sure—and whether it was disorientation, finding herself halfway across the world, or the sheer size of the impressive city, she couldn't get a clear grasp of where she was.

When the car finally slowed down, it was near a wide, two-story building. Unlike those around it, which boasted shops and restaurants on their pavement levels, this one was somber, its facade purely practical. The only entrances to the reddish-brown brick building were a door and a truck-size entrance from the main street, the latter of which their car now drove through.

Ivory, an environmental protection company, was one of several such companies set up in a number of regions around the world by IBH World Synergy to understand their environmental needs and find solutions that could help create a sustainable existence, and through which it could provide resources for areas hit by natural disasters. As such, Ivory was different from the corporate heart of Ian Blackwell Holdings in a number of aspects. One of them was that it was separately audited, along with the rest of IBH World Synergy's subsidiaries, later in the year.

But not only that. All of Ian Blackwell Holdings' subsidiaries were connected to a central system that allowed their resources and specific sector-relevant and region-relevant performance parameters to be monitored by the international company's Blackwell Tower headquarters, to ensure its efficiency and long-term stability. All but IBH World Synergy and its subsidiaries, which had their own independent monitoring system. Eight months earlier, the two systems were linked by a virtual connection that was still in the pilot program phase. And that pilot program began where the company that created the connection was, Australia. Hence, IBH Ivory.

Which explained why Brett had chosen it. Working from inside Ivory gave him a layer of separation between him and Ian Blackwell Holdings' corporate heart, reducing the chances of anyone who might notice what was happening tracing it to him while still affording him the access he needed.

As such, it was perfect for his point of origin.

It was also his weakness. He must have been certain what he was doing would in fact be invisible to external scrutiny, other than perhaps for someone who knew what to look for. Someone like Tess, whom he had recognized as a threat, but was now convinced was no longer around. And he must have thought he would know if anyone tried to go after him by entering Ivory remotely through the new virtual connection, which he had made his gateway between Ivory and the rest of Ian Blackwell Holdings, and that he was monitoring.

But Tess was still there, still after him. And she wasn't planning to get into Ivory remotely. She was right there, in its building. This was her turn. IBH Ivory was a remote corner Brett used thinking he was hidden in it, and she was about to break into it without him ever knowing she was there. She was about to go directly to his point of origin, and to the algorithm he had prepared that was designed to trigger the domino effect that would destroy Ian Blackwell Holdings in a way that would point the finger to the man she loved as the culprit. But she was no longer going to simply unravel Brett Sevele's work.

She had a different idea in mind.

Ivory was dormant, some of its dedicated staff in the field, poised to help in the dry weather that was threatening wildfires, and most of the others off for the weekend. Ian didn't have an office there, and the CEO readily offered them his. They declined. Tess asked to see the company's computer room, under the pretext of curiosity about the new system being tried there, and since the person monitoring it wasn't there, she suggested she would gladly do so by herself, she did after all have the necessary background. Ian, in the meantime, chatted with the CEO, suggesting he wanted to see some more of Ivory's work while he was there, thus making sure everyone present would focus on him, not his wife.

But the pretense wasn't necessary. The CEO was ecstatic that Ian was there. It had been a long time since Ian Blackwell himself had visited the company, and he was not one to miss such a rare opportunity. And so Ian found himself being given the tour by Ivory's eager employees, while in the cool computer room Tess connected her laptop to the mainframe and went to work.

By the time Tess began to feel the jet lag, she already had her own system connected to Ivory's in a way that would not raise any suspicions. The way it looked, Brett had indeed never considered the possibility of anyone actually connecting to Ivory directly. By his own admission, he himself had only done so remotely, through whatever system he had set up in his home, fully trusting his cunning and expertise. Hubris, she thought, was never a good thing.

"Where are we staying?" She stifled a yawn. They were sitting in the back of the car, which picked them up from Ivory and was now driving among modern skyscrapers through the bustling streets of the city's central business district.

Ian glanced at her. She'd been through too much and had been pushing herself too hard. As resilient as she was, it worried him. "We have an apartment here in Sydney," he said. "Graham is already there." Ivory was not his only company in Australia or in the region and having the privacy of his own apartment was valuable to him.

She settled back and closed her eyes.

"We're here," Ian said just moments later, and Tess opened her eyes as the car entered the private car park of a skyscraper, not really taking note of her surroundings as they walked into a private elevator up to the penthouse.

"Mrs. Blackwell, Mr. Blackwell," Graham greeted them enthusiastically when the elevator door opened again. Tess was glad it was him there, and not someone she didn't know.

"Would you like anything to eat?" he asked. "I can make anything you want, we're pretty much set for a siege here."

"I just want to sleep," Tess said, stifling another yawn.

"I concur," Ian said and guided her inside. She looked around her in astonishment. The place was huge, spanning the entire top floor of the skyscraper, and certainly not like any apartment she'd ever seen.

"You'll stay in the master bedroom," Ian said. "I'll sleep in one of the other bedrooms."

"No." She turned to him. "You stay in your bedroom, and I'll take one of the other rooms."

"But . . ."

"It makes the most sense, Ian. You should sleep in the bedroom you're used to. And we're just staying here temporarily, it doesn't matter." She yawned again.

Ian let it go, more than anything wanting her to get some rest. He motioned to Graham and led him to the bedroom closest to his, going inside with him to make sure it would be made comfortable for his wife.

Chapter Twenty-One

She came out the next morning to find Ian Blackwell himself in the kitchen, making breakfast. "Aren't you jet-lagged?" she asked him, coming to sit on the other side of the kitchen counter.

"You get used to it after a while." He handed her coffee, hot and strong with half a teaspoon of sugar, the way she liked it.

"And you're making breakfast." Scrambled eggs were sizzling in a pan, and the juicer in the corner was making fresh orange juice.

"I didn't always have people to do things for me, you know," he said, placing before her a plate with an assortment of heated rolls.

"I didn't think about that." She sipped the coffee. It was good. "Where's Graham?"

"Having some jet lag issues. I thought I'd let him sleep in."

"You don't usually take him with you, do you?"

He shook his head. "Rarely when I travel on business, unless it's for a duration. I do take him, and sometimes Lina, too, when I spend time in some of my other properties. But this apartment is normally maintained by someone arranged for by Ira."

"You brought him because I'm here."

"You're used to him taking care of us at home, I thought this will make traveling easier. Especially since this is your first time."

"That's thoughtful of you."

Her smile made his heart accelerate, trip, then try in vain to gain its footing again. He had to put some effort into focusing again. "You sure you don't need to go back to Ivory?" he asked her.

"Not for now, no. Maybe not at all. I used the direct connection to create a link I can use to work remotely without going through the virtual connection and without him knowing I'm there." Her brow furrowed in concentration. "I want to map exactly where and how he's working inside Ivory, and then comes the tricky part. Backtracking through the virtual connection into Ian Blackwell Holdings' corporate monitoring system and through it to all the subsidiaries he's touched, and mirroring what he'd done up to a point I can let my own ghost-web form against his. Same as his web but with the opposite effect. And, of course, I need to get to his points of origin, his real one and the one he's set up to implicate you, and then I need to disable them so that they won't crash your company."

"Both origins?"

"Yes, just in case he has a way to work with only one of them if the other one doesn't work."

"What's first?"

"All at the same time, intertwining in each other's dead intervals, that is when each task is doing something it doesn't need me for."

He nodded. That didn't sound simple, but she didn't seem at all worried.

"Robert says Brett doesn't suspect anything," he said, coming into the living room, his phone in his hand. "He came to look for me at the office, and Becca referred him to Robert, who told him I didn't want to involve anyone in this delicate situation so I left to make the necessary arrangements myself."

"To dump me." She was sitting on a sofa with her laptop. Relaxed. With every day that passed the bruises were increasingly no more than a background reminder of what had happened to her, no longer needing numbing.

"Pretty much, yes." He contemplated her. "Are you comfortable here?"

"I miss the library." She looked at him. "And my soft, comfy reading chair. And the fireplace." Which he'd started having on in those autumn evenings that were already cool.

"That last one at least I can do something about," he said. He went to the closest console and turned on the air conditioner, then came over to the fireplace and started a fire.

She followed what he was doing with a wide smile. "I'm speechless."

"It's the little things, you know," he reflected with a grin of his own and returned to sit on the sofa nearest hers, and to his own laptop. He'd spent the day working with his East Asia audit teams through his Tokyo-based assistant, continuing what he'd left in the middle of.

They worked quietly, comfortable together. As the sun set, painting the sky outside in brilliant colors, Ian finally emailed his comments to items he wanted included in some of the audits to his assistant, with notes to Becca in San Francisco, and then sat watching the remarkable woman who was intent on saving his company and him. Her strength amazed him. To have gone through what she had and still become the woman she was. He wondered what she had been like as a child. Naive, that's what she had said. Protected, as any child should be.

Suddenly something occurred to him. "Tess, do you have anything left of your parents? Anything of what you had when they died?"

She raised her eyes to him, surprised. After some time, she shook her head.

"What happened to it all?"

"I don't know. I have no idea. All I know is that my parents were buried in Montaville, I checked the records later."

"What were they like?" he asked, his voice soft. He wanted to know, but he didn't want to hurt her.

She clearly hadn't expected the question. It took her a bit of time to answer him. "They were nice.

Just my mom and dad." Her gaze was quiet. "They were very protective. They . . . loved me." She shifted restlessly, pained, and he regretted asking.

"What were *your* parents like?" She needed to deflect the next question that might come, push away the memory of the family she used to have.

He saw it. But he would have answered her anyway. "My parents still live in the same town I grew up in, in California. They're schoolteachers."

"Are?" She was surprised. "There's no mention of your parents anywhere."

"Unfortunately, this day and age their life and mine need to be kept apart in order to protect them. Robert and Muriel know them, and Graham has met them, and that's it. My parents like their life, and I don't want it disturbed."

He saw the questions in her eyes. She cared. And he wanted to share this with her, what he had never shared with any other woman. "I was a small-town kid, probably would have been something like that myself, a teacher or something. I was even all ready to start college with that in mind. But when I was eighteen the community bank my parents were in changed its policy, because of a new manager who wasn't happy with the bank's profitability. Their mortgage was called in without warning, as were those of other families in town, good, hardworking people. My parents tried to fight back, but they didn't have the power to go against a bank, and no one gave a damn enough to even listen to them.

And these were people with jobs, with two modest but certainly stable salaries."

She saw the anger, the pain in his memories, and wanted to be there with him, to sit beside him. To touch him, she realized with shock.

"The house I grew up in was foreclosed on. Too many other houses were also already empty, so it couldn't even be sold. It just stood there. My parents tried to convince the bank to let them stay, continue paying the mortgage. After all, it would benefit the bank, and it was better than letting the house run down. But they were refused. The head of the local branch, a guy sent from Los Angeles, and bitter for it, made things worse." His eyes were on the fireplace, but it wasn't just a reflection of the fire burning in it that she saw in them. "With all the stress, my father got a heart attack and couldn't work for a while, although the school was kind about it, the only kindness my parents saw back then. Instead of starting college, I ended up getting a job outside town, and I swore I'd get them the house back. But even after my father had gone back to teaching, and with the additional money I earned, the bank didn't budge, and I became angry. For the first time in my life I understood the reality of this world."

He raised his eyes to hers, pure force in them. "I did everything I could to earn as much as I could, and two and a half years later I bought the house back and moved my parents back in. But I never

returned to that town, to the life my parents wanted for me. I pushed on. Three years later I took
over the bank, got the town back on its feet. Then I
tore the bank apart, sold it in pieces, made sure those
I wanted gone would never work again. Including
that branch manager. That's the only company I ever
completely destroyed."

"And that's how you became Ian Blackwell."

"Yes. And, by the way, my parents aren't called
Blackwell. Once I decided not to go back to my old
life, I changed my last name to that of an ancestor
of my mother's. A name that died off somewhere
along the line, a man who did exactly what I did but
in different times, and in less . . . lawful ways."

She considered what he'd told her, and he saw
the realization down on her. "Us. This marriage. Your
parents know."

"My parents have been happily married for more
than thirty-eight years. Nothing of what I did with
my own marriage suits them. But they know my life,
and they accept my reasons for doing what I did,
even though it saddens them. They wanted me to
have what they do."

Contemplating this, she tucked her feet under
her and curled up comfortably on the sofa, her soft
hair spread on its back, the fire a flickering gold in
her eyes. She looked, he thought, so very alluring.

And no longer quite so forbidden to his touch.

He pushed the thought away. This wasn't the
time. Not until she was ready for it to be. "I will

arrange for you to meet them when this is over," he said. "They will be happy to finally meet you."

She shook her head. "How can they be? I'm not what they wanted for you."

She was everything they wanted for him. She was everything he wanted for himself. Her eyes were on his, her gaze sending emotion throughout him. She would be his, he knew there was no other way for him. He would do whatever it took to have her, no matter how long it took.

"They will love you," he said softly.

She only spoke again after her heart settled a bit. "How do you meet them?" she asked.

"They spend all their vacations in my properties worldwide, anywhere they choose but the house you and I live in."

"Not where you are watched most."

He nodded. "Imagine what would happen if it became known they are Ian Blackwell's parents."

Her brow furrowed as she considered this, him. "You're trusting me."

"*You* are trusting me," he answered.

The furrow deepened. "Why did you do this, enter into this contract? I mean, really. Why?" It was her turn to ask.

He was glad she did this, ask him personal questions about himself. It meant, he hoped, that she was finally allowing the distance between them to close. "My parents have been married for so many years," he said, "and they are still so very much in love with each other. They can't really do without each other. I ended up comparing every relationship to what they have."

"Was there no one?" It wasn't like he'd had the life she had.

He shook his head. "Once I began building myself, that was my focus, not a relationship. I was driven by anger, a sense of injustice, the knowledge that I need to be able to protect my parents and myself. And once I became, well, Ian Blackwell, that's what the women I met all saw. I imagine if someone would have caught my attention earlier I might have given it the time, made the effort, but no one had."

Earlier. She noticed that.

"And then, in the months before you and I met, I was targeted as the eligible, desirable bachelor, and that type of attention quickly became disruptive." He shook his head in distaste. "Women coming at me from every direction, my every move being watched by every person with a smartphone and a social media account. It's one thing to get the attention I do because of who I am. It's another to get *that*."

"You let Robert choose."

"I had no time and I trust his judgment. Or at least did." He smiled.

"Yes, he got us both, didn't he?"

"He was supposed to get me an unromantic socialite who cared more about her social status than marriage to play the part."

"Instead he got you . . ."

"Instead he got me my wife," he said, and she felt herself blush. "That's the one thing I never expected."

"Neither did I," she said, her voice barely audible.

Her laptop beeped twice, and she turned her eyes to it and adjusted the parameters again. Good. She was now Brett's shadow.

"It occurs to me that the woman doing what you're doing there has never finished high-school," he remarked.

"Good thing the only ones who know that are you and Jayden."

"It certainly hasn't stopped you. I'm impressed." He thought a bit. "It also occurs to me that you're younger than you said. You told Jayden you were seventeen, but you weren't even sixteen yet."

She shook her head.

"You told him you were seventeen in January. That's when you escaped, isn't it?"

She was quiet for a long time. "I was sixteen the following May. May twentieth," she added softly.

He did the math. "You'll be four months shy of twenty-eight next January. Not thirty." Which was what her employee record and Robert's report had indicated.

She nodded.

"And you had a birthday shortly after we got married," he said gently.

She said nothing.

"I'm glad you told me."

She lay her head on the back of the sofa again, her gaze on him.

The decision was Ian's, to remain in Sydney. Not because they might have needed Ivory again—Tess had decided she no longer needed the direct access. But he thought it was safer to stay there, where she would be less visible.

By the end of the next day Tess had Brett's real point of origin figured out and knew exactly what he was doing, and she could set algorithms to begin tracking his web, to prepare to reverse what he had done. With nothing to do but wait until her trackers gave her what she needed, she let Ian convince her to go out to dinner at least once while they were there.

He took her to the Sydney branch of Antonio Torelli III, her favorite restaurant. This, at least, was simple. It was easy to ensure their privacy in the restaurant that he owned. The car stopped at a side entrance and they were ushered into a private room. They never saw the other diners, nor were they seen by them.

"Mmm," she said, tasting the exquisite food.

"Something wrong?"

"Something right," she said. "This tastes exactly like Antonio Torelli III."

"We are at Antonio Torelli III." He smiled.

"Our restaurant, the way Antonio himself cooks for us." She loved his cooking and could easily tell. "But it can't be, he's in . . ."

She stopped and looked at Ian, who was looking at her with an innocent twinkle in his eye.

"He's here. You flew him to Sydney."

He nodded, enjoying her surprise and pleasure.

"You flew him all the way here for me?" The astonishment on her face was everything to him.

He called their waiter, and a short moment later Antonio walked in with a smile that widened when he saw Tess's obvious pleasure at his food and at seeing him there. He joined them for a coffee and the dessert he himself had made, telling them happily that while he was cooking there for them that night, and was glad at the chance to visit one of his restaurants, he was mostly happy that he could bring his family along with him to Australia for an extended vacation.

When Antonio had left, Tess looked at Ian, laughing. "You're something, you know."

"I'm sorry we can't do more than this. In other circumstances I would have taken you to see the city, but since we're not supposed to be here . . ."

"This is enough. It's more than enough." She couldn't believe he'd done this for her.

He did have the driver drive around the city in the dark of night, and when they returned to the apartment he took her up to the skyscraper's rooftop, where she could stand on top of the world. She walked around the rooftop balcony, her gaze on the sweeping view of Sydney Harbour and the magnificent city stretching before her, taking it all in. It was breathtaking. She had never seen anything like this, never stood in such a place, never imagined that this, here, could, would be her. Finally, she stood in the middle of the rooftop, turned a full circle, then stopped and smiled at the man who stood not far from her, watching her, mesmerized by her.

She didn't move as he walked toward her, his steps slow but not measured. Didn't move as he came close to her and put his hands tenderly on her waist. Never moved away as he leaned in and gently touched his lips to hers. When their mouths parted, his brow remained on hers.

"May I do that again?" he asked softly.

She nodded.

His arms tightened around her and he kissed her again, deepening the kiss softly, parting her lips with his as she responded to him, as she tentatively put her arms around him. They stood on top of the world for a long time, their arms around each other, neither of them wanting to let go.

His arm was around her as they returned to the apartment, and as he kissed her good night, lingering, before they went into their separate rooms.

Chapter Twenty-Two

"Gotcha," Tess said.

Beside her on the sofa, Ian raised his head from his own work. "You got him?" She had worked the entire day—and the day before—without indicating what she was doing and without needing any information from him. It was her and the data, her and Brett Sevele's tangle of webs that she was intent on destroying. Ian just stayed close, working beside her, leaving her only when he had a call to make.

And to prepare Robert for the eventuality that had now, apparently, arrived.

Tess nodded. "Him, his webs, and his inter-web links that he's using to make up the encompassing web. And"—she typed some more, then looked at him, her eyes bright—"my webs are now forming alongside his in your subsidiaries."

"How long will it take you to finish building them?"

"It no longer matters," she said. "They're there just to counter what he's done so that nothing will remain, not a trace. They will be a mirror image of every change he's made. What's more important is that I've also already put in place my own point of origin."

"What does that mean?"

"It means that from now on, if he decides to trigger his point of origin he will no longer be activating the secondary one that implicates you, or the web that he already has in place. Instead, he will be triggering my point of origin, which will in turn activate my webs that are designed to counter his, to undo everything he's done. And as for that secondary point of origin, yours, he will be destroying it, it will be gone without a trace. It's a dead end for him." Her eyes were golden ice. "Ian, he no longer has control of what he's done to your company. You're safe."

God, he thought. It's scary, how smart she is. "Won't he know it?"

"No. He receives diagnostic feedback from his thread-forming routines while his webs are being built throughout Ian Blackwell Holdings' subsidiaries and as they interconnect to form the encompassing web. I've made sure that feedback is not disturbed, and that it doesn't register and report to him what I'm doing."

He nodded. "Thank you," he said.

"I still have to watch him as long as he's free, and see what he does when he realizes his plan has failed. He's smart enough and mad enough to do something that could hurt you." The ice her eyes deepened. "And there's something else I still want to do." She wasn't done with Brett Sevele.

"And yet, thank you." Ian's brow furrowed. "I never imagined, when I came up with the idea of this marriage, that the woman who would be my wife would end up saving everything I've built. But then, there's much I hadn't expected that this marriage is proving to be." He got up, a finality to his movements. "We're not going to let Brett decide when to pull his trigger. I've placed some triggers of my own, and now that you've neutralized him it's time to pull them." He took out his phone and left to make a call. As he passed by her, his hand brushed hers, holding it for a lingering moment.

Tess came out of her room early the next morning to find Graham alone in the kitchen, humming to himself. The breakfast table was set for two, not three.

She stopped and looked at it. "He left," she said.

Graham turned around. "Mrs. Blackwell! Good morning. Didn't hear you there."

"Mr. Blackwell has left," she repeated, her brow furrowed.

"Yes, just a few hours ago. He flew back to . . . eh, take care of Mr. Sevele, he said." Graham went to the living room and returned holding something in his hand.

"Why didn't he tell me? And why does he have to do this himself, can't Robert do it?" And why didn't he take me with him, she didn't ask. There was no longer need for her to remain in Sydney.

"Mr. Blackwell said he'll call to explain." Graham handed her what he was holding in his hand.

She took the long box and opened it. There was a flower inside, a single, beautiful, fresh red rose. A note lay on top of it. She took it out and read it.

"I already miss you," it said.

He called a half an hour later from the jet. She wasn't angry, he saw. But then he hadn't expected her to be. She did look at a loss, though, and that he had expected. He'd simply disappeared, leaving her halfway across the world from home.

"I expect to land in San Francisco at around midnight there," he began. "Robert will pick me up at the airport and I'll be staying at his and Muriel's place, it will reduce the chance of Brett finding out I'm back."

She said nothing.

"Brett will be picked up in the early hours of the morning. He's already being followed so he's not likely to run, but he might have time to try to cause the damage he wanted."

"He won't succeed. I'll be watching him."

"I know," Ian said. "Tess, I'm sorry I left this way, without telling you." It burned in him to say this, to be personal. He would have started with the personal, but this was a first for him, too.

"Why did you?" Her voice was quiet. And she really was just asking.

"Because you would have wanted to come with me. Tess, he'll be picked up, and I'll give my official statement at Robert's house, everyone who needs it will be there."

Which meant, she knew, the relevant authorities, and Ian Blackwell Holdings' legal team, whoever Robert would decide to use. And, naturally, Robert would also be acting as Ian's personal attorney, since Brett's attack was aimed not only at the company but also at Ian personally, and at her—

At her. Now she understood.

"Once it's over, I will issue a public statement. This way it will come directly from me. Of course, no one will ever know how far Brett has ventured into Ian Blackwell Holdings, or his exact plan. There is more than enough without it, you've taken care of that with the evidence you've prepared along the way, and in the days since we've known he was behind it I've had people uncover additional illegal activity rigged toward what he was doing. And—"

"And power goes a long way toward getting what you want."

"Yes," he said evenly.

"Toward keeping me out of this. Toward protecting me."

He said nothing.

"This is all about protecting me," she said incredulously.

"Just as everything you have done has been about protecting me, Tess. That was the first thing you thought about after he attacked you. It was what you've cared about all along." His voice was quiet.

"I guess we're the same," she said.

"I guess we're the same for each other." His eyes were on hers. "I'll be staying in San Francisco for as long as I'm needed, to make sure the authorities have what they need to hold Brett and that there are no speculations that can hurt the company. I'll let you know what's happening, I promise, and when it's over I'll come back. In the meantime, please stay in the apartment with Graham. The news is bound to get there, even though Ivory's involvement won't be known. Ira has people watching the apartment, so don't worry about anything."

She nodded.

Just before he ended the call she spoke again, more than a bit shy. "Ian, I liked the flower." She didn't need to tell him it was her first.

"Like I said." His voice was soft. "I already miss you."

It went smoothly, but that didn't surprise Ian. It was a carefully set out, meticulously executed plan. He knew how to protect his own and had everything required to do just that.

By sunrise in San Francisco, Brett Sevele was in custody, away from too many questions, and that would remain the case. At the last minute, he had tried to use the elaborate system of computers he had set up in his home to trigger his point of origin. But instead of activating the part of the encompassing web he had had time to create within Ian Blackwell Holdings, his action triggered what Tess had set up, leading to his point of origin becoming just that for him, a point, a very dead end unable to do anything but activate the destruction of his own work.

Tess had effectively disarmed all of Brett's threads, the foundations of his web of webs, unleashing a domino effect to undo everything he had done. Her own webs weren't all in place yet when Brett was arrested, but as soon as he was and she no longer had to worry that he might find out what she was doing, she could freely harness the entire power of Ian Blackwell Holdings' main computer systems to accelerate what she had begun, so that all original numbers were quickly restored and not a trace of Brett's plot remained.

Except in IBH Additive Manufacturing. Tess had left enough, manipulated enough, to make it look as if Brett had been embezzling money and stealing trade secrets—only within the subsidiary he worked in, of course—and making sure it would all point to Ian in order to deflect blame from himself. Thus, she had effectively exposed his plot against Ian but in a way that did not throw a shadow on Ian Blackwell Holdings' integrity or on its perceived ability to protect itself, its subsidiaries and its business partners. What she had left, together with the documentation she had prepared as evidence and had given Ian, he could safely provide to the authorities to prove Brett's illegal activities. It also showed that an internal investigation had been going on for almost as long as Brett had been implementing his plan, proving that Ian Blackwell Holdings had discovered Brett's actions at a reasonably early stage and had taken steps to protect itself, while continuing to monitor him at all times to understand his intentions. That part she had done too.

But that wasn't all she had done. And this, only Ian and Robert knew, in retrospect. Mimicking what she had done to her assailant almost thirteen years earlier, she had used the time between Ian telling her that Brett would be arrested and until that had actually happened and had copied his entire home system, the one he had used to carry out his plan, sending it all, the entire proof, to the one place no one would ever find it in. Just in case she ever needed it.

Then she deleted from his computers anything that could hurt Ian or his company, and everything Brett had created to hurt her, the materials he had threatened, and then tried, to use against her. Everything, in a way that could not be restored. And then she made it look like it was Brett who had deleted it all, in fact leading to speculations being raised about the true extent of his plan, his true intentions, making him look, in the eyes of those who now held him, like the villain he really was.

Throughout it all, Ian Blackwell Holdings was never compromised, and Tess Blackwell's part in preventing what had almost transpired—the little the outside world was allowed to know—remained hidden to all but a few. As was the attack on her.

In his jet, on the way back to Sydney three and a half days after he had left, Ian leaned back in his seat, perturbed. The damage Brett had caused had been fixed, largely thanks to Tess. Everything, except she herself. That was the greatest, most terrible damage he had caused, and it was a scar that would take much more than Ian Blackwell's money and power to fix.

It would take Ian Blackwell himself, and that's exactly what he intended to do. If she let him.

He glanced at the clock and calculated the time left until he got to her, dreading the one thing he still had to do.

Tess was sitting on the sofa, staring at the dark fireplace, the one her husband had lit just a few days earlier to make her happy, when the elevator door opened and he came in. She had known he had landed, had known he was on his way, and still her heart accelerated, then stumbled, when he walked into the living room, where she now stood.

He had done this countless times since they were married, come home from his office or from a business trip, and the way he came toward her, the look in his eyes, the words he said, had changed over that time. And yet it was never this way, the way it was just now. The way he stopped in the doorway, the way his eyes fell on her. The way they softened and his lips curved up just a little. The so obvious way he had been waiting to see her.

It was over now, what they had been doing together these past weeks. It was now again just this, just them, the man and woman who had married in such an unlikely way. She wondered what he would do. Would he kiss her? She missed that, his touch, his kiss, in the days he was gone.

Overwhelmed by her own reaction, her own emotions, and at a loss as to what she should do, she took her laptop from where it was still sitting on the sofa and placed it on the table, then brought up the news broadcast from San Francisco, from the day Brett had been arrested. With some difficulty, Ian turned his gaze from her to what she was showing him.

"Brett Sevele, CTO of Additive Manufacturing, an Ian Blackwell Holdings company, was arrested today on fraud and embezzlement charges. The investigation, conducted by the parent company itself, has been ongoing. Sevele has already been replaced by—"

352

She muted the volume, focusing on the images that showed Brett being taken into the police station, his attorney beside him, the press hounding him. He looked haggard, terrified—and the way he moved, the way he flinched when a police officer prodded him on, and the beginning of a bruise on his jaw, were clear signs to anyone who knew him, who knew what was going on.

Tess turned to her husband, whose eyes were still on the screen. He looked at her and gave a slight shrug.

"You failed to mention that you intended to beat him up."

Ian had known she would figure it out as soon as she saw Brett. And yet he had set it up. No one objected. Very few, only those who needed to know and who would protect the secret, knew why. And that was the way it would remain.

When he spoke, his voice was calm and very much countered by the darkness in his eyes. "He hurt you. He's lucky I didn't kill him. Lucky that you asked me not to. Lucky that Robert was in the room with me." He raised an eyebrow. "A lucky man, all in all, I would say. Except for the fact that he has nothing left and is going to prison for a long time." His gaze turned to the muted broadcast.

She looked at him, at this fine man of business and calculated moves who flew halfway across the world to beat up the man who had attacked her. Her eyes flickered over him, seeing in her mind the

353

muscles she knew were under that finely cut suit, which she had fleetingly seen the night she had come into his bedroom. Her heart tripped over itself again, and she told herself it was because of what he had done for her. And it probably was, to an extent.

"I don't know if I should throw something at you or kiss you," she remarked.

His gaze turned to her in surprise. He didn't expect that. Nor did he expect what it did to him.

"Kiss me," he suggested with his eyebrows raised.

She considered him. Then she walked up to him and touched her lips to his, of her own accord for the first time. He put his hands on her waist, holding her gently. When she began to move back he held her to him, holding her eyes for a tender moment before leaning and kissing her. He deepened the kiss slowly, keeping it gentle even as he let passion dictate, as he felt her respond. When their lips parted he stayed close. So did she.

"What happens now?" she asked him.

"Legal and Public Relations prefer that we stay away for a couple of weeks, until they clear us to return. They want to be free to handle the situation their way. Robert concurs strongly, he says it would be best if he could say we're on a well-earned vacation, maybe even hint that we've finally gone on our honeymoon, since the Brett affair is now completely resolved."

"So—" she began, then fell silent. He was looking

at her intently, hesitation on his face. She's couldn't recall ever seeing him hesitating.

"Ian," she said. Waited.

He let go of her and moved away. He didn't want to do this. But he had promised himself that he would, had been talking himself into doing it for some time now. It was the right thing to do.

He came to lean on the fireplace, his eyes lowered. "I have an island in Fiji. I bought it before I bought the Woodside house, when I still lived in San Francisco and wanted a place no one knows about or at least can't get to without my permission. I would like to go there for the duration. It would be the best place to disappear to, and it would certainly be a welcome reprieve." He looked at her. "For both of us."

Her heart took on a life of its own.

"I would like you to come with me." He watched her. "But I'm also offering an alternative. For you only. My jet will take you anywhere you want, anywhere in the world. I will annul this marriage and ensure no one knows where you are. You are a rich woman and can do as you please. Free of me."

He stopped. He didn't want to continue explaining this option that had tormented him for many a night now. An option she deserved to have. She had the right to be free, to have the life she never had. And she had, he thought, every right to leave him. And while he would otherwise chase her across the globe until he won her back, circumstances, what he had allowed to happen to her, might just dictate otherwise. For him, her happiness was all that mattered.

Her silence following his proposal was excruciating for him.

"Which would you prefer me to do?" she finally asked him, her eyes on his, her voice quiet. She knew what she wanted, what her choice would be, a choice she never would have imagined she would make. But she needed to be sure of his, needed to hear him say it.

Her heart beat hard as the look in his eyes changed, becoming that which she was learning was meant only for her.

"There is nothing I want more than for you to come with me," he said, his voice soft. "Nothing I want more than for you to be my wife."

She walked up to him and he waited, bracing himself, as she stopped before him, standing close, almost but not touching him, her eyes never leaving his.

"Ian," she said with that now familiar tilt of her head, a gentle glimmer in her eyes, "I *am* your wife."

He took her in his arms and held her to him, held tight as relief flooded him, allowing love to follow in its wake, allowing what he wanted, what he had in him for her, to come out unchecked. His mouth locked on hers, his arms tight around her, and she answered, letting him in, leaving them both breathless when they finally parted.

"I love you, Tess," he said, holding her close, so close to him.

"Say that again," she said, wonder in her voice.

He embraced her, feeling her arms around him, a sensation he had no idea could do so much to a man, to him. "I love you, Tess, my wife," he repeated, never letting go.

They stood together, their arms around each other. She marveled at how good it felt to be held by him. Loved, by him. A tug of apprehension followed, at what she knew this meant, what was still to be between them, but for the first time she pushed it away. It, and not him.

"Can you just leave this way?" she asked.

"I've taken care of most of what I needed to since we've arrived here, the main audits are pretty much done and my people are perfectly capable of dealing with the rest. And if I'm needed, I can be reached. The island has satellite communication service and Robert and Becca know where I am." He smiled. "It may come as a surprise to you, but I don't work all the time."

"It seemed that way since us."

"I couldn't take time off without you, and I couldn't take time off with you."

She laughed. "Good point."

"I can now, and I am. We are."

"When are we going?"

"In the morning, after the crew gets some rest

and the jet is prepared. I still need to tell them where we're going, I had to speak to you first." He eased back to look at her. "Graham will be the only one on the island with us while we're there. Do you mind him?"

"No at all, not Graham."

"Good. He likes it there." He looked toward the kitchen. "I'd better go talk to him. I told him earlier what I intended to do, and he's waiting, rather anxiously I should say. He's angry at me for even suggesting I might let you go."

"You did the right thing," she said quietly, and let herself be pulled close to him again.

Chapter Twenty-Three

Staying out of the public eye for a little longer suited Ian. He wanted the time alone with his wife, and he didn't want anyone to even think they might be in this part of the world. Even IBH Ivory—which still had no idea about its role in everything that had transpired—thought he was back in the United States, having seen him there on the news.

They made their way unseen to the building's car park, and from there to the private hangar that housed the jet at Sydney Airport. Tess and Ian sat together in the back of the car, while Graham sat beside the driver, chattering happily on the way.

"You will love the island, Mrs. Blackwell," he said for the hundredth time as the car entered the hangar. He was in a good mood, delighted to see how close together Mr. and Mrs. Blackwell were sitting now, that Mr. Blackwell was holding his wife's hand. Finally. These two were driving him mad. He loved them both, but they were seriously driving him bonkers.

Tess took her seat on the jet, still listening to Graham enthusiastically describe their destination.

After speaking to the pilots, Ian came to sit in his seat opposite hers. As the aircraft taxied and took off smoothly, his eyes came to rest on Tess's, and hers on his.

"See? I knew you'll end up together. But who ever listens to me?" Graham, sitting on the other side of the aisle, grumbled.

"What's that, Graham?" Ian said.

"Two hearts with a shared destiny will always find each other, is all I'm saying."

"I had no idea you were a romantic."

"You've never given me a reason to be," Graham grumbled some more. "And after seeing you two skirt around each other for so long, I'll be taking some liberty with that, Mr. Blackwell. If you don't mind my saying so, sir."

"Skirt around each other?" Ian looked at Graham incredulously.

"I should say. You fell for each other like five seconds after you met, even Mr. Ashton said so."

"I seem to have missed some occurrences around me," Ian noted with interest.

"Doesn't matter, it's all good now. But you'll understand if I keep an eye on you two for a while, just to make sure, won't you?"

Ian stared at his loyal house manager and Tess stifled a laugh. He glanced at her and smiled. Anything was worth seeing her like this, finally being with her this way.

They landed at Fiji's Nadi International Airport, and from there it was a short distance to where a seaplane waited to take them to the island. Tess sat beside the pilot, looking around her elated. It was her first time ever in such a plane, in such a place, with the most beautiful view she had ever seen. Ian sat behind her, and beside him sat Graham, muttering at the boxes of extra supplies that had waited for them in the seaplane when they embarked on it. The island, which was maintained by a specialized property caretaking crew arranged for by Ira Gold, was always prepared in advance for Mr. Blackwell's visits, but Graham liked to decide at the last minute what else he wanted there. This time he'd planned what he said were his romantic island meals for Mr. and Mrs. Blackwell, making it clear to both of them that he was not about to let the matter of their finally being together drop.

At Ian's request, the pilot flew around the island, giving Tess a full view of it, before the seaplane descended gracefully and landed on the water not far from the palm-lined beach, then docked at a mooring that led into a natural cave. Ian helped Tess disembark, and she walked along the mooring to the cave. Inside, a speedboat bobbed on the water, and to her right, on a patch of sand that led outside, stood a granite-colored open-top Jeep Wrangler. She stepped around the Jeep, shaking her head in wonder, and went outside again. She stood on the beach under a sunny blue sky, breathing in the sea air. It had been years since she'd been to the beach, hadn't seen the sea since she was a kid, in another life. Had certainly never been to a place like this.

At the sound of the seaplane taking off, she turned to see that Ian and Graham had already finished taking everything they had brought with them into the cave. She was about to go back in herself when she heard a car start, and the Jeep came out, driven by Ian. He stopped near her and waited while she climbed in beside him, with Graham sitting in the back, his focus still on his cherished supplies.

They drove along a well-kept path that wound through thick woods and high vegetation, and stony terrain at times, until they came to a hill where a cabin stood, its slanted roofs and its colors blending in with the terrain around it. Tess got out of the Jeep and walked around the cabin, while Ian helped Graham bring in their bags and the boxes of supplies. He came out again as she stood in front of the cabin, looking up at it dreamingly. She turned around slowly, taking in the peace around her.

"This," she said, a smile on her face, "is a good place to bring a woman to."

"The only woman I've ever brought here is my wife," was all he said.

She looked at him, her smile making place for an expression of wonder.

He reached his hand to her.

She took it.

He led her into the cabin. If it could even be called that, Tess mused. It certainly had that cozy, calming feel to it, which fit the island it was on, but it was still Ian Blackwell's cabin, and it showed. The want for nothing, albeit understated, hidden under comfort and quaintness, was here, too.

To their left, a flight of stairs led down, Tess couldn't see where to. And up ahead, at the end of the hallway, she could see a living room that opened to the clearing in the woods that surrounded the cabin. As they walked toward it, something fell not far from them on their left, and they heard Graham curse.

Ian winked at her. "Graham? Are you okay?" he called out.

"Fine, fine, just a difference of opinion," Graham called back, and they peeked into the kitchen that opened both to the hallway and to a dining room that led to the living room on its other end.

Leaving Graham to argue with a kitchen cabinet that was adamant on opposing him, Ian led Tess to the living room, the glass wall of which opened to the outside when Ian uttered a command, and then to a flight of stairs on its far right.

"The cabin uses the slope of the hill to create three levels," he said. "This is the main level. On the cabin's left are the bedrooms, you saw the stairs going half a level down to them near the front door. Graham has his room there, it opens to the side of the cabin and has a porch he likes to sit on, watch could.

ame out involuntarily, full of feeling.
it could feel this way."

did come into the room, covered
her in long strides, caught her in his
her, unable to stop, not wanting to.
intake of breath as his hands moved
to her hips, molding. He felt her
his and his hands tightened, want-
, needing to have her, needing—
nself to stop. Slowly, he had to do
time and in as many more times
ed, slowly. Show her how it should
d be with him, love her until she
but him, what he could give her,
her.

k and breathed. "I'm sorry, I had
slow."

She was overwhelmed, but only by
ouch, the kind of need behind it,
ver known, and her need for him,
asily, so impossibly easily.

had felt the change in her, her in-
esitant acceptance of the growing
them, since he had first kissed her.
her respond to him just now. "I
d, and touched his lips to hers.

downstairs and they both jumped,
ing.

see if we still have a kitchen," Ian

his favorite shows." He led her up the stairs. "The
cabin and the entire island, by the way, are secure.
There are security consoles scattered around the cabin, including in the kitchen, in the living room, in
Graham's room, and in the master bedroom."

He stopped at the top of the stairs, finding himself feeling uncharacteristically awkward. He felt as
if he was a teenager again, on a first date with his
sweetheart. "That's the master bedroom," he said,
indicating a door immediately ahead. "It's the only
room up here, on this level. That's where you will
sleep, I've already put your bag there. I'll be in one
of the bedrooms on the other side."

She couldn't take her eyes off the door to the
master bedroom.

"Tess."

She looked at him.

"We've got time," he simply said, and she loved
him for it.

This time she didn't argue with him about him
giving her the master bedroom. It was different, it
felt different, and she couldn't bring herself to talk
about the bedrooms either of them would be sleeping in. Instead, she went in and looked around.

The master bedroom was large and airy, boast-
ing the same quiet coziness as the rest of the cabin,
as befitting this island heaven. Wooden walls, comfortably hued furniture, a door that opened to a
spacious bathroom and another on its left that led
to a closet. Her suitcase sat on the ottoman at the

foot of the bed, facing a big fireplace with wood stacked high beside it. She walked into the closet, curious. One side held some clothes, casual, his. Of course, she thought, he kept clothes here, shed off the suits and the business world's Ian Blackwell with them, or at least partially—she imagined he never truly stopped. That part of the closet was sparse, though, enough to make her realize he must have moved some of his clothes to the room he would be staying in.

The other side had her jaw drop. Clothes, fitting for where they were, for a woman. Her colors, her fit. She turned to look at Ian. He was still standing at the doorway, hadn't set a foot inside.

She loved him for that, too, for doing that even though there was no longer need for it.

"These clothes," she said.

"I had Juno and Hubert make them some time after we started working on what was happening in Ian Blackwell Holdings. You were working hard, I thought I'd send you here."

"Just me."

"You, Lina and Graham."

She looked at him with those beautiful eyes of hers, and he cleared his throat and put his hand in his pocket, the fingers of the other brushing through his thick black hair. Sheepish, she thought with wonder. He actually looked self-conscious.

"I was supposed to . . . I had planned to take you out to dinner the evening after I would have

returned from
back, to do
To allow me
erly. Had yo
here at som
Had you sai
come here v
would like

"You we
eventually c

"Yes. Dif
but yes. I
time, Tess.

"He's ri
under his
to say, wh
open door
view of th

He saw
not comin

She wa
ening red
hair. A ge
her face

He co

She ca
and saw

And
finally lo
for him

what only love
The words
"I had no idea
And then h
the distance to
arms and kisse
He felt her soft
down her back
body respond t
ing to take mor

He forced h
this, in their fir
as she would n
be, how it wou
had no though
when he touche

He eased ba
meant to take i

"I trust you."
the feel of his
which she had n
which came so

"I know." He
creasing, albeit
intimacy betwee
And he had fel
know," he repea

Something fe
then started lau

"I'd better go

said, still laughing. He touched his lips to hers one more time, keeping his hands light on her, and left.

Tess breathed in and sat down on the bed, then immediately stood up again and looked at it with new eyes. Realizing she was blushing, she forced her attention to her bag, and unpacked.

She took a long shower, letting hot water wash over her, wishing the past days, the past, to be just that, hoping that what she wanted could be. Going into the closet, she knew what her choice would be as soon as she saw it. One of her new dresses, a white, knee-length summer dress with thin straps and a perfectly fitting bodice, its skirt gradually flaring out from the waist down. With a plunging neckline, true, which was more of a cleavage than she normally wore, but Juno and Hubert knew what she was comfortable with, and this one fit in a perfect way that was not too revealing. She glanced at herself in the mirror and let her hair down, did nothing with it but let it fall to her shoulders. She loved it this way, and so did Ian.

She went downstairs and followed the sounds to the kitchen. It sounded like Ian Blackwell and his house manager were busy.

"You boys need a hand?" she asked, amused at the sight before her.

Ian began to answer, turning to her with a smile, but at the sight of her the smile disappeared and all his words were forgotten. She had expected the look, the gaze that took in her body, the way she looked in the dress. What she hadn't expected was the tingle of pleasure it gave her.

"We're good," Ian said, collecting himself, still bewildered that she could do this to him. Bewildered, but not at all displeased.

"Sorry, Mrs. Blackwell." Graham looked abashed. "I tried something new for your first time here and I had a bit of a mishap."

"A lot of a mishap, but you know what," Ian came toward Tess with a shirt that had some sort of sauce, she guessed, spluttered all over it, and glanced behind him at Graham, "I think it came out very well, Graham."

"Think so?" Graham's face brightened.

"I'm sure so. We'll see what Mrs. Blackwell says about it at dinner. I'm going up to wash this off me." Walking by Tess, he touched his lips to hers, keeping a careful distance, but strictly because of the state of his clothes. "You look beautiful," he said.

She followed him with her eyes as he walked down the hallway, but had to look away when he took his stained shirt off on the way. Feeling the color return, she escaped into the kitchen.

"No, please, not the way you're dressed, Mrs. Blackwell," Graham said, horrified. "We've got this all sorted out, I'll just finish here. Can I get you a drink in the meantime?"

"Don't worry, Graham, I'll get one myself." She smiled at him and got out of the way.

She chose a bottle of wine and poured two glasses, leaving Ian's in the living room and taking hers outside. She stood in the warm breeze, not thinking, not having to in this place that called for nothing but peace, just letting it be for the first time . . . ever, she realized, enjoying the feeling, enjoying herself.

"Thank you."

She turned to see Ian coming out with the drink she had poured for him in his hand. He had showered and was dressed casually, looking more relaxed than she had seen him in weeks. And far too good looking. Sexy, she thought and knew the color had returned. She turned back to the falling darkness, just that bit frustrated. She was too inexperienced, far too new at this, and with a man who was everything but.

He surprised her by coming up behind her, moving her hair aside and gently touching his lips to the nape of her neck, lingering. He had promised himself that he would, after earlier, keep his distance, but he couldn't, he simply could not stop touching her.

Her reaction, leaning into him, letting him, trusting him, made his heart just that little bit more, impossibly more, hers.

"Dinner is ready." Graham was far more pleased now than he had been before, but that was because of the way the couple was standing together. "I prepared the table for you inside."

"Or, the three of us can eat out here," Ian said.

"I thought it fitting. Our bedroom, our fresh start."

"How long did you plan it? This is perfect, it's . . . us." She looked at him. "Yes, it has us written all over it."

"I made a few calls before we left Sydney."

"After I said yes."

"After you said yes to coming with me to the island, to staying with me. Before you said yes to fully sharing my life, and my bed," he confessed.

"And if I hadn't said that second yes?"

"I would have used one of the guest bedrooms until I would have convinced you. This is meant to be *our* bedroom."

"You thought about everything," she said.

"Yes, I did. Come see." And he led her down an internal corridor on their left to two walk-in closets, side by side, both filled with their clothes, then to a double bathroom, where her things were laid out alongside his. It was, in every way, their bedroom.

"Lina will now take care of this room together with Graham," he said.

"Won't he mind the intrusion?" Things had been a certain way in this house, in Ian's life, for as long as Graham had been with him.

"Intrusion?" Ian laughed. "He meant it when he said he's been waiting for us to be together. Do you know he actually told me I was a fool for not admitting I love you much earlier?"

She looked at him in astonishment.

"I'm with him," Tess agreed. It was beautiful outside, the evening comfortably warm.

"But it's supposed to be a romantic dinner, I put candles and everything."

"There are all kind of romantic," Ian said. No frills, no pretenses. Not with Tess. This he would do his way. Love her, his way. "We'll all eat out here together."

"Graham," Tess went to him and put an affectionate hand on his arm. "You've worked hard on this dinner, enjoy it with us."

"And you and I always eat together when we're here," Ian said.

"We're always alone here. You finally brought . . ." He looked from Ian to Tess and back. "Oh, I give up."

Ian laughed. "Good." He tapped Graham heartily on his shoulder. "Come on, we'll help."

Dinner outside was indeed pleasant. It was also relaxed. After clearing the dishes, insisting on doing so alone, Graham excused himself, claiming the wine made him sleepy. He left Tess and Ian sitting comfortably beside each other, looking out at the woods, at the starlit sky above them.

"I've never known anyone to hold his liquor better than Graham," Ian observed after a beat, and Tess laughed. He looked at her. The smile remained on her face and she was looking out at the gentle night that had fallen over the island.

"He loves you," she said.

"Yes, he does. He's family."

At that, she glanced at him, at this amazing man. Her husband, she mused, and her heart picked up speed as she became conscious of this place, this night, with him.

"He likes Lina," Ian remarked. "He's always chosen to be alone, but he really likes Lina."

"Why doesn't he do anything about it?"

"He feels clumsy around women."

"But he's been around you," she said, and he threw her a glance.

"I meant that he must have learned something, picked up some moves." She fumbled it again.

"Picked up some moves?" He turned to her in his chair, raising both eyebrows.

"Oh, never mind." She laughed. "Either way, she likes him too."

"She does?"

"Yes. Very much. But she's shy about it. She actually asked me for advice." Tess shook her head incredulously.

"What did you tell her?"

"I had no idea what to say. I mean it's not like I know what to do."

"You mean now that there's a man you like." His smile was a bit wicked.

"What, no!" she protested, then laughed again and hid her face in her hands. "Oh, God. That's it, I'm not talking to you about this. But," she added after a thought, "they like each other, and we need to help them. They're good people."

"We will. We'll figure a way to set them up."

She nodded, and they sat silently.

"But maybe not like Graham just tried to set us up," Ian said, and they burst out laughing again.

Chapter Twenty-Four

The night was deep and silent by the time he walked her up the stairs to the master bedroom. He had no intention of doing anything that night and she knew that, just as she knew that he wouldn't come near her unless she wanted him to. At the bedroom door he caressed her cheek, his fingers gentle, then touched his lips to hers, just a touch, though lingering just a little, just a bit longer. When she went inside, he turned and left.

He walked into the guest bedroom he had chosen. Across the house from her, too far from her, but still. He would sleep here tonight, and his sleep would be calm. After all, she had come here with him. That was what had kept him up more nights than he cared to admit, unbearably so since she'd been attacked, and since he had learned her secret. The wondering, would she stay with him? Would she let him be who he wanted to be for her, would she let him give her the life she deserved? And she had chosen him, had chosen to stay. So now he would give her time. Move slowly. True, much had changed between them, it was so right now, so right for him too . . . Still, it was best this way. She was so close, just a few strides away. Still. He should wait. He would.

He stared at the bed.

Tess closed the door behind her and stood inside the room. The night was warm, the breeze coming from outside comfortable. She looked around her, at where she would be sleeping. Her eyes stopped at the bed. Abruptly, she walked over to it and turned down the bed covers, then the top sheet. There. Now it was ready for sleep, the bed.

His bed.

The thought came out of nowhere. This was Ian's bedroom, Ian's bed. He had slept here, would be here now, in this bed, between these sheets, if she wasn't here. Unexpectedly, her mind brought up the image of him in his bedroom in their house, when she had woken him up the other night. Getting out of bed, near naked. Of course she knew he was well built, it was clear no matter what he wore. And he worked out, she'd seen him in the gym.

She snapped herself out of it, out of her thinking about him this way. She had never thought about any man this way. But then, she had never been in love before. And no one had ever touched her like he had, kissed her as he had.

She couldn't stop thinking about him. Shaking

her head, wondering at herself, she came to stand at the doors to the balcony. To calm herself, take a refreshing breath. But standing in the well-lit room made the darkness outside simply dark, and so she returned inside and dimmed the lights, low enough for her own comfort, dim enough not to mar the night outside. She returned to the balcony and stood on the seam between inside and outside. It was comfortable, standing this way in the dimness. Easier in it, to deal with herself, with that part of her that was changing, that was still between what was and what was to be.

She knew sex would come. Lovemaking, that's what it would be. She had never thought about it in these terms, certainly never for herself. But she did now. Dared to think about it, about what it would be like with him. She wasn't afraid of him. But she was afraid of it. No, she corrected herself. Not just afraid of it, afraid of her ability to experience it, the act itself. She was acutely aware of the sensations in her body when he touched her, felt something new tug at her. Need, need for him. An urge she had never felt. With him, she wanted the touch. And earlier that evening—

Earlier that evening she hadn't wanted him to stop. But after what had happened, what was done to her, would she even be able to . . . ?

Movement in the corner of her eye snapped her out of her reverie and she turned around. The bedroom door was open, and Ian was a shadow in the doorway. Her heart leaped, then again, refusing to settle, and she didn't, couldn't, move.

He took a step forward, a single step. He could see her clearly in the dimness of the room, framed against the darkness outside. Saw that the bed was turned down but she was still in the dress. He closed the door and walked over to her. Slowly. Giving her time to react, to decide if she didn't want to, if she wasn't ready. Coming close, he leaned in and brushed her lips with his, his hands on her waist, his touch light. She put her hands on his arms, but she didn't push him away, and as the kiss deepened her arms came up around him, even as his tightened around her, holding her to him.

He eased back, met her eyes. His had a question in them.

Hers answered, her heart pounding.

He picked her up, and, standing in place, kissed her, lingering. Then he walked to the bed, laid her down gently, and lay beside her, fully clothed. His need did not dictate patience, it dictated passion, taking, but this, tonight, was hers. He knew she was inexperienced, and he knew her fears. And before coming into this room, coming to her, he'd vowed she would think of nothing, feel nothing, but him and his love for her.

He propped himself up on his elbow, his body alongside hers, careful not to put his weight on her. Keeping his hand light on her hip, he leaned and touched his lips to hers. Hers answered, parting to meet his as he deepened the kiss. He eased back just enough to look at her, to let her see his eyes, what they had in them for her, before his lips covered hers again, his hand moving up along her side, his touch tender through the soft fabric of her dress. She felt him linger at the swell of her breast as his mouth left hers, as he softly nuzzled her throat, his kisses slow and tender, moving down to where the dress did not cover, a bare shoulder. It was in his way, the dress, what she wore was in his way, but he removed nothing, not yet, wanting to let her feel his touch without being, feeling, exposed. All he did was continue to touch her, slow, so very slow, with a gentle brush of his fingers, minding where he touched, where he kissed, heeding her every reaction, every intake of breath, every parting of the lips, her eyes never wavering from his, watching him, never truly relaxed as her body fought memories even as her heart had already pushed them away.

He lowered his hand to her thigh, his fingertips touching bare skin and feathering down to her calf, then back up, lightly brushing the back of her knee. He felt her gasp softly, then again as he circled to her inner thigh, just that much up under the dress, enough to feel the heat but nowhere near touching it. He lowered his mouth to hers, his hand moving back up, on the dress again, his touch light, gently gliding on her, becoming more pronounced as he deepened the kiss, as need threatened, as he felt her body respond to him.

Letting go of her with one last touch of his lips to hers, he moved back, got off the bed and undressed, showing himself to her as she lay there, baring himself before he bared her. He saw her eyes on him, saw them widen fleetingly with old fears as her gaze flickered down his body, saw the anxiety disappear again when she raised her eyes to his, saw him. Saw *him*.

He keeps doing that, she thought. Showing me I'm safe, even now, when he knows I trust him—

The thought, all thought disappeared as he returned to lie beside her, naked, his body touching hers, but still without putting his weight on her. His eyes left hers and followed his hand as it traced her body again, his touch less delicate now, meant to be felt. As he leaned in to kiss her this time his hand slid to her back and he opened her dress, his movement slow, his fingers caressing bare skin as he did. His touch, where he had never touched her bare before, was caring, tender, so different, so amazingly different. The way he touched her, the sensations he awakened in her body, she had no idea it could be that way, had no idea anyone could do this to her, bring so much to life in her. His fingertips caressed every soft spot he bared, his lips following them tenderly down her shoulder, her chest, the soft skin of a warm breast.

At that, at the intimate touch, his mouth on her bare breast, she instinctively raised her hand and pushed against his shoulder, pushing him back, away from her body that was already too exposed, but he only raised his head and took her hand in his, stroking her fingers. He kissed her fingertips, his eyes back on hers, waiting, patient, giving her time. She breathed in, lay back, let him. Wanted him.

He said nothing, did nothing until he felt the tension leave her body, saw her focus back on him. He trusted this, that he loved her, that she knew it. That she loved him. His mouth was soft, so soft on hers when he kissed her again, taking his time before he trailed down, lingered on her breast, his lips brushing over soft skin and teasing around the nipple, and when he finally touched it, his tongue gentle, she arched against him, her body responding, reacting to nothing but him, letting him pull the dress down, slip it away, slip it all away. His eyes roamed over her body and she saw the look in his eyes, filled with need, saw him breathe in, restraining himself, and trusted him as she finally lay naked with him.

His hand moved on her body again, on bare skin, tracing her hip down to her thigh, and he did not stop this time, his eyes never moving from hers as he approached her. He lowered his mouth to her breast as his fingers lingered, his tongue teasing as they brushed through soft curls, sliding down, gentle. She strained against him, cried out as what he was doing to her took over, as every inch of her body reacted to his touch, and there was nothing in her but him, them, now.

He aroused gently, swamping her with sensations that drowned old life past, replacing it with new life present and the promise of a new future. She did not realize she opened up to him, had no idea she arched up against him, no longer felt anything but him as he gave her what she needed, keeping his own need excruciatingly in check until she was ready. Her body was taut and her hands reached for him, but he did not let release come. When it did, this time, her first time, it had to be with him inside her, showing her what it should be, what it would be with him.

He shifted on top of her, their bodies finally fully against each other, his eyes holding hers so that she would see him, see it was him even as she felt him. Her arms came up around him, her fingers digging into his back as his entry shocked her body into re-acting. She gasped as he moved deeper, filling her, his movement slow, gradual, knowing how hard he was, how gentle he needed to be. She watched him as he watched her, saw the struggle of need and restraint in his eyes, felt it in his every move, and let herself be with him. Holding tightly on to con-trol, his own body unbearably strained, he moved in long, deep, pleasuring strokes, each thrust feed-ing need yet creating a new one in its wake, until finally their bodies moved together in unison. He did not let go, did not let himself climax until he saw the surprise on her face, heard her cry out as the shock of the release she had been so sure was impossible came, piercing through her, breaking through nightmares past and washing them away forever.

As his heart settled, he raised his head and kissed her, then shifted off her, gathering her to him. He closed his eyes and tightened his arms around her. His. She was finally his.

She let herself be drawn to him, inching closer. There was no pain, had been no pain, although she had been so afraid there would be, worried that she was forever scarred. There had been nothing but his hands, his mouth, his body on her, in her, the need he had awakened. The way it, the way *he* had felt, touching her, being with her, she couldn't believe it, hadn't thought it was possible. But then she hadn't thought she could fall in love, either.

Her body felt different. Different than she was used to. Everything in her felt different than she was used to. And lying in bed with him, wrapped in his arms, his body naked against hers, it felt right. It felt amazing.

As her mind calmed along with her heart, she let out a soft, wondering breath.

He felt it and shifted a little so that he could look at her, never letting go of her. "Are you okay?" he asked gently.

She blushed under his gaze. "Yes, I was just . . . I didn't think it could be this way, for me." Her blush deepened. "Or that I could be . . ."

He touched his lips to hers. "In love and in bed."

She laughed softly.

"In love and in bed with me." His kiss deepened.

She let herself just be with him, feel him against her as if in a sensuous dream. Except that it wasn't a dream, it was real, so amazingly real.

It was the small hours of the night when they finally slept, and a bright sun was up when Ian opened his eyes. The woman he loved was asleep beside him, on her back, and he remained still, not wanting to awaken her, wanting her to stay just as she was, so peacefully at rest, so trusting in him. His gaze moved over her. Her body was half-covered with the same sheet that no longer covered him, her chest rising and falling with each soft breath that came out of her slightly parted lips. His eyes flickered down, to the curve of a breast, to a long leg, the sheet covering just enough, exposing just enough. His wife, he thought with wonder. The first time he actually wanted to wake up beside a woman in his bed, and it was his wife.

It had been her since that first day, he realized, and knew he could never let her go.

She turned to him in her sleep, the sheet slipping off, baring her, the movement bringing her body against his, almost but not quite touching. He fought the urge to close the distance, to touch, to take. And waited.

She opened her eyes, feeling him close to her.

Her eyes met his and focused. She didn't move back, didn't distance herself from him. Instead, she moved just a bit closer and touched her lips to his.

In an instant he deepened the kiss, bringing his body against hers. He rolled her to her back, and she ran her fingers through his hair, every inch of her body responding to his. Remembering, caring, he held back, began to shift his weight off her, but she stopped him.

"Don't, Ian, don't hold back," she said, her eyes on his, wanting him to destroy all remnants of what had been, what had kept her from a life, from him. There was nothing of the resistance, the fear, none of that, only strength in the eyes that met his.

"Tess." He shook his head. He wanted, still wanted too much, was afraid he would ravage, worried he shouldn't.

She held his eyes. Hers were intense. "It has to be real for both of us. Not just for me. And I want you to take it away, take it all away for good, all but you. It should only be us when we're together, Ian. No one else. Nothing else."

His eyes darkened, need taking over, and he shifted back to her, his mouth closing on hers, the kiss open, taking, taking everything he wanted. His lips moved down her neck, her chest, nothing slow, nothing tender about them now, closing on a warm, firm breast even as his hand moved down her body. His groan mixed with her intake of breath as he touched her, found her wanting him. She arched against him, wanting to feel it again, what she had already had with him, but he raised his eyes to look at her.

"Not yet," he murmured as he kissed her again, his tongue teasing, "Not this time," and he lowered his head back to her body, wanting, needing more. His mouth pleasured her, roaming her breasts, moving slowly down a firm belly, and she gasped in surprise as he continued down, parting her thighs, as his tongue glided gently, skillfully, took her. She began to call out his name but was left breathless, unable to do anything but grasp the sheets she lay on. Her body screamed with what he was doing to her and she couldn't, simply couldn't hang on, and when he stopped, moved back up her she fell back, breathed, tried to breathe, but his fingers replaced his mouth, brought her over the edge, then up again, this time bringing her just short of full release. Her body was tense under his mouth and his hands, sensitized to an edge, and there was nothing, nothing but him when he finally drove into her, filling her with a single thrust, her fingers slipping on his back as he thrust into her again and again, as he raised her hips to enter deeper, not holding back, neither of them holding back, freedom taking them both all the way to powerful release.

She finally found the energy to shift under him and he raised his head and looked down at her with the eyes of a man who for the first time truly had it all.

"Good morning," he said softly.

"Hi." She colored a little, a lot, and he laughed and covered her mouth with his.

They came downstairs to an empty kitchen. The coffee machine stood ready on the counter and brunch was laid out on the dining room table, but Graham was nowhere around. Ian busied himself with making their coffee, then handed Tess hers and leaned back on the counter, sipping his, looking at her. He'd given her a robe after they'd gotten out of the shower, and, as he'd hoped, she had stayed with it, not putting any clothes on. Neither had he.

"Where is Graham?" she asked.

"I'm guessing he knows and is giving us some privacy."

"Good," she said softly.

He smiled.

When they did go out of the cabin, it was to a small beach north of it, not the one they'd arrived at but an exquisite wild stretch of golden sand at the end of a tree-flanked path from the back of the cabin. They stood on a knoll overlooking the beach, watching as the gentle sea rolled in playfully, as if trying to get the attention of the man lying on the sand. But Graham was too busy with his supersized tablet, watching a movie again, of all things.

"Graham vacationing," Tess mused. "A contradiction in terms."

"He loves it here. As long as he has enough of his movies and favorite shows with him."

386

"Too bad Lina isn't here."

"Next time. She had some things to take care of in the house and is then going away for a few days to visit her family, something she's been wanting to do." Ian nuzzled her neck, his arms wrapped around her. His kisses sent delicious sensations deep down her and she leaned back into him, her eyes fluttering closed. Groaning, Ian tugged her gently away from the view and back into the lush forest. There was a natural waterfall pool further inland, a lovely, peaceful place. Peaceful and private, and that's all he wanted, needed right now, more of that privacy with her.

Twilight had fallen by the time they returned to the cabin, wrapped up in each other. Graham was in the kitchen, muttering busily to himself. Going upstairs, they found Ian's clothes organized beside Tess's in the closet of the master bedroom.

"Subtle," Ian remarked, and Tess caught her lower lip between her teeth and buried her face in his shoulder, color rising in her cheeks. I didn't know this could be, she thought. I had no idea I could be happy.

"I can't believe we're going back tomorrow." She stretched leisurely on the warm sand, clear blue sky high above her as far as the eye could see.

"We'll come back here." Beside her, Ian rolled

over, bringing his body alongside hers, no longer thinking twice about the contact, about putting his weight on her. "Tess," he said, and she turned her gaze to him. He caressed her cheek. "When we go back home, will you move in with me?"

"Ian," she said softly.

"Share my bedroom. My bed. Be my wife and let me be your husband as should be, as should have been from the beginning. I know we haven't done things in the conventional order, but we've still arrived at the right place." He stopped, waited. He had phrased and rephrased the question in his mind over and over again in the past days, hoping she would say yes. He needed her, loved her. God, he loved her.

"I love you, do you know that?" It came out before she even knew she meant to say it, and what she saw on his face made her bring her arms up around him and draw him down to her.

Chapter Twenty-Five

Tess got out of the Bentley, her husband holding the door open for her, and stood looking at the house as she had that first time, six months earlier. And as he had that first day, her husband waited patient-ly, giving her time. But unlike on that day, this was home now. She was returning here as Ian Blackwell's wife in every sense of the word.

She turned to the man whose eyes now had so much love for her in them, and he touched his lips to hers, knowing what she was thinking of. They walked in together, their arms around each other, as Graham, who had returned more than a day be-fore them, held the door open.

"Welcome home, Mr. and Mrs. Blackwell," he said, trying with little success to maintain a formal expression.

"What are you doing up so late, Graham?" Ian asked. It was well past midnight.

"Oh, I don't know, sir. Closure maybe?" Graham allowed himself a smile. "Lina wanted to be here to welcome you home, Mrs. Blackwell, but I talked her into going to sleep. She wants to make some of the jam you like early in the morning, and fresh bread."

Tess smiled. "It's good to be home."

Bidding them a good night, Graham left them, walking away with a hum.

They walked up the stairs hand in hand. Upstairs, Tess looked left, toward where her room used to be. She thought about the long way she had come, the long way both she and the man who was now truly her husband had come. Beside her, Ian stood quietly. When she turned to him he nodded and led her to the master bedroom.

He opened the door, but didn't go in, instead stopping in the doorway and waiting for Tess to go in before him. She took a surprised step in. The room didn't look the same as it had the one time she'd been in there. Gone were the dark, masculine colors, the ambience that accompanied the room of a man. It was now made up in creamy, cozier shades, down to the walls, the soft carpet, the separate sitting area before the closed balcony doors, with its comfortable chairs and sofas, the marble of the fireplace opposite the bed. The bed. It wasn't the one she'd seen in here last time.

"When did you have the time?" she asked incredulously.

He smiled and came into the room, closing the door behind him. She still wasn't used to all that money could do.

"You even replaced . . ." She indicated the bed.

"His words. In Sydney, when I told him that I intend to offer you the option of leaving me. And then he threatened to go with you if you do decide to leave."

Her jaw dropped.

"I'm not kidding." He took her in his arms and kissed her.

She answered his kiss, but then took a step back, away from him, as she realized something. "Oh."

His brow furrowed. "What's wrong?"

"He knows . . . he and Lina, they know we're here. I mean, here." For most of her adulthood she had been a private person in an isolated life that hadn't included quite a few things others were used to, had a chance to get used to.

Ian stared at her, then swooped her off her feet, laughing, and strode to the bed.

"No, no way."

"Yes way. We need to try our new bed."

"Fine, we'll sleep. Just sleep."

"You know, we're married. People have assumed we have sex for quite a while now."

That, she hadn't thought about. "That's different. They assumed, we didn't. And people in this house knew we didn't."

"I think they already know we do. I remind you Graham knew what we were doing on the island."

"That was different, too. It was . . . Never mind, I don't care. We're not doing it again. Not here. We're not. Ever."

"We are. A lot." They tumbled together on the bed.

"I'm not doing this while people know we're doing this."

"Okay, but I will." His mouth locked on hers and his hands were already on her, finding her under her clothes. She started to speak, but her thoughts had no chance against what he could so easily do to her now.

By the time her skin was bare against his, nothing else existed.

"You still thinking about them?" He was lying prone on top of her, feeling her heart racing against his chest.

"About whom?"

He raised his head to look at her, grinning. Suddenly remembering, she pushed at him. "Oh my God. Get off me!" she said, and started laughing.

He buried his face in her neck, nuzzling, feeling the laughter reverberate through her. I'm happy, he realized with astonishment. I really am happy.

He shifted off her and sat up, and reached into the top drawer of the nightstand on his side of their bed. When she saw what he had in his hand when he turned back to her, she sat up too, perplexed.

"I ordered this when I came back here, while you were still in Sydney," he said as he opened the small box he was holding.

Tess's hand came up to her mouth.

He took her left hand in his and fingered lightly the two rings she had on. "I thought," he said, "that these were no longer right. We are more now, as is our marriage. It's real, *we* are real, while these rings are a lie."

He slipped off both rings, then did the same with the one he had on his own finger and put them all on the nightstand. Then he took one of the two exquisite rings from the ring box, not a simple band anymore but a delicate weave of white and rose gold, intertwining perfectly, as they themselves had. "This ring," he said, looking at her, "is my choice, as you are." And he slipped the ring on her finger, then kissed it.

She could barely see through the mist in her eyes. As he proceeded to take the ring meant for him out of the box, she took it from him and slipped it onto its rightful place. Saying nothing, unable to say anything, she kissed him.

"The other rings I will keep, I think," he said, kissing a tear away from her cheek. "To remind us."

"Our story," she said.

"Yes. Our story." He found her lips with his.

She woke up in the morning with the new day playing gently on her face through the delicate curtains, and opened her eyes to see Ian propped up on his elbow, watching her. She reached out and touched his cheek.

"Good morning, Mrs. Blackwell," he said in a

way that made her heart sigh.

"Good morning, Mr. Blackwell," she answered softly.

Buttoning his cuffs, Ian walked to the bathroom. He stopped in the doorway. His wife was checking her makeup in front of the mirror. She let her hair down, shaking it lightly, and he watched her, mesmerized. She caught his gaze in the mirror, walked over to him and kissed him, a long, sensual kiss that had his heart and his mind reeling. He held her to him, her body a perfect fit to his.

"Let's go back to bed," he murmured against her mouth.

"We have Robert and Legal and Internal Security and who knows who else in less than two hours."

"Screw them."

She laughed and kissed him again, her hands running down his back. Nothing was more tempting than him, being with him.

"This isn't helping," he grumbled, then sighed reluctantly. "Fine. We'll talk to whoever, then come back here and get some more of this."

"Are you okay?" His arm was around her, and he felt her tense up as the Bentley cruised lazily through the San Francisco traffic to Blackwell Tower.

"I am," she said, but inched closer to him. She needed to feel him. She stayed close to him as they went inside the building, and even more so in the elevator, the memory of what happened the last time she had been there too vivid.

"I had the security team that was here that night replaced," Ian said quietly.

She raised her eyes to his. "You promised me they wouldn't know."

"They don't. All the security guards in all of Ian Blackwell Holdings' subsidiaries, and the guards in this building, work for IBH Internal Security, and Ira simply rotated them elsewhere. They will be fired at some point, so that no connection can be made to what happened here. They can't be trusted to do their job."

Tess nodded, distracted. "How . . . Do you know how he got in, how Brett got to your office without anyone knowing?"

"He used this elevator. He created a footage loop that continued long enough for him to get to the top floor, not from the lobby but from my private parking in the underground car park. The security guards weren't watching the screens like they should have been, and they didn't notice the passage to the loop and back to real-time monitoring. They didn't make their rounds, so no one heard the elevator, and they never noticed Brett go back down—Ira found another loop after you left. He used the elevator again, but then he wouldn't have expected. . ."

"He didn't expect me to call for help, because of his threat."

Ian's arm tightened around her. After a while, she spoke again. "So Ira knows."

"He's a trusted friend, and he had to know because I wanted him to make sure Brett is watched and to oversee his eventual arrest."

The frown remained on her face, and he added, "He knows, but he hasn't seen what happened. All he's seen is the CCTV footage from outside my office, the elevator and the lobby. And I'm the only one who has that footage now, everything from that night." That, and the clothes she had worn then. She had never asked what happened to the clothes she had thrown in the corner of her bathroom.

Tess breathed in. Robert knew, he had to, and so did Muriel, she herself had agreed to that. Muriel was a good friend. But other than them, what happened to her would not be revealed to anyone, not even when Brett Sevele went to trial. And yet Ian had assured her it would be reflected in his punishment. Power goes a long way, he had said, and this was something he had no intention of letting go of.

Neither could she.

The worst of it, of the dread Tess had felt from the moment she had seen Blackwell Tower from the Bentley's window, was when she finally walked into Ian's office. She stopped just inside the door. Noticing she wasn't beside him, Ian turned. And saw it. Understanding, he began to walk to her. But then he halted and watched her. Her gaze moved from the spot where she was attacked to him, focusing on him. Her expression changed from the memory to now, to herself here in this office with this man who wanted nothing but to stand by her, to protect her. To love her.

He walked to her and she met him midway.

When they came out of the office again, Tess found before her a graying man, her height, his face stern. The eyes that scrutinized her were dark brown and dead serious.

"Tess," Ian said, putting a hand on her back, "this is Ira."

Tess had known she would be meeting Ira Gold, it was one of the reasons she was here. But, finally meeting him face to face, she felt uncomfortable. This man knew what had happened to her here, in this building, on this floor. What he knew, and what he had seen, even though it was only a little of what had happened, was, for her, personal. And he was a stranger, a man she didn't know.

She said nothing, but he stepped forward and offered his hand. A brief hesitation, and she shook it.

"A firm handshake. Of course. I wouldn't expect any less." He nodded once. "It's an honor to finally meet you in person, Mrs. Blackwell."

Tess was taken aback.

"Your discomfort, by the way, is unwarranted. I'm the one who should feel uncomfortable, I'm the one responsible for what happened to you. No one was there to stop him from getting to you that day, or to help you, and that's on me. And, just so you know, I've changed the security protocol in this building. In all IBH sites, in fact. You'll be safe in them now." He frowned and stopped speaking.

"What happened to me is not your fault," Tess said quietly.

"But it is my responsibility. This will never happen again." His voice was low, and Tess tried to discern what it was she was hearing in it.

Anger, that was it. There was an undertone of anger there. And that's what made her change her view of the encounter with him, or rather of her place in it. His respect, and his anger. What happened to her, it wasn't her shame. In no one's eyes, the few who knew, was it her shame. She wondered about her own perception. On her back, she felt the hand of the man who loved her. She remembered what he had told her, that day in her bedroom. You fought, he had said, and then you fought some more, and look what you've made of yourself.

Deep inside her, a weight she had carried for weeks, and that which she had carried for over a decade, finally eased.

"I expect you to stand by your word," she answered Ira, "but not with regard to me. Anyone who sets foot anywhere in this company should be safe. And I also expect you to call me Tess, I think you and I are past the formalities."

His brow furrowed. "You really are one hell of a

lady, aren't you? Well then, Tess, I have your back, that's all I have to say." He cleared his throat. "Right. I understand that while all that was happening, you also saved this company. I'd like to understand how, and what we can do to prevent what Sevele did from happening again."

She nodded and led the way to the conference room. This time it was Ian who worked in his office, catching up after his time away, while Tess had the meeting about the breach into Ian Blackwell Holdings and what Brett Sevele had almost succeeded in doing to it. It was her, Ira and the head of his cybersecurity division in the conference room, after which Ian joined her for the meeting with Robert and two of the company's legal experts.

Outside, Muriel stood watching Tess. She had come here thinking that she might have a chance to take her friend out to lunch. Other than speak to her on the phone, she hadn't seen her since Tess and Ian had left for Sydney. She was dying to hear about their time alone. But all she'd managed to do so far was go to Tess after her first meeting and hug her tightly, something she'd wanted to do since she'd first learned of the attack. Tess had been glad to see her, but she was nowhere near able to leave and had then gone on to her next meeting, together with Robert.

She was sitting on the same side of the massive

table as Ian, on his right. Just then, he leaned toward her and said something, and she smiled and
looked at him, answering. Muriel couldn't hear what
she'd said, but Ian laughed. They stayed close together, and Muriel was struck by how much they
had both changed.

Not inaccessible, nor untouchable. Not to each
other, not anymore.

"What do I do with this?" Robert asked, following
Tess and Ian into Ian's Office, Muriel beside him,
and making sure the door was closed behind them
before he spoke. He had a folder in his hand.

"What is it?" Ian asked.

"Your contract."

Ian exchanged a look with Tess. "We tore up
our copies weeks ago."

"You did?" Muriel beamed.

"We did," Tess confirmed.

"When we had that fight," Ian remarked with
some amusement.

"Oh yes, we certainly did," Tess confirmed again
with a small smile.

"Unfortunately, I can't do the same," Robert said.
"It is a binding, duly witnessed legal contract and
it has to be properly voided. Since I absolutely and
completely agree with your recent actions, I will happily draw up the necessary documents."

Ian went to him, took the folder out of his hand

and put it on the desk, then pulled a pen from his friend's inner jacket pocket and scribbled something on the contract. Then he offered the pen to Tess. Coming over, she read out loud what he wrote.

"This contract is hereby voided. I love my wife and consider this a true marriage. Ian Blackwell."

Smiling, she took the pen from him and wrote, "Ditto. Tess Blackwell."

"Poetic," he said with a short laugh.

"Was that an objection?" She turned to him, giving Robert his pen back.

"Hell no." And he pulled her into a kiss.

Robert raised an eyebrow. "Yes, well, I suppose this will also do." And he witnessed their signatures with his, with Muriel as an additional witness.

"I would just like to say, for the record, Ian, I told you so," Robert said, pleased that for once, finally, he'd outthought Ian Blackwell.

"Robert!" Muriel looked at him, appalled.

"No, he's right," Ian said to her. "He did. He told me the day I came up with the idea of this marriage that I should give myself a chance, find the woman for me. He was right. And he found Tess." His gaze turned to Tess. "He found me my wife."

When Tess and Ian came out of Blackwell Tower that day, it was through the front entrance, with the Bentley waiting for them up ahead. No hiding, no avoiding the media that waited outside the building in anticipation after the unusually lengthy absence of Ian Blackwell and his wife. The questions they had, those that had to do with the Brett affair and those that had to do with simple curiosity, he answered, calmly, patiently, with Robert and the head of Ian Blackwell Holdings' public relations department behind him, unneeded. He was Ian Blackwell, and he did what he'd been doing since the day he first started the company whose headquarters were in the towering structure behind him.

"Mr. and Mrs. Blackwell," a reporter called out as he and Tess were about to continue to the car, Jackson already waiting with the back door open. "Is it really true that you've just returned from your honeymoon, or was this just a way to disappear and let things quiet down?"

"How about just telling us, while we're at it," another chipped in, "is your marriage real?"

Ian halted and looked at his wife. She smiled, and he drew her to him, held her close. Their kiss left no place for any doubt.

Ian and Tess Blackwell got into their car and drove away.